HIS FINAL ACT

Emily Slate Mystery Thriller
Book 10

ALEX SIGMORE

Dark Woods Press

Prologue

EVEN THOUGH THERE'S no timer, she knows the explosion is coming.

Chloe sits at a bank of monitors, watching the events unfold. Each screen is the viewpoint from a different operative, the cameras on their helmets transmitting the scene to her milliseconds after it happens. She watches as the lead operative removes the small rectangle of C4 from his pack, sets it on the large rolling door, and inserts the firing pin, which is connected to a remote detonator.

The leader calls for the group to fall back, which they do, to a safe distance. Chloe checks the feeds. In addition to seeing everything from the team's perspective, she has another six cameras on the yard itself. So far, so good. No one has tripped any alarms and the guards remain incapacitated. She wishes they hadn't been so hard on the two guards when they breached the yard, but there was little she could do about it from here. It was her job to let the team know if they'd been compromised in any way and so far, the op has gone about as clean as she could have expected.

The only problem was every bone in her body was screaming at her to stop this while she still could. But orders were orders, and the word from above had been to make sure everything goes off without a hitch. She just hoped they knew what they were doing.

A man's voice crackles through the radio. "Chloe, are all the emergency suppression systems disabled?"

"Still off," she replies. "But remember the halon system will immediately activate as soon as the room detects a breach. Make sure everyone has their masks on before you blow those doors."

"Yes, ma'am," the man chuckles. She knows she doesn't have their full trust yet. But at least she has their respect. She came into this organization less than two weeks ago and already she occupies a significant position, witnessing the group's biggest heist so far. Not only that, but as far as she can tell, she's the only woman who has managed to join Simon's ranks. Until now there had been a lot of talk and preparation, and part of her thought they might not actually go through with it.

But Simon recognized talent when he saw it, and appointed her to run things from their headquarters. The man was a zealot; and he had no idea who he'd just entrusted his entire operation to. She'd wanted to take it all down right there, to expose them all. But again, that wasn't her call to make. So now she was here, watching as Simon's men were about to blow the doors off a highly secured facility outside of Baltimore.

"Fire in the hole," the lead yells.

Chloe watches intently as they all turn away from the doors which are still visible on her security feeds. A second later all six feeds flash bright white before returning to normal, showing a large hole where the door had been. The concussive blast hits the team's radios a split-second later, and she catches a few of them curse at the strength of the explosion.

How ironic, using explosives just to get more explosives.

"A team, move forward. B team, stand by," the leader on

the radio calls. Chloe checks the feeds, as well as the local police chatter. No one had been tipped off yet, though that blast would have been heard by some of the surrounding businesses, if anyone was still working. That was part of the reason Simon had chosen to go in at night. The other was there would be less people to deal with.

He'd been right on that much, at least.

Chloe watches as the A team pushes forward, then makes their way through the still-burning hole, not slowing down. A member of the B team steps forward, and using a small fire suppression canister, sprays down anything still burning. The last thing they need is to blow themselves up while trying to retrieve the material.

"We're in, stockpile is here, just as described."

Chloe leans forward, like she can see into the building, even though she has no cameras inside. "Good. Just what Simon said, remember? Nothing else. Don't waste time on things you don't need."

"You think we're amateurs, little girl?" the team leader jokes. Omar. He's been hitting on her the past few days, but she hasn't let it get to her. But this comment does. They all might know she is a genius, but they still see someone barely older than a teen. While it irritates her, Chloe knows it's better this way. Better to let them think they always have the upper hand; that they're in control. As long as they continue to underestimate her, she's not in as much danger.

"Chloe, come in," Simon says over the radio.

"Go," she replies.

"Status from there."

Simon is nothing if not a little paranoid that everything won't go exactly according to plan. From the way he describes it, this is only step one. "A team is on schedule; B team is on standby. Just like the practice runs."

"Any word from the outside world?"

"Not—" An errant flashing on one of her screens catches

her attention. "Hang on, looks like someone nearby might be calling out. It's headed to the local precinct."

"Intercept it," Simon insists.

"Already on it," she replies, before cutting him off and answering the call. "Baltimore 911, what's your emergency?" she says in a sweet, but calm voice.

"Hi, I…uh, I just heard what sounded like an explosion?" the man on the other end of the line says.

"Sir, can you tell me your name and where you're located?" Chloe asks. He relays the information, and she can hear the uncertainty in his voice. He's not sure he should have called or not.

"Did you see an explosion, a flash or any kind of residual cloud?" she asks.

"N-no, I just heard it. I'm down here working late tonight, trying to finish up the end-of-year reports for my company."

"Do you know what direction it came from?" she asks.

"Yeah, sounded like the munitions yard down the street."

"All right, sir," she says, adding an extra amount of sweetness. "I'm notifying the local units who are already on their way now. Would you like us to follow up with you once we assess the situation?"

"Oh, n-no," he replies, like he doesn't want to bother her. "That's okay. I just thought I should let someone know."

"The Baltimore PD thanks you for your help. It's citizens like you that make this community what it is." Maybe she's laying it on a bit thick, but the last thing she needs for some onlooker to get involved. Simon may be a paranoid zealot, but he's also a deadly psychopath. She has no doubt he'd kill this man if he ever thought he was a security threat.

"Thanks." She hears the smile in his voice.

"Have a good evening, sir." She hangs up and goes back to Simon on the radio. "One call-out. I intercepted it before BPD had a chance to respond. As far as they're concerned, it's a nice, quiet night."

"Good, keep it that way," he replies before cutting the channel.

Nice talking to you too. To be honest, she doesn't like being around Simon. The man gives her the creeps. He looks at everyone like they're either an instrument to be used or an obstacle in his way. Chloe has done everything she can to stay on his good side. But this wasn't supposed to take this long, nor was it supposed to get this far, at least not when she first approached this group.

She can't help but wonder how much longer she's going to have to play this role before the cavalry comes in.

"Team A clear," the lead says as he and the rest of the unit leaves back through the blown door.

"Are the packages in hand?" Simon asks.

"All accounted for," the lead says, making his way back to where Team B is waiting. Chloe notices they still all have their weapons pulled. She checks all her feeds again. Everything is still clear.

"Teams A and B, you are clear to move back to transport." Part of her can't believe how smoothly it's all gone. She thought for sure something would get screwed up somewhere, given the people running this operation. But she must hand it to them, they have been cool and professional the whole way. Given that some of Simon's men have military backgrounds, that's not surprising. But it does shoot an undercurrent of fear down her back. If they're this good now, what happens next week?

Hopefully by then this will all be over, and she'll be out of here; headed back home where she can relax. She's tired of wearing this persona, tired of working undercover. The psychological pressure alone is enough to crush her. She thinks about the other operative stationed in the group. Even though they've never spoken, they know each other through the Bureau. It would have been madness to just send one person in, though Chloe is newer than he is. He's been in with them a good two months. She's only been here a few weeks.

"Team A is secure, Team B is en-route," Simon says over the radio. "Chloe, is our exit clear?"

She pulls up the pre-planned route they'd decided on two days ago. "You are clear to go," she replies. "No obstacles, no—"

Before she can finish, she registers the sound of two gunshots over the radio. "Team B, come in," she says. "Identify aggressor." How could someone be on them already? Her data is flawless. No one could have gotten past without her seeing.

"We haven't been compromised," the leader from B replies over the radio. "That was Simon, taking care of the two guards."

Chloe swallows down the sick feeling bubbling up inside her. "I thought they were incapacitated."

"They were," Simon replies, back on the radio now. "But now that we've been successful, I'd rather not have any witnesses."

"Was that always the plan?" she asks.

"Do your job, Chloe, and let me do mine." Simon cuts the radio before she can say anything else. On one of her screens, two small dots representing the two sprinter vans they used to transport both teams to the site are leaving via a side alleyway. They'll be back here in less than half an hour.

Frustrated, Chloe has the urge to call the local cops and set up a roadblock; end this already. But given what she knows about him, Simon would engage the police before letting go of his "master plan". And given how heavily Teams A and B are armed, it would take more than a few local cops to stop them. Right now, Chloe can't put anyone else in danger. Maybe it was naïve to think this could have gone down without any bloodshed. Then again, she told her boss how dangerous these people were; that they needed to be stopped now, before things got any worse. And all that ever came back was for her to keep going. To stay, observe, and continue to report back.

Well, after tonight, she's done. Let him fire her if he wants to. She can't just sit here and watch as a psychopath with access to military-grade explosives decides to target the Pentagon, or worse. This has gone on long enough, and it's time to end it. Now.

As she's waiting, anticipating Simon's return, Chloe clones all of the data she's recorded tonight, storing it on a jump drive she slips inside of her bra. It should be more than enough to put Simon and all of his men away for a long time. But she has to get it to the Bureau first. Maybe Wallace didn't think Simon would actually be able to pull this off. She'd tried warning him, telling him that Simon Mangus was smarter than he'd been giving him credit for, but her orders had been to wait.

Wait for what?

By the time the teams return, Chloe is anxious, ready to be done with all of it. She's not even going to bother trying to maintain cover after tonight. She'll just disappear, leaving Simon more suspicious, yes, but at the same time, he won't know what happened to her. It's hard to track someone who doesn't really exist.

With the thumb drive hidden discreetly away, Chloe heads for the doors, just as the teams are pulling into the garage. The men are boisterous as they exit the vans, enjoying the spoils of a job well done. She can't wait to rain on their parade. If she has anything to say about it, all of them will be in custody forty-eight hours from now.

Simon gets out of the passenger side of the first van, not joining in the festivities with all the others. He ignores everyone else, Chloe included, and goes right for his office. That's fine with her; she doesn't need to be here any longer; her job is done.

"Hey there, Clo-clo," Omar says, a big grin on his bearded face as he approaches. "I've got a massive boner from fucking the federal government right up the ass tonight. Gonna need someone to take care of that for me," In his hand he's holding a sample of what they just "procured".

Inside, her guts turn, but she doesn't let it show. "C'mon, Omar, we all know there's nothing you won't fuck. Go find a small hole in a tree somewhere, I'm sure that will be more than sufficient."

The rest of the men behind him begin howling as Omar turns red in the face. He never has been able to take a joke, especially when he's the butt of it. "You little bitch," he says.

"Yep, and trust me. You don't want to test it. I'll snap that thing off before you can—"

"Chloe! Get over here," Simon says.

Omar grunts as she heads back to Simon's office. She shouldn't be surprised he wants a full rundown of everything she saw. He put a lot of faith in her to make sure everything went off without a hitch, which she did. Regardless, she's not worried. But she can't help but feel a sense of trepidation as she approaches the man, standing in his doorway, his face like a block of marble.

"What's up?" she says, keeping it casual.

He holds the door open for her, allowing her to come inside. She hears the click behind her, and her exposed skin breaks out in goose pimples. What's going on?

"Everything go smoothly?" Simon asks from behind her.

"You know it did," she replies. "You made it back in one piece."

"Nothing you want to tell me?" he presses. "Nothing…out of the ordinary?"

Can he know? How? She's covered her tracks so well. The best thing she can do in this moment is keep calm. Panic won't do anything but make the situation worse.

"You're being paranoid. Everything went according to

plan," she says, feigning irritation in her voice in hopes that it will throw him off. She's supposed to be a sullen twenty-something. Why not play the part? But before she knows it, she's reeling and heading for the ground, her vision having gone white for a brief second.

When she looks up through blurry vision, she sees that he's hit her in the back of the head with the butt of his gun. "Wha—"

"Don't," he warns, getting down on his haunches as he stares at her with those black eyes of his. "You've got some explaining to do." The gun is loose in his hand, but he's holding it in a manner that he could shoot her at any second if he wished. "Don't you, Zara?"

Chapter One

I HATE THIS COUCH. It's supposed to be comforting, but it's itchy and feels like it was purchased back in the seventies, which, given the age of its owner, wouldn't surprise me.

"This is a waste of time."

The man sitting across from me crosses his leg, leans back in his armchair and gives me a pointed look over his glasses. Dr. Kurt Frost is the perfect picture of a stereotypical psychologist—if there exists such a thing. His salt and pepper beard matches his clean-cut and perfectly-styled hair, and he normally wears a pair of reading glasses, though those are on the desk beside him. He's also wearing a green sweater today, over a button-down shirt with pressed slacks and loafers. For some reason I hyperfocus on the fact his sweater is almost the same color as this horrendous couch I'm sitting on.

"What's that, Emily?" he asks. Like he doesn't already know.

"The fact that I'm sitting in here with you, when there are about a million other things I could be doing right now," I huff. I only just got back from Fernview yesterday, after having been there for a good two weeks attempting to solve a twenty-year-old murder investigation. Though, that hadn't been my original reason for going back to my hometown. I had been there hoping to find out more about these mysterious letters that keep appearing at my doorstep, but I kinda got sidetracked.

That happens sometimes. Actually, it happens a lot, it seems.

"What's so funny?" he asks, his own mouth quirking.

I wipe the smile from my face. "Nothing," I reply. I forgot how closely therapists watch body language. I really need to be more careful around him.

"That's all right," he says. "No need to talk about it if you don't want to."

"Then I can go, right?" I'm sure to him I look like a mess. It took them four days to discharge me from the hospital down in Fernview, after only receiving one hit from Brodie Tyler—the aforementioned murderer who'd been operating in the town unchecked for years. Unfortunately for me, Brodie had packed a lot of heat in that punch, causing my brain to swell, along with a broken nose and a fractured jaw. I just had the brace removed yesterday and got the all-clear to start eating semi-solid foods again, which is an adjustment. It's going to take a few weeks before I'm back in fighting shape again, and until then, I've been ordered to take it easy.

Frost glares at me, giving me a stern look that also somehow holds an inch of disappointment. For a split second I feel a pang of guilt because I know he's only trying to help, but then I remember I didn't hire Dr. Frost. He was appointed to me by my current boss.

"I think we can do a bit more with our remaining time." He reaches over and picks up a pad from his desk, along with his reading glasses, slipping them on. "Why don't you tell me about your trip back to the town where you grew up?"

I shrug. "What's there to tell? It's pretty much the same place I left back then. Not a lot changes in a town like that."

"And that's why you left." He looks over his glasses at me.

For a second I'm surprised by his insight, but then I remember this is his job. "I left because there was nothing keeping me there."

"Your father was still living there when you moved away, isn't that right?"

"And? Lots of people move away from their hometowns."

"That's true," he replies. "I'm just curious how you felt about going back. From what I know about you, you're not the kind of person who reminisces a lot on the past."

I stifle a chuckle. Maybe that was true once, but more recently my entire world has been consumed by my past, ignited by these letters coming from my "mother". Though that's impossible, because she died when I was twelve. And unless zombies have started walking the Earth and I haven't been notified, she's still where I last saw her—being lowered into a hole in the ground.

"It was fine," I say. "I reconnected with a few old friends."

"And you solved a murder investigation going back twenty years." He reads down his page of notes. I'm sure he has all my case files tucked away in that desk of his. No doubt Wallace is funneling them to him the minute I finish my reports.

I cross my arms. "It was a personal matter."

"Your friend's sister," he says, his eyes scanning the pad. I haven't told Frost about receiving the letters, nor do I plan to. My experience with Camille last year has taught me that getting my workplace involved with my personal life only makes things more complicated. I need to take care of this myself. Fortunately, while I was in Fernview, I got a lead from the same friend I managed to help. The name of another therapist—coincidentally. Though from what she said, I don't think this is any conventional therapist.

Still, all of that has taken a backseat to more urgent events, which is the entire reason I insisted on coming back to DC as soon as possible.

Frost glances up and at the same moment I realize my leg is bouncing. I will it to stop, but not before he's seen it. "Anxious?" he asks. I blow out a frustrated breath, though my jaw is still sore. Frost removes his glasses and sets his pad back on his desk. "Okay. Why don't we talk about the real reason you're here."

I arch an eyebrow. "*Real* reason?"

"Agent Foley."

The mention of her name causes everything in me to tighten, and I almost hug myself in response. "What about her?"

"From what I understand, she hasn't checked in from her assignment in almost six days."

My leg starts bouncing again, though this time I don't do anything to stop it. I don't want to give him the satisfaction of seeing me rattled, but it's almost like I can't control my own body. I have been worried sick ever since Wallace walked into my hospital room down in Fernview to deliver the news. "Yeah," is all I say in reply.

He takes a deep breath, like he's gearing up for something big. "Let's talk about what happened…in the hospital."

"Oh, you mean when my boss forcibly had the nurses knock me unconscious?" I say, more heat seeping into my words.

"From what I've read, you didn't take the news well."

I scoff. "That's putting it lightly. How was I supposed to take it? I love Zara more than anyone in the entire world. And instead of helping to find out what happened to her, I'm sitting here with you, like a lump, trying to talk about it."

"Believe it or not, this is good for you," he replies.

"Look," I say, glaring at him through hooded eyes. "You're not the only one in here with experience in psychology. I know the benefits of therapy. I've worked with many people to get them the help they need. The difference with you is that *I* didn't choose you. My boss did."

"And you think because SSA Wallace brought us together that I have some ulterior motive?" The implication is buried in his words, even though he doesn't need to say it: he thinks I'm being ridiculous.

"The point is, I have a hard time trusting you, not knowing the entire story," I reply.

He nods. "That's fair. And I can see where you're coming from. Let me assure you, I'm only here to help you, Emily. Our conversations remain completely confidential, and I have no communication with SSA Wallace about you or any other patient. That would violate both my personal and my professional code of ethics." He pauses, assessing me. "But I understand trust takes time to build. So I'm willing to be patient. I just ask that you keep an open mind."

· "Fine," I say, finally uncrossing my arms. "I'm sure you're a great therapist. But right now, my best friend is missing— maybe even dead. But instead of looking for her, I'm stuck in here. You can imagine how that makes me feel."

"Like you're wasting your time," he replies. "Like if you could just join in with the rest of the Bureau, you could find her, is that right?"

Now that he says it, it sounds a little more ridiculous than it did in my head. Logically I know adding one more person to the search is unlikely to change the outcome. But emotionally I also know that if I would just be allowed to help that I'm sure I could find her.

"Agent Foley is very important to you, I understand that," he says. "And I really do hope she is all right."

I wait for him to continue, but he doesn't. He's left something hanging out there, waiting to see if I'll take a hold of it. "You're wondering if I've considered the possibility that she's dead."

"I didn't say that," he replies, uncrossing one leg and crossing the other.

"But you were thinking it." I stand up. Even though I'm

on painkillers, I can still feel the blood rushing to my face when I make a sudden movement. It makes everything ache all over again. "You want to know if I'm mentally prepared to deal with the possibility."

"Emily, I think you are an incredibly strong person," Frost says, leaning forward. He nets his hands together, looking up at me. "I have no doubt you could survive just about anything."

A flood of emotion hits me, and it takes a considerable amount of willpower to stop the tears from breaking the barrier. "Not with this." I'm surprised how soft my voice sounds.

"Why not?" he asks, sounding genuinely curious.

"Because I can't take any more loss," I finally say. He wants me to have an open mind? Okay, well here goes. Nothing ventured. "Zara is my lifeline. She was there when I lost my husband. And she's always been there, no matter what happens. If something has happened to her…" I trail off, unable to finish without risking the flood. Instead I turn from him and pace to the far end of the room.

"Let's not dwell on what we don't know," Frost replies. "You've often spoken about how Agent Foley is competent and smart. Trust those qualities will keep her alive."

I've been telling myself the same thing, but honestly, sometimes situations spiral out of your control. So far Wallace has refused to give me any information about the undercover operation she was running. It's like he's deliberately keeping me out.

"And no matter what happens, as difficult as it may be, you will get through it," he adds. I know he's trying to make me feel better, but I don't *want* to "get through it". If Zara really is dead then I don't see how I could ever move past it. With Matt it was a little easier, mostly because I had work to keep me busy. But being in that building, in that *job* with her ghost always over my shoulder—I couldn't do it. And as great as

Liam has been, I'm not sure even he could be there for me like she was.

I turn back to Frost, doing my best to reset myself. "If you say so." I glance at the clock and note we only have another ten minutes in the session. "I know you said I need to use my time here, but I really do need to go. I still have a lot of work to catch up on."

Frost purses his lips and leans back, as if he were expecting this. "Emily, this isn't a prison. You can leave whenever you want. It is your time to use as you wish and as much as I would hope you'd want to stay, I can't force you to do anything."

"In that case," I say on my way to the door. "Right now, my time is at a premium and I just don't have any to waste." I leave him sitting in his chair as I make my way back down the hallway for the elevators. If there was one thing I got out of the session, it was that I need to be focused on one thing, and one thing only: finding my best friend.

Chapter Two

I SPENT the rest of the evening going through every communication I had with Zara right up until she stopped responding to my calls and texts, which was almost two weeks ago now. I lost a lot of time in that hospital recovering, which didn't do much for my mental state. Liam tried to help comfort me and keep me up to date after Wallace returned to DC, but until I know her exact whereabouts, nothing will make me feel better.

Liam came by last night to help me fix a few meals for the next few days and to help take care of Timber, who has been a lot more rambunctious since I returned home. I'm not sure if it's because he knows I'm injured or if it's because I was gone for so long, but he's been on edge as much as I have. I need to remember to schedule some more time with the sitter for him, just to help wear him out during the day.

I know Liam was just trying to help, but ever since Fernview, things have been a little strained between us. I expected him to give me a heads-up about Wallace, instead of just showing up with him at the hospital unannounced. Not to mention he didn't stop Wallace when the man insisted I be knocked unconscious because I was "a danger to myself".

That little stunt has me wondering if I have any legal rights against my boss. But I will deal with that *after* we find Zara.

Needless to say, Liam didn't stay the night.

This morning it took me a little longer than normal to get ready, but I'm getting used to working around my injuries. For the most part the swelling has gone down in my face and without the jaw brace all I have is a splint that still covers my nose. The other bandages are gone too, though I'm still on about six different types of drugs for another two weeks.

With all the injuries, lack of sleep and stress, the woman in the mirror is a stranger to me. My hair has lost some of its luster, and dark purple bags still hang under my eyes. Some of that is from the fight, but a lot of it is stress and worry. Still, I do my best to make myself presentable and professional, and tie my hair back to keep it out of my face.

Because of my injuries I haven't been cleared to operate heavy machinery yet. Which means there's an Uber waiting for me in my apartment parking lot when I lock up, having fed Timber his morning treat. Yes, it's humiliating not to be able to drive my own car to work, but it's better than getting in a wreck I suppose. Unfortunately, the Uber driver isn't as proficient as navigating the streets of DC as I am and by the time we pull up to the J. Edgar Hoover building I'm already running late.

I get through security with a few curious looks from the guards—no doubt at the big white thing on my nose holding it in place—before making my way up to my floor. I've spent all morning winding myself up for this and yet I still don't know exactly what I'm going to say to my boss. Though I realize whatever it is could very well get me fired, which means I need to temper myself, at least until this business with Zara is done.

But before I can make my way to Wallace's office, Liam falls in step beside me, matching my pace.

"Morning," he says, all business.

"Morning," I reply. I don't like how we left things last

night, but right now I'm on a mission and I don't want Liam to get caught in the crossfire. "I—"

"Listen, there's a meeting in the conference room happening right now. Wallace called in me, Kane and Sandel. I thought you should know."

I stop, looking up at him. Liam has about six inches on me. "About what?"

"What do you think?" he asks.

Zara. "And he didn't call me in?" I ask, checking my phone for any missed messages. There are none.

"C'mon," Liam says, taking me by the shoulder and leading me away from the bullpen and toward the conference room instead. Before I can object, I catch sight of Wallace speaking to a few of the other agents in our division, though his back is to us. Liam and I slip past him and into the conference room where Agent Elliott Sandel and Agent Nadia Kane, both of whom look up with wide eyes as soon as we enter.

"Emily," Kane says, partially standing. "My God, I didn't realize—"

I wave her off. "It's nothing," I say. "Just a broken nose." Liam and I take the seats furthest from the doors.

"I read your report," Agent Sandel says. "That man must have been as strong as an ox."

"Kinda felt like getting hit by one," I reply.

"Did Wallace add you to the itinerary without telling us?" Kane asks. There's no accusation in her question, only confusion.

"No," I tell her. "I'm here unofficially."

Her eyes go even wider and she quirks her mouth. "Cool."

Not more than two seconds later Wallace strolls in, a couple of folders under his arm. Before he even gets the measure of the room his gaze lands on me, glaring at me through those signature horn-rim glasses of his. I see surprise, shock, fury and about a dozen other emotions cross his face all at the same time. He takes a few measured breaths before going to the small podium at the head of the room, right beside the projector. After setting up, and seemingly once he's got his emotions under control again, he finally turns back to me.

"Slate. You're not scheduled to be here."

"I know," I tell him. "But this is about Zara, isn't it?"

His gaze flashes to Liam then back to me. I'm sure Liam is going to pay for that one. Wallace opens his mouth again but before he can utter another word the door to the conference room opens and Deputy Director Janice Simmons strolls in. She doesn't acknowledge any of us, only takes a seat at the far end of the table, opposite Wallace.

All of us seem frozen in place, especially Wallace, who clearly didn't expect his boss—the woman who previously held his position—to show up. "Deputy Director Simmons," he finally says. "Is there something I can do for you?"

Janice slips a vape pen out of her inner jacket pocket and takes a long draw. "No. Proceed."

Wallace glances from her to me and back again, and I can't help but wonder if he thinks I had something to do with her being here. But I haven't even seen Janice in almost a month, though I think her impromptu appearance might have just saved my ass.

Wallace clears his throat, obviously thrown off his game. No doubt he was planning on coming in here to outline the situation with Zara to everyone else, but hadn't counted on needing to deal with me or his boss.

I wish I could hug Janice right now, but she's not the hugging type.

"Today, Mr. Wallace." Janice takes another pull on her vape pen. "I have a busy schedule."

"Yes, ma'am," he replies, clearing his throat again. "This is an update on the operation we've dubbed *counterstrike*, which until now had been classified level five and above. However, seeing as both the agents we've had working on this case have failed to check in or respond to repeated attempts at communication, the deputy director has authorized the classification be lowered to level four. But that means what you learn in this room does not leave it, not until I say so, are we clear?" He looks at me as he says it and I just stare right back.

Operation Counterstrike? Sounds like some bad eighties movie.

Wallace takes my silence as a win and activates the projector in the room, which throws up an image of what looks like incoherent writing on the screen beside him. I take a minute to study the words, reading them as best I can, though they come across very preachy and somewhat unhinged. The next image is of a group of men, all with lined faces, and short haircuts. Half of them are wearing sunglasses and looking off into the distance. The image looks like it was taken from a telephoto lens.

"Six months ago we began monitoring a group of people we have come to start calling the Simonists."

"The *Simonists?*" I ask, forgetting that I probably shouldn't be speaking.

Wallace doesn't stop, though. "We've been tracking them across the dark web, watching their activity and doing our best to keep tabs on them. As far as we can tell, they are a group of homegrown terrorists, led by a man who calls himself Simon Magus. We suspect this is a pseudonym, as Simon Magus is a biblical figure, colloquially known as a sorcerer of some sort."

"Who is he really?" Sandel asks.

"We don't know yet. And we don't have any images of the man. Whoever he is, he's working hard to cover his tracks. But his following has grown significantly in the past few months. Enough that it was decided we needed people on the inside, keeping tabs on this group. We sent in two agents: Foley and Crowne. Both of them stopped checking in at the same time. However—"

"Wait, you sent Zara in and *don't* have a picture of the

guy? How can that be possible? Wouldn't that have been the first thing she did?" I ask.

Wallace narrows his gaze at me. "Magus is known to be highly paranoid, not allowing any of his followers phones or any other electronic equipment. Agent Foley provided a description, but that's all." He resets himself. "Before we lost communication with both of them, we learned that Magus and his followers were due to strike an explosives storage facility in Baltimore two weeks ago."

"Wait, I think I heard about that," Kane replies. "The Lockheed storage yard, wasn't it?"

Wallace nods. "Our original plan was to wait until we knew how they planned to use the explosives before going in to take them out, coordinating with our men on the inside to ensure the least amount of casualties possible."

"You mean you let them obtain explosive material? On *purpose*?" I ask, practically yelling.

Wallace screws up his face, and it goes a shade of crimson. But before he can answer, Janice pipes up. "It was decided that without the explosives, any charges we brought against the group would be inconsequential in the long run. We realized these were dangerous people and we needed to strike in the short amount of time between when they obtained the explosives and when they planned on using them. Had we hit them too early, Magus would have rallied and just come back stronger."

I turn back to Wallace. "So what happened after they hit the Lockheed storage yard?"

"We don't know," Wallace replies. "That was the night both Agents Foley and Crowne failed to check back in. We haven't heard from them since."

"You think they were compromised," I say.

"We don't know what to think, Agent Slate," he says, frustration seeping into his words.

"Send me in," I say. I've done my fair share of undercover work. I can find out what happened to her.

Wallace adamantly shakes his head. "Absolutely not. We're not sending anyone else in. If either agent was made, then the group would perceive any new member as a threat, and it's too much of a risk. Plus, after the raid, they packed up and moved. We no longer have any intel on where they're operating from." He clicks the remote in his hands and images of what look like an abandoned underground bunker come up. The walls are all gray brick, and the floor is littered with trash, dust and debris. "We sent a team in sixty hours after we lost contact. This was all we found."

Shit. I sit back. The evidence is there. They *were* made. Otherwise why move locations right after the heist? "What about the hit on Lockheed? Were there any stragglers? Anyone who didn't make it out?"

"No. They were fast, clean, and professional, which leads us to believe at least some of their members are former or current military. They killed two guards."

"So then what are we doing here?" Liam asks, saving me the question.

Wallace levels his gaze on him. "You, along with Agents Kane and Sandel will be heading up a task force designed to find and stop the Simonists before they can use the explosives they've stolen. You'll be working hand-in-hand with the ATF on this one."

"Because of the explosives, right," Liam says, nodding to himself.

It doesn't escape my notice that Wallace has neglected to mention me being part of this "task force". "We don't know what the Simonists plan to do, but it's a good bet they're going to want to blow something up. Familiarize yourself with the online rhetoric. A lot of it talks about the evils of capitalism and the destruction of the modern world, but it's dense, and a lot to wade through. Also keep in mind we're not sure if

Simon Magus himself is responsible for these…manifestos, or if they're coming directly from his followers. What we do know is they are armed, dangerous, and not afraid to get their hands dirty. This takes top priority as of right now. Any additional resources will need to be approved by me," he pauses, then looks at Janice. "Or the Deputy Director."

Liam raises his hand as Wallace is closing his folder. "I request we add Emily to the task force. She knows Agent Foley better than anyone and it would be foolish to leave her out of this investigation."

Bless this man. Despite everything, he's still on my side.

Wallace looks like he wants to argue, but one stern glare from Janice shuts him up. "Fine. Approved—provisionally."

"What provision?" I ask.

"Mental readiness. You're coming out of a traumatic situation. I want one last neurological examination before I put you back on active duty."

I move to protest. "But—"

"I don't think it's an unreasonable request, given what you've just gone through," Wallace says, shooting Janice a look. She doesn't look at me, only nods once. Great, that means I get to go *back* to the doctor. Hooray.

"Okay then," Wallace says. "Get started going through what information we have. I'll have the information for your liaison with the ATF later today. Remember, our goal is to find these people and interrupt their plans at any cost."

"And our agents?" I ask.

"Pray they're still alive," he says."

Chapter Three

"YOU KNOW damn well I don't need a mental readiness examination," I say, storming into Wallace's office after the meeting is over. Liam, Kane and Sandel all went to work on the investigation, but I've got a bone to pick with my boss and I can't put it off any longer.

Wallace throws the folder he was using in the meeting down on his desk. "Damn it, Slate, can't you see I'm doing you a *favor* here?"

"A *favor*?" I feign a laugh. "You mean after that stunt you pulled at the hospital? That kind of favor?"

He glares at me. His expensive suit isn't pressed like it normally is. Instead, there are actual wrinkles in it. "That *stunt* was to keep you from ripping your IV out of your hand. I spoke with your doctor afterward. He said more than likely some of the drugs were causing you to act irrationally."

"Right, because I can't just be concerned for my friend," I say.

He places both hands on his desk and leans on it. "That's exactly what I'm afraid of. Coll is right, you do know Foley better than anyone. And I *want* to bring you on this investigation. But I'm not sure I can trust you'll put the investigation first and your friendship with Agent Foley second. Which was why I didn't invite you to the briefing this morning. I *was* going to speak about this with you in private."

"Well, I saved you a lot of trouble. Because unless you're planning on firing me, there's no way you can keep me off this case. I *will* find her." I'm usually not this combative, but this is Zara we're talking about, and I still get the feeling like Wallace is stonewalling me.

He rubs his temple. "How was your appointment with Dr. Frost yesterday?"

"What, he didn't send you the transcript?" It's out of my mouth before I can stop it. I'm walking a very fine line here and even I know that was over it.

Wallace, to his credit, takes a deep breath and waits for my real response. "It was fine. Normal session."

"He didn't have any objections to you coming back to work?"

"It never came up." I must admit, if Wallace were receiving information from Frost, he probably wouldn't be asking this. He'd probably just shut me down and put me on desk duty. But that doesn't mean I'm automatically going to start trusting the good doctor.

"And how is your head? Any additional headaches? Any dizziness?"

"Are you my physician now?"

"Slate," he says, his voice flat. "You didn't see what I saw. I looked at your charts, at the photographs they took when they brought you in. I'm not sure you realize just how close you came to buying the whole farm."

I purposely haven't been thinking about it very much, instead I've been focusing more on Zara, and before that, this issue with my mother. Both have been very good distractions to what happened to me. "It was bad, I know."

"Bad? He could have killed you. I saw the man. Built like a tank, with hands the size of paint cans. It's a wonder that hit didn't kill you. Probably because of all your conditioning. But it could have. It's barely been a week and already you're chomping at the bit to get back to work. I'm just not sure that's the best idea, and were it not for these circumstances, I'd chain you to a bed, since you obviously can't take time off without getting into trouble."

"I promise I will take some real time off once all this is over. But you have to let me find her. *Please*," I say, hating how desperate I sound. I hadn't meant for it to come out that way, but I can't help but think he's right. That blow from Tyler could have killed me. If he'd hit me at a different angle or knocked me out and I'd hit my head on a rock or something— I'm not good thinking about my own mortality. Probably why I've been trying so hard to avoid talking about it.

"Show me that you're fit for duty," Wallace says. His mind is made up. Which means I need to go back to my doctor. No excuses.

"Fine." I turn and leave before he can say another word.

Outside his office, Liam meets me before I can get to my desk. "What happened? What did he say?"

"He's not budging," I reply. "He wants proof I'm mentally fit to work. Which means I need to take a trip downtown."

"Can you really blame him?" Liam asks.

"How can you say that?" I ask.

"Because I'm worried about you!"

My initial reaction is to lash out at him, but something in the back of my mind tells me to take a step back and assess the situation. I put my hand on his chest, close my eyes and count to five. "Thank you for going to bat for me in there," I say. "You didn't have to do that. And I know you're just looking out for me. But I am fine. It was scary, but I made it through."

He places both his hands on my shoulders, the first real physical contact we've had since I got back. He holds me like that long enough for me to see the concern in his eyes. Maybe

I've come back into this whole thing stronger than I should have, maybe I should have been less raging bull and more careful otter. He's always been there for me, even in times like this, when maybe I don't deserve it so much. "Liam—"

"Emily, you are the most important person in my life right now," he says, bringing his forehead down to touch mine. It's like he's reaching out with his soul. "You don't know what it's like seeing the person you love connected to a dozen machines in the hospital. I wasn't sure you were going to make it out of there."

"Wait," I say, pulling back. "You *love* me?"

His eyes go wide. "Did I say that?"

I nod. "You did."

For a brief moment he seems mortified. I'm not sure he wanted to make that declaration here in the building where we work, in the middle of a manhunt. But then something in his face changes and he smiles. "Good. I'm not ashamed. I *do* love you. I think I have for a while now."

"Liam—" I'm speechless, but as I search his eyes, I can see there's no deception, no ulterior motive there. I don't think he meant to tell me, but at the same time he's not ashamed of it.

"It's okay," he says. "You don't have to say it back. I know I kind of sprung it on you." He takes a step back, releasing me. But before he can even think of letting embarrassment set in, I jump forward back into his arms, and my lips lock on his. I'd been away for so long and I've been so distracted by all these other things I'd forgotten just how good it feels to *have* someone.

I don't know how long we kiss, but it's long enough that I realize the chatter in the office has quieted substantially. When I pull away from him, I don't even bother looking around—who cares what these people think? Instead, I look deep into those hazel eyes of his before running my hand through his hair. "Thank you," I whisper.

He chuckles. "Anytime."

I finally let him go. "You better get to work. I'll be back in a few hours."

"Already looking forward to your return," he says, grinning.

What did I do to get this lucky? I swear he has the patience of a saint. I'd start calling him Saint Coll, but I know he'd hate it. Maybe I will anyway. I give him one final smile before heading in the other direction, feeling a lot better than I did when I came in the office this morning.

THREE HOURS LATER I'M BACK IN ANOTHER UBER ON THE WAY to work again having just seen my doctor. One nice thing about being in the FBI—I can use a little of my influence to get seen same-day, especially in situations like this, when there could be lives on the line. Thankfully, after her assessment, Dr. Perrin believes I'm fit for full duty. There's no evidence of residual damage from the swelling and most of my vitals have returned to normal. To say she was a little more than shocked to hear about my exploits in Fernview would be an understatement, but she also knows the kind of person I am. It's not the first life-threatening injury I've sustained, and I doubt it will be the last.

But she emphasized *light* duty, no jumping over fences, chasing bad guys and *definitely* no hand-to-hand combat.

Saying I can't go out there and fight if I need to is like telling me not to use one of my legs. My fighting prowess is one of the things I'm most proud of. I didn't spend years studying martial arts just for it all to be wiped out because of some stupid injury. She assured me I could start training again, but not for another few weeks. My body apparently can only take so much, and I need time to heal. Seems like I'm not invincible after all.

My second Uber of the day pulls up to my work and I go

through security again, though this time I feel less anxious than I did this morning. At least now I have some understanding of what Zara was involved in, and I'm looking forward to working on the case. It will help to have Liam there by my side; he's more of a calming presence than I gave him credit for.

"Here," I say, slapping down the report I had Dr. Perrin print out for me so Wallace couldn't claim he never received an email. "Everything's fine. Like I said."

Wallace glances up at me for a moment before taking the report and reading over it. "You're not to take point on this, hear me Slate? Sandel is the lead agent. I don't want to have to explain to your doctor why you have another concussion. Understand?"

"Completely," I say.

"Good. Then best of luck." He hands the report back to me and I head back to my desk, feeling vindicated. When I arrive I notice there's a message waiting on my landline. Strange, usually if a call comes in on my phone here it immediately transfers it to my cell. I look around for Liam and the others, but don't see them right off. They've probably set up a makeshift command center somewhere to begin pooling information.

I pick up the receiver and play back the message. "*Slate, it's Simmons. I need to see you as soon as you're back.*" Janice? What could she want?

Heading to the elevators, I can't help but wonder why if she needed to talk to me, she didn't just call my cell. Also, this is highly irregular. SOP would be for her to send me an email to make an appointment. Not to mention she and I have barely spoken in the past month, ever since she received her promotion and has been working up on the top floor.

Funnily enough, Janice took the old office of James Hunter—my husband's father and member of the Organization that nearly brought this place down. Had it not been for

Liam, Zara, Janice, and me working together, he could have very well succeeded.

"Is she in?" I ask the man sitting at the desk outside her office.

"She's expecting you. Go on in," he replies without looking up from whatever he's typing.

I've always been a little intimidated by Janice. She's not the kind of person who shows a lot of emotion. I believe that helps to make her an effective leader, but I've also never seen her rattled, even when she was on the chopping block. That intimidation has only increased tenfold now that she's the deputy director in charge of our division.

As I enter her office, she's seated, writing what looks like a handwritten note and my mind immediately goes back to the letters I received. But a second later I dismiss the possibility. No way would Janice have anything to do with that—and if she did, why show her hand by inviting me up when she's clearly in the middle of something?

"Slate, take a seat," she says. "Give me one moment, I need to finish this up." I do as I'm told, taking a look around her impressive office. It's a far cry from the office she used to occupy down on our floor. Large wooden shelves hold volumes of books, trinkets, awards—things important to her or that she's accomplished over her career. Janice is in her mid-forties, which means she still has a good ten years with the Bureau. I fully expect her to become the director one day.

As I sit, the only sound is that of her pen on the paper, scratching, and I find myself wishing she had the radio on or even a fan. *Something.*

She finishes up, folding the letter and placing it in a standard envelope. "Letter for my niece," she says. "She needs a reference for her college application."

"Oh," I say. I didn't realize she had a niece. "Where did she apply?"

"Stanford," Janice says, dropping the letter in her "outgoing mail" box beside her desk. "How did your medical exam go?"

"Perfectly fine," I say. "Dr. Perrin cleared me for full duty."

She arches an eyebrow. "No restrictions?"

I purse my lips. Lying to Janice is like taking your life into your hands. "Light duty for the next two weeks. She doesn't want me training until everything fully heals."

Janice nods. "And the nose?"

I feel the splint attached to my face; I'd forgotten it was there, honestly. "Fine. Should be off in less than a week."

She stares at me a few minutes longer, to the point where my leg starts bouncing again, just like in Dr. Frost's office. "Was there some reason you wanted to see me?" I finally ask.

"Foley," she says, then looks away. It's a strange move from her—usually she's so confident, so unflappable. "I may have made an error recommending her for this operation."

"*You* recommended Zara for the job?"

"I did. She's had an impressive track record so far. Promoting her to field agent was one of the smartest moves we could have made." But I can see the regret in her eyes. I've never seen that from Janice before. Not like this.

"Whatever happened to her, she didn't screw up, trust me." I know Zara's capabilities. She's not that sloppy. Something else must have happened.

"She hasn't been undercover before," Janice says. "Perhaps…"

"Maybe not, but I've seen her undercover," I say. "When we were up in Vermont, chasing down all those men who were getting killed towns apart. She had one hell of a poker face, never broke character. I was the one who messed up. Trust me, she's got one of the coolest heads in the Bureau. Whatever happened wasn't because she made a mistake."

Janice takes a deep breath, then turns and looks out her window. "I've always felt somewhat…responsible for the two of you. Especially after what happened with the kidnapping ring. Keeping you on duty was an error in judgment on my part. I should have given you more time. It's been almost a year now, hasn't it?"

It's as if someone has poured cold water down my back. A year. The one-year anniversary of Matt's death is in a few days. I'd almost forgotten. "Y-yes, in a few days."

"Ever since then I've tried to keep a close eye on you and Foley. I feel like I owe it…to the both of you."

"I didn't know that," I say.

She turns back to face me. "You weren't supposed to. As agents-in-charge we're not supposed to have favorites. But sometimes it's hard not to."

I think back to all those times when Janice paired the two of us together. At the time I thought it was just because we worked well together, now I see it was something more. She was watching out for us, because she knew we'd never work as hard with another partner as we would with each other. And that keeping us apart could potentially lead to distractions.

"I'm *going* to find her," I say.

She leans forward. "Emily, you need to be very careful here." I'm frozen to my seat. I don't recall her ever using my first name, unless I was being dressed down, in which case it would come along with my middle and last name as well. But this is something different. More…intimate. "From what we know Simon Magus is a *very* dangerous individual. Those two deaths Wallace mentioned? The men were executed, point-blank. The coroner determined they had been knocked out, probably never even saw it coming. Magus could have left them there and no one would have been the wiser. But he decided not to take any chances. If he's discovered who Zara really is…"

She trails off, not needing to finish the sentence. I get the implication. Odds are she's already dead. But I'm not going to stop until I find out for sure. If there's even a one in a ten-thousand chance that she's alive, I'm not about to leave her out there.

"I will do whatever it takes, I swear it."

She appraises me for a moment, then leans back in her chair. "Then go do what you have to do. And don't worry about Wallace. He's not as bad as you think."

I give her an appreciative nod and head back for the door.

"And, Slate," she says as I turn the handle. I glance back. "When you find the bastard…kick his ass for me."

I can't help but grin all the way back down to my office.

Chapter Four

"HEY," I say, weaving my way back into my office and finding Liam, Agent Kane and Agent Sandel have set up shop in one of the adjacent offices. Kane already has the photo of who we believe to be Magus followers up on a pinboard, along with print-outs of what look like the manifesto we saw earlier.

"Hey," Liam says, looking up. "Everything okay?"

I nod. "She just wanted an update on my progress." I pull him to the side. "Has anyone told Zara's boyfriend what's going on?"

He glances back at Sandel and Kane, both of whom are involved with their work. "Raoul? I don't think so. No one has mentioned it to me. What does he do again?"

"I can't remember, Architect maybe?" We've only met Raoul a couple of times, and the only times he hasn't been standoffish with us is when he's drunk. But he seems to adore Zara, so I haven't said anything. "But he must know something's going on, right? She's been gone for weeks now."

Liam shrugs. "Maybe she told him she had a work thing and wouldn't be back for a while. He's an odd guy, he may not think anything about it."

He's probably right. And we don't need to go making

more waves where they don't exist. The last thing I want to do is raise Raoul's suspicions about where Zara might be. Though I am surprised he hasn't tried to call me to ask what's going on.

"Okay, you guys have a head start, get me up to speed," I say before throwing Liam a little wink to make sure he knows I haven't forgotten about what he said earlier.

Agent Kane swivels in her chair. On the screen behind her I see the manifesto again. I have a feeling I'm going to be reading a lot of that over the next few days. Kane is on the smaller side, about as tall as Zara, but she comes across as much more shy. On the few occasions we've interacted outside of work, I've noticed she tends to keep to herself. But when she's in work mode, she's as good as they come. I can't forget how helpful she was in sussing out Brodie Tyler down in Fernview. "Here's what we have," she says before Agent Sandel can say anything. "We suspect this Simon Magus person began collecting followers about a year to a year and a half ago. But he didn't begin making his presence known until much more recently. Apparently he used that time to not only recruit, but also build up his funds."

"Funds?" I ask.

"We believe he's not only completely funding his operation but providing for the needs of his followers as well," Agent Sandel says. His pronounced chin is unwavering, and those deep-set brown eyes of his act as a mask to what he's really feeling. He's one of the few people I have a hard time reading. "Before they disappeared, Agents Foley and Crowne independently verified that food, water, and basic needs were all being provided to the followers of the group, so they didn't need to leave in order to get what they needed."

"They couldn't leave?" I ask.

"They could, but were encouraged not to," Sandel replies. "Still, you can't expect to control the actions of thirty or forty people. Foley regularly reported members would come and go when nothing big was going on. Of course, every time they came back, they were stripped of all personal devices and effects."

"Nothing big…like the Lockheed hit," I say.

Kane nods. "Exactly."

Mercifully, they have set up a desk for me in here. I take a seat, finding I'm a little more tired than usual. "How many of these operations did they have?" I ask.

"This was the first. We believe the rest Foley reported on were just training ops," Kane replies. "In preparation for what's coming."

"Which is?"

"No one knows," Liam says, taking a seat at his own desk. "Foley and Crowne could only provide so much intel because their access was restricted. But she did report that after the night of the hit on Lockheed, she would have complete access to everything." He glances down, reading from the same file folder I saw Wallace with earlier. "I guess it was some kind of loyalty test."

I rub my hands together for a moment. "Do we know the identities of any of the rest of Magus's followers?"

"Nothing concrete," Kane says, turning back to her computer. "I'm running ID's on the image we have, along with brief descriptions from our agents, but that won't do us a lot of good without their actual names. I've started scouring the dark web to see if I can find anything else on Simon Magus or the Simonites."

"That has to be the worst name I've ever heard of," I say, blowing out a long breath. "I bet Zara got a kick out of that." While the rest of them have had some time to digest all this information, I need to catch up. "Can you send me over everything you have so far? Including that damn manifesto?"

"It's already on your computer," Sandel gives me a pointed look.

"Great, we may want to take another look at the site they

abandoned. You never know, they might have left something behind the strike team missed."

"Already in the pipeline," Sandel replies, though this time there's a bit more edge in his voice.

I grit my teeth. "Sorry, Agent. I'm so used to—"

"—to being the case agent, I know."

"I didn't mean to step on your toes." I shoot Liam a look, he just gives me a quick smile.

"I know, it's all right," he replies. "You've been through a lot in the past few weeks. Try to take your time with it. We won't do our people any good by rushing into things."

"What time are we supposed to meet with the ATF?" Liam asks.

Kane checks her watch. "Wallace said they'd be here within the hour."

"Then I think it's best we're all caught up *before* they arrive," Sandel replies. That's about as clear of a directive as I think I'm going to get. Head down, shut up and figure out how to find these people before they start blowing things up.

No problem.

IT'S ALMOST ONE BY THE TIME I FINALLY EXTRICATE MYSELF from all the data Zara, Crowne, and everyone else has already compiled about Simon Magus and his followers. I've completely skipped lunch, but sometimes that's how rabbit holes go. And this one is *deep*. Magus strikes me as one of those falsely humble types, as in he'll reluctantly take up the mantle of leadership without telling you he's the one who killed everyone else who was in the line of succession before him. His *manifesto*, whether written by him or his followers in response to what they've learned from him is something else. Full of rallying cries against the modern world, talking about how the evils of capitalism are destroying life as we know it, how corporate greed and insider deals have eroded away the fabric of all developed nations.

I have to admit, not all of it sounds completely irrational, but then Magus dials it up to eleven. Talking about how we as a society need to turn the clock back a couple thousand years, stop relying on medicine and electricity and all the conveniences of modern life. He's especially adamant about the concept of money, which I believe has something to do with his pseudonym. I've done a little research. In the Bible, Simon Magus attempted to profit off the church, to turn the concept of spirituality into something that could be bought and sold. From what I can tell, *this* Simon is looking to do the opposite. He wants to remove money from all aspects of human existence. He believes it has only led to the corruption of our species.

And while a part of me can see how a philosophy like this could have evolved and formed over years and years of anger and fury, I'm worried just what he has in mind for accomplishing his goals. With the explosives he stole from Lockheed, he's got enough to level entire city blocks if he wants.

"Ugh," I say, leaning back in my chair and rubbing my eyes. "This stuff is so dense. It's like wading through molasses."

"This your first religious nut, Agent?" Sandel asks, not looking up from his own station.

"It's my first one that's still out in the world. I interviewed a few members of *The Arrow of Guiding Light*. Fun bunch."

Kane lets out a low whistle. "Oh, yeah. I've heard of them. What was the leader's name? Big boy or something?"

"*Papa*," I say, recalling sitting down across from the man. "But he wasn't like this. *The Arrow* was all about the purity of people, not society as a whole. I don't think they ever thought this big."

"Magus certainly does have some big ideas," Kane says. "Fortunately, I've been able to narrow my search using excerpts from the manifesto. I'm trying to find out how these people communicate with each other. I think if we can do that, we can find one of them."

"And then they can lead us to Magus," Sandel adds.

It's a good plan—at least it's the direction I would have taken had I been lead agent, which makes me feel a little better. I still haven't fully committed to trusting Sandel and Kane yet, but I'm close. I also have to admit that I may not be able to find Zara without their help.

Wallace appears at the door to our "command center", knocking once on the door before sticking his head in. "Look alive. ATF is here."

We all exchange looks. Having been in this job as long as I have, I know how well inter-agency operations tend to go. Typically, everyone is trying to out-dick each other; either that or they're afraid the other side is going to take the case away from them and take all the glory for themselves. It's all just a bunch of posturing by man-children in my experience, which is why I'm really hoping our ATF liaison is a woman.

We file out and head to the conference room, coming face to face with three men in dark gray suits.

"*Shit*," I say under my breath. Wallace shoots me as look as I realize probably half the people in the room heard me. The lead agent, a stocky guy with a goatee and a crew cut eyes us, his gaze landing on me and staying there for a few seconds longer than everyone else.

"This is Special Agent Cohen, along with Agents Larson and Escobar," Wallace says, indicating the three men resembling gray statutes. "Gentlemen, this is Lead Agent Sandel." Sandel steps forward and takes Cohen's hand and I can see both men straining to make it the hardest handshake either of them has ever endured. "And these are Special Agents Kane, Coll and Slate."

The tension in the air is practically crackling as no one

says anything. We just stare at the ATF agents, and they stare right back.

Wallace turns to Agent Cohen. "Thanks for coming in so quickly. I think we all want the same thing here, don't we? A quick resolution without any further loss of life."

Cohen nods without saying anything else.

"Well, I'll leave you to it," Wallace adds before shooting Sandel a final look and leaving. We stand there in silence for a moment. I hate how Sandel is drawing this out. If I were the one in charge all of this posturing would be over already, but it seems like we're going to have to endure it regardless.

Finally, Kane elbows Sandel in the side and he winces. "We might as well begin. How much do you know so far?"

"Just that the FBI allowed a dangerous terrorist to escape with over sixty pounds of high-grade explosives," Cohen says.

Oh this is going to go swimmingly.

"Look, we just learned about this operation ourselves," I say, piping up. "If you want to be pissed at someone, be pissed at our bosses who made that call. We've got two agents out there whose lives are in danger, and we'd like to find them before they end up at the bottom of the Potomac."

Cohen eyes me for a minute. "Slate…did you work down in Charleston last year?"

I narrow my eyes. "I did."

He nods. "My father is good friends with Stan Farmer. I understand you made quite the impression on him."

I arch an eyebrow. "Your father?"

"He moved down to Hilton Head a few years ago when he retired, but he and Farmer still keep in touch. He was a career agent in the ATF."

"Good to know I made an impression. Farmer's a good agent." I guess I shouldn't be surprised that Cohen knows who I am; that story down in Charleston last year was a big case. Still, it's a little unnerving knowing he knows more about me than I do about him.

"Yeah, he is," Cohen finally says before turning back to Sandel. "You need to look at this from our perspective. Your operation allowed a lot of dangerous material out there in the world. And now it's our mess to clean up."

"Like Agent Slate said, it wasn't our operation. We just learned of it this morning." Another point for Elliott. But I don't expect him to side with the ATF over his own team.

Cohen eyes us all once more. "Very well. Show us what you've got and let's get started."

Chapter Five

WE SPEND the next couple of hours pooling our resources and setting up spots for Agents Cohen, Larson, and Escobar in our command room. It's getting crowded, but not so much that we all can't work around one another. Fortunately, the ATF has already started some of their own work regarding this case. They give us the details on the explosives themselves, what they could be used for and how much damage they could do. It seems Lockheed was storing some pretty potent stuff in that yard and Cohen admits the company didn't have it locked up as well as they should have. He also admits that's another rabbit hole he'd rather not go down, as it's more political than anything.

Regardless, someone at Lockheed is going to have to answer for this one way or another. The question is, how did Magus find out about the stockpile in the first place?

"I think I've got something," Nadia says, turning to look at all of us. Everyone stops talking and gives her their attention. "I've been combing through a bunch of different sites looking for anything that might be related to Magus or his particular coda." She points to her screen as Sandel gets up to see what she's found. "I think I've got a guy—goes by the username

DarkStar505. He's spouting a lot of the same rhetoric, but none of it mentions Magus specifically."

"A copycat?" Liam asks.

"Maybe. He could be a Simonist who has decided to create his own little sect," she says. "It looks like he's talking to anyone who is willing to listen."

"Do you know who he really is?" I ask.

She gives me a sly smile. "C'mon Agent Slate, I know we haven't been working together very long, but give me a little credit." She taps a few keys, and the image of a man comes up, which she then transfers to the projector, throwing his image up on the wall. "Leo Bolton." The man is unshaven, his dark blonde hair wild and unruly, like it hasn't been washed in weeks. He's also wearing filthy clothes and his lips are cracked and dry.

"Homeless?" I ask.

"When this mug shot was taken, yes," she replies. "He's been in the system for about a decade for minor offenses, shoplifting, loitering, a B&E, but stopped showing up about eight months ago. Before that he had been a regular, picked up at least once every month or so."

"Are you thinking he fell in with Magus?" Sandel asks.

"He fits the type," Cohen says, crossing his arms. "At least if what you've told us about this Magus guy is accurate."

"His online presence is also relatively new," Kane replies. "Which means he's sloppy and inexperienced. That's how I found him so quickly."

"Why would Magus allow one of his followers to hijack his own teachings?" Larson asks. It's the first words I've heard out of the man.

"Either he doesn't know, or Bolton could have left the Simonists," Kane replies.

I clear my throat. "Or he could be using the man as a recruiting tool, which would allow Magus to stay in the shadows. You said yourself we don't know if this manifesto is from

Magus himself or not. It seems to me the man likes pulling the strings from behind the curtain. What better way to gain new followers than to get your current followers out there to recruit for you? It's what pyramid schemes do."

That elicits a chuckle from Liam.

"Do we know where Bolton is?" Sandel asks. "I imagine he has to be easier to find than Magus."

"He never had a home address on file," Kane replies. "But from what I've gathered from his posts, he always attends 'freedom rallies' that pop up around DC and Baltimore. There's one scheduled this afternoon at four. He doesn't say he'll be there specifically, but he alludes to it. I can't imagine a better hunting ground for someone trying to recruit."

"What are you thinking?" Cohen asks. "Go in undercover, try to get recruited?"

"Our boss has specifically forbidden us from any undercover work," Sandel says. "But if we can locate Bolton, we could at least tail him once the rally is over. We could end up leading us back to Magus."

I check the time; it's already closing on two in the afternoon. "We don't have a lot of time to get out there and get set up."

Sandel nods. "We can make it. Our directive is to find these assholes as soon as possible. We don't want to miss this opportunity."

"The rest of my team is on standby," Cohen says. "I can have them mobilized in thirty minutes."

Liam turns to them. "I thought this *was* your team?"

Cohen narrows his gaze. "You think I'd just bring two other agents with me to this fuck-up? No, we're just the guys in the suits. The rest of my team is back at ATF HQ, waiting on my orders."

"Good," Sandel says, though I know this has to be news to him as well. "Get them over to the rally asap. I'll coordinate with local PD Coll, you're with me. If we leave now, we can get over there in time."

I clear my throat, as if to remind him I'm still here. But Sandel doesn't seem fazed. He never does—I've never seen him anything more than slightly uncomfortable, which was how he looked at my birthday party. Of course, had I been invited to the birthday party of a fellow agent I didn't know very well I would have been uncomfortable too. "Slate, you and Kane monitor the situation from here. You'll help coordinate, keep our teams working together."

Liam shoots me a sheepish look. He knows I want to be out in the field, but Sandel isn't about to send me out there after Wallace made such a big deal about my condition. Not to mention I still have this big white thing on my nose and that doesn't exactly blend into a crowd very well. "Understood."

"Very well," Sandel says as everyone else but me gets up. "Let's get to it."

"HOW WELL DO YOU KNOW AGENT SANDEL?" I ASK NADIA AS we sit in our command center, watching the monitors. Cohen's team is marked by small red dots on our situation map, while Liam and Sandel are marked in blue. We have a high-altitude drone circling above the rally, far enough up that most people won't even notice.

Kane looks over, then back to the monitors. "We've worked together for a year or so now. You know how it is. Work spouse."

I glance at her finger even though I know I won't find a ring there. But I look for the outline of one anyway. "Are you married in real life?"

"Nah, never had the time for it. The job…the hours…you know. You?"

"I…was," I say. "It ended almost a year ago."

"I'm sorry to hear that." She sounds sincere. The more time I spend around Agent Nadia Kane, the more I see what Zara was talking about.

"Thanks. The reason I ask is because I want to know if Sandel doesn't think we can handle ourselves out there. I mean, I know I haven't been cleared for full active duty yet, but—"

"Nah, Elliott's not like that," she says before I can finish. "He knows I can do a much better job here than I can out there. He's more of a 'get his hands dirty' kind of agent whereas I like to sit back and take a more global view." She smiles.

"Okay." I didn't want to say anything, I just happen to find it convenient the only two women on the team have been left behind while all the boys are out trying to find our perp. "Thank you, by the way. Not only for your help with my last case, but also for not opposing me working on this case."

"Wouldn't have it any other way," she says. "Foley is a unique individual, and I know how important she is to you. I honestly believe you are the best person to help find her."

"And these explosives," I say. "I just can't believe they thought allowing terrorists access to the explosives in the first place was a good idea. Why didn't they come in and switch out the stockpile with replicas?"

"You should know better than to question the motives off the all-mighty-bureau," she says, though there's some disdain in her voice. "It doesn't always make the right choice. I'm not sure they took the Simonists as seriously as they should have before the operation. Otherwise we would have been waiting for them there, ready to take them all down."

"Seems like that's becoming rarer and rarer these days." And now we have an unholy mess to clean up. We watch as the sets of dots converge on the rally which is happening on the lawn of the Mall, between the Washington Monument and the Capitol building. It's not a huge rally—there's probably less than a hundred and fifty people in attendance, and it's not the only one happening today. There's another one a few hundred feet away. It seems like there's a rally almost every day now. Back when I was young and we'd come up to DC for field trips, I never remember seeing rallies like this. But then again maybe I wasn't paying attention back then.

"Looks like they're moving into position." Kane taps her earpiece. "Come in?"

"We hear you," Sandel replies. "Cohen?"

"Here, my team is on standby," Cohen replies.

"Cohen, position each of your men on the outskirts of the rally. In the event he decides to leave, we want to make sure we catch him," Kane says.

"Ten-four," Cohen replies and relays a series of orders to his men. The dots on the satellite map move toward the edges of the group of people, but not making a formation. They're keeping their presence somewhat random, which is good. The last thing the attendees of the rally need to see is a bunch of military-looking guys touching their ears.

"Searching now," Sandel replies. "Anything on your end, Coll?" Kane and I watch as the two blue dots make their way through the crowd. I can hear a person yelling through a megaphone through Liam's earpiece, but it's still muffled.

"Don't see him yet—you'd think he'd stand out. Most of these people are at least wearing clean clothes."

"Don't forget, he may have changed his appearance since his last mug shot," I relay to the group. "A hot meal and a couple of showers will do wonders for a person."

"Good point, everyone keep a sharp eye," Sandel says.

I lean back, watching them move through the crowd, inspecting everything. Then I hear it: a booming voice, like someone else has taken the megaphone.

"*Are you sick and tired of the rich only getting richer?*" It's meant as a rallying cry, but because it comes out of nowhere with no build up, there isn't a lot of response to it. But then the owner of the voice yells it again and this time a din of yells responds.

"*Are you sick of your life being controlled by the few at the top?*" This time an even louder response comes back.

"*No generational wealth! No nepotism! No quid pro quo!*" This really gets the crowd fired up and they're all yelling and screaming in the affirmative with the man.

"I think we may have something here," Sandel says, though I'm not sure if he's talking about the speaker or someone else.

"You have eyes on someone?" I ask.

"I think it's him," Liam says. "The guy with the megaphone."

"He doesn't even look like the same guy," one of Cohen's guys replies, though I'm not sure which one. Might have been Larson.

"Look at his eyes, I'm gonna get a picture." A second later my phone buzzes with the image Liam just took of the man. He's standing at the front of the crowd, and Cohen's guy was right—he looks nothing like the mugshot of Leo Bolton we saw earlier.

"Let me see that," Kane says, and I hand her my phone. She zooms in on his eyes, then pulls up the picture of Bolton. She holds them side by side and when she does, it's obvious they are the same man. The new one might have cut his hair, gotten nice, new clothes, and shaved his beard, but it's still him.

"Bolton confirmed," I say. "He's our man."

"Moving in," one of Cohen's men says.

"No!" Me, Kane, and Cohen all say at the same time.

"*Shit,*" Sandel adds.

"What's happening?" I ask but I can already see on the satellite view some of the crowd beginning to disperse.

"He's running!" Sandel says. "Agents in pursuit, Coll, try to flank him on the left!" The crowd is a mess of bodies now, people going in every direction. Liam and Sandel are heading south, toward Jefferson Drive, with two of Cohen's men in pursuit. The rest of Cohen's guys are still in the crowd, dispersing in all different directions.

"Sutton, Terrell, he's headed for the metro! Get your asses over here!" Cohen yells. Liam and Sandel have some distance on him, but without Bolton marked on my map I'm not sure which one of the men they're pursuing is him.

"You have to cut him off before he gets on the train," I yell.

"Contact the Transit Authority," Sandel yells. "Get them to stop any trains from leaving the station."

"On it," Kane says, pulling up information on another one of her computers before dialing the number on her phone. "This is Special Agent Nadia Kane with the FBI. I need you to shut down any trains in the Smithsonian station. This is a national emergency."

"Shit, he's *fast*," Liam says and both he and Sandel disappear into the metro station entrance, with Cohen's men not far behind.

"I've relayed the situation to the transit authority," Kane says. "But it's going to take them a minute to get in contact with the drivers."

Static comes over the comm as Cohen and his men descend into the station as well. Without a line-of-sight signal, we don't get much other than bits of static as the men continue to pursue Bolton. Unfortunately, Nadia and I have no choice but to sit there, waiting for something to happen. I've never been in this position before; I'm always the one on the ground, always the one in pursuit. This sitting and watching computer screens is the worst kind of torture I can imagine.

"I can't believe you and Zara used to do this all the time in Intelligence," I mutter.

"We never had the chance to work together," Kane replies.

"But yeah, this is kinda what you do. Wait and see what happens."

"Cohen's man jumped—he spooked Bolton," I say.

"Sounds like it. Not much we can do about it now, though," she replies. "Except hope Elliott and Liam caught up to him in time."

It takes an excruciating six more minutes before Liam and Sandel emerge from the tube station again. It's hard to see from this distance, but it doesn't look like they have anyone in custody.

"It's over," Liam says, out of breath over the comm. "We lost him."

Chapter Six

By the time I pull into the parking lot of my complex, it's almost eight p.m. Liam sits beside me in the passenger seat, looking worn out from the day. Both of us are exhausted, but I wasn't about to send him to his place alone tonight. Not after what happened this morning.

I open the door to my apartment and am almost run over by Timber, his tail wagging so hard it sounds like someone is knocking on the doorframe from where it keeps slapping it. In my kitchen sits Tess, playing on her phone. When she sees us, she gets up and scoots the chair back in under the table.

Once I manage to get Timber off me and stop giggling from being licked so much, I reach into my wallet and pull out a fifty, handing it to her. "Thank you, I really appreciate the overtime tonight."

"No problem," she says. "He's already had dinner, so don't let him tell you otherwise." She grins and bends down to rub his head a few times, but he's still slamming his body up against me. "Anytime you need me to stay late, I'm available."

"Thanks again," I tell her as she grabs her keys and heads out. She gives Liam a wide grin before leaving, though she doesn't say anything to him.

"I think she likes you," I laugh once he's closed the door.

"What? No, she doesn't." He seems genuinely confused by my comment.

"Your obliviousness is adorable."

"If you say so." His tone is somewhat joking, but I can also tell I've insulted him.

"Hey," I say, pulling him close to me as he tries to pass. "It's been a long day. I was just messing with you."

He lets out a breath. "I think we're both exhausted. I was going to try and fix something for dinner, but honestly I'm too tired. I think it's either pizza or skip dinner and just wait for breakfast."

"Pizza works for me." I plant a small kiss on his lips, careful to turn my head so the contraption on my nose doesn't hit him before releasing him and heading into the kitchen in search of a bottle of wine I know we opened a few days ago.

"I was about ready to kill Cohen this afternoon," Liam says, taking a seat at the kitchen table as Timber comes up and nuzzles against him. He gives Timber a good pat on the side.

"I think he was about ready to kill…what was his name? Larson?"

"Yeah," Liam says. "If he hadn't been so gung-ho, we could have tailed Bolton, no problem. Now, thanks to his incompetence, we've alerted Magus that we're on to him."

I pull the wine out of the side drawer of the refrigerator. There's only about a quarter of a bottle left. "Which doesn't bode well for any of us. I'm afraid it might make him do something rash."

He pauses. "I'm worried about her too," he says.

I pour what's left of the wine into two glasses and hand him one, clinking it before downing my entire glass in one gulp.

"Is there something else bothering you?" he asks, setting his glass to the side.

"You mean other than the fact my best friend might have been murdered by a sociopath?" I ask, trying to lighten the mood, but it doesn't work. He just continues to stare at me with those hazel eyes of his, like he's looking into my soul.

I sigh. "The one-year anniversary of Matt's death is in a few days. I honestly hadn't thought anything about it until Janice brought it up this morning. I think after everything in Fernview I felt like I had moved on. Or…at least I was getting there."

"I knew it was coming up, I just didn't know when." Liam takes a sip of his wine.

I'm sure he's getting tired of hearing me talk about this. I know I'm tired of talking about it—but it still occupies a significant part of my brain. At least, it has ever since Janice brought it up. "I honestly can't believe I forgot…or maybe I just didn't want to remember. I really want to move on with my life, I don't want this to keep popping up, to keep haunting me."

Liam gets up and wraps me in a warm embrace. "Sometimes grief just doesn't work like that. Sometimes you have to go through it at your own pace. It's not something you can rush."

"I just feel like it's going to be like this forever sometimes. Like no matter where I am or what I do in life I'll always come back to that moment where I found him in the kitchen. I wish I could just erase it." I can feel myself beginning to tear up, but that's the last thing I want right now. I bury my head into Liam's shoulder to try to stave off any tears.

"Did I ever tell you about my grandfather?" he asks softly.

"You told me he was one tough son of a bitch."

Liam chuckles. "That he was. He was tough in his job, but he was always gentle with us kids. He'd always make sure that we were taken care of, and any time we came to visit, both my grandparents would just lavish attention on us. Of course, I didn't get to see much of him because he died when I was eight. I remember thinking that I would never stop feeling horrible. It was like someone had carved out part of my life and all I could think about was how that piece was now missing." He's quiet for a moment and I can't help but wonder if he's lost in memory like I am.

"Wasn't it like that with your mother?" he adds.

The question surprises me. I take a step back to look him in the eye. "My mother's death was difficult, but not the same. I think I always knew, even as a child that I would outlive my parents. I never expected to outlive my spouse. Mom's death was unexpected, yes, but it felt more…natural. That sounds weird, but it's how I think about it. Maybe if he had died from natural causes, like I first suspected, then I wouldn't be thinking about this so much. But—"

"You can't keep blaming yourself, Emily. You have to let that go. There was nothing that you could have done to save him. And if you'd been home at the same time, Camille would've killed you too." He bends down and lifts my chin with his hand placing a soft kiss on my lips. "At least, she would've tried."

That elicits a small laugh for me, and it's like the emotions come pouring out. I find myself trying to laugh and cry at the same time and not really succeeding in doing either.

"Come on," Liam says. "It's been a long day." He sits me down at the kitchen table and hands me the rest of his glass of wine. "Give yourself the time to process it. I know the anniversary will be a big deal, but we'll go through it together, okay?"

I hate feeling like this, like a lost little child. But it's nice to have someone near who I know will take care of me if I need it. "Yeah, okay."

"Great. Let me get that pizza ordered."

Even as he's tapping away on his phone I find myself staring off into the distance. "What if it happens again?"

Liam looks up. "What if what happened to Matt happens to Zara?"

He puts his phone on the counter and crouches down in front of me. "We're not gonna let that happen."

"But what if it's already too late? What if Magus has already killed her?"

"Give Zara a little credit, she's tougher than that."

He's right, she *is* tougher than that. All we can do is hope she can hold out until we find her. It's always possible that she went into hiding and that's why she hasn't made contact. I just wish I could've been undercover with her. At least then I would know.

Liam places a hand on my cheek then gets up and continues ordering the food. Timber comes over and plops himself right on the floor at my feet. I reached down and give his head a good scratch and he looks up at me with those big brown eyes of his. "Think good thoughts for Zara, okay buddy?" At the mention of Zara's name, Timber's ears perk up. It's almost enough to cause an overflow of emotions, but somehow I keep it together. Instead I just keep scratching him behind the ear as Liam rummages around the kitchen.

"Want something stronger?" he asks, nodding to his now-empty glass.

"Just a water," I say. I'm not going to be able to relax until I know she's okay. And I want to stay sharp, in case something develops.

I can't afford not to be ready.

Chapter Seven

IT FEELS like she's been locked up for days. But Zara knows that's probably not the case. She's studied countless cases of prisoner testimony, especially prisoners that have been used in hostage negotiations or have been kidnapped. Almost universally they all perceived time moving much faster than it actually was. Minutes would feel like hours, hours would feel like days. It had something to do with how the brain was in such a state of hyperactivity that it tried to take in all the details of a given situation and thus slowed down the perceived passage of time. Often times, when asked to look back, victims could recall their situations in vivid detail, as well as their captors, if they ever saw them. It had been a fascinating read, though Zara had hoped she never would have been among those who experienced it.

The fact is she has screwed up her first undercover assignment—well, second if she counts that little stint up in Vermont, but that had just been her and Emily doing what they did best: following the trail of evidence. This was an actual assignment, coming down from Janice as Zara understood it. Which meant she had taken it as seriously as a car wreck. And until now, she thought she had succeeded. She'd ingratiated herself to the damn Simonists, found a way in, made friends, gotten them to trust her, and then it had all fallen apart. How? What had she missed? Was it really because she was the only woman, and they just hadn't trusted her? There was no way they could have traced her gathering the evidence the Bureau would need to put them all away; she'd been more than careful in that area. And even though some of these Simonists were good, none of them were *that* good.

Something else must have happened. That was always a possibility with undercover work—things could go wrong for no reason. It didn't help matters that Simon was a paranoid psychopath. She's been extra cautious around him, making sure he's never had a reason to suspect her.

She rubs the back of her head where he'd hit her with the butt of the gun. There hadn't been any blood, thankfully, but it was still very tender, and she feels a lump forming. She needs some ice. And some water. But instead, she'd been thrown into the back of a van and driven for at least an hour before being black-bagged, removed and tossed into this small room. Whereas before she knew she was still just outside of DC, now there was no telling where she was. She could be halfway to Pittsburg, or halfway to Chicago for all she knew.

That was the worst part. She'd lost any edge she'd had about where Simon and his followers had holed up. Had he detained her back at his base of operations, she probably could have figured a way out, having spent the week going over every inch of that place, looking for vulnerabilities she could report back to Wallace.

But this new place...she has no idea. She doesn't even know if Simon has left anyone here with her, or if he's just left her here to rot away from lack of food and water. Why hadn't he just killed her on the spot? Magus isn't the kind of man who leaves loose ends—which means he wants to keep her alive for some reason. And while he's cruel and calculating, she hasn't seen him as the kind of man who likes to draw things out. He prefers to get it over with and move on. He's "practical" in that way.

She's had plenty of time to study her new surroundings, however. The walls are barely ten by ten, cinder block on all sides, and there's nothing but a bucket in the corner and a light above her, dangling from a wire. Plus one ominous chain that hangs along one of the walls from the ceiling. The door to the room is reinforced steel and the concrete floor is covered in dirt and smells vaguely of peat.

It's taken her a while to stand up without feeling dizzy, but after testing it a few times, she's found she's able to walk around the small room with only a small headache throbbing in the back of her head. They've taken everything from her— fake ID, belt and even the data drive she'd stashed in her bra —which had happened some time on the drive when she'd been in and out of consciousness. She bet it had been that dickhead Omar—he was always looking for an excuse.

If only she'd been able to anticipate what set Simon off. It didn't look like anyone else had suspected her—and the operation had gone exactly to plan, just like Wallace ordered. But now she was here, instead of back at the Bureau helping to coordinate the strike that would capture and arrest Simon and his men. They must be losing their minds over there. Everything had hinged on her ability to get out, get the evidence to the Bureau, and finally move in on Magus and the rest. She'd been looking forward to the assignment being over—to being able to tell Emily all about it once she got back from Fernview.

How many times had she considered leaving her a message, even though it would be breaking protocol? She knew Emily had probably been worried—but hopefully Wallace had filled her in on what was going on. But now that Zara hadn't checked in—she worried about what her friend might be thinking or feeling. Not knowing what's going on—it can be hell to a person. God knows she's been on the receiving end of that situation more than once. She hopes she and Emily will have a laugh about it…if she ever sees her again.

Just as she's about to get up and pace the room some more, in order to keep her blood flowing, the bolt on the door shoots, and it opens inward to reveal one of the Simonists— though it's one Zara has only seen a few times before. *At least it's not Omar*, she thinks.

"Here to deliver my last meal?"

"Get up, come with me," the man says. He carries a semi-automatic weapon wrapped around his shoulder with his hand on the trigger, though it's pointed at the ground.

"I need some water," she replies.

He points the weapon at her in response. *Well, that's more like it.*

With a grunt, Zara gets up, rubbing the back of her head. "You wouldn't happen to have an ice pack would you? Or maybe just some frozen peas?"

The man grabs her by the shoulder, yanking her out of the room and pushing her forward, into the hall ahead of him. No doubt his weapon is trained on her back.

"Okay, jeez, all you had to say was no." She walks forward, taking in the musty air. While it's good to be out of that room, the hallway isn't much better. They seem to be in an underground bunker of some kind, based on how the lights are strung along the cinder block hallway. They pass a few other metal doors in the cinder block wall, but he doesn't stop her at any of them. Instead, he urges her on, until they reach a metal staircase that goes up one floor. Funny, she doesn't remember being taken down this staircase when they brought her here, but then again, she still wasn't fully conscious then either.

The man forces her around the corner once they get to the top of the stairs, where the room itself opens up into a larger space. It looks like a larger version of the room Zara had been in downstairs, except this one is full of people, equipment, and supplies. Along all the walls hang maps of different cities, though she only gets a cursory look before the muzzle of the gun is pressed into her back and she's moving forward again. Folding tables take up a lot of the space, and cinder block columns hold the ceiling up in a grid pattern. Camo military netting hangs in some areas, covering some of the supply boxes while more of it hangs from the ceilings. In the far corner the cinder block frames out two large garage doors, both with the sprinter vans parked in front of them. The vans are in the middle of receiving a new paint job from some of the Simonists.

Zara catches the eyes of some of the people she knows, people who were working on the operation or who have been part of the group for a while. No new faces among them. Though she does see Omar, whose face is practically curled into a snarl as she passes. It looks like Simon has moved everyone and everything to this location. Which means any hope for a rescue is out the window. The Bureau had Simon's previous location and part of her had hoped they would close in on him there, and eventually force him to tell them where they moved her. But that had been back when she'd assumed she had been here alone.

"Looks like the gang's all here," she mutters.

"Quiet," the man behind her orders. She can't quite remember his name. Miles? Micah? She'd ask but fears she'd get nothing but a bullet for her trouble.

At the far corner of the room, opposite the garage doors and the sprinter vans, an office sits, sectioned off from floor to ceiling. It's made of the same cinder block, but has a green glass window, though Zara can only see light coming from inside the room; the glass is too foggy to see through. There's also another one of those metal doors leading into the room.

A wave of dizziness passes through her, and she almost stumbles but manages to stay on her feet. Any sudden move and Rambo back there might accidentally shoot her before he's supposed to.

Without direction, she opens the door to the office, since that's obviously where they're going. As soon as the door is open she's hit with the smell of something rotting, which almost causes her to gag.

"You'll get used to it." Looking up, she sees Simon at the far end of the room, behind another folding table which he's turned into a makeshift desk. Behind him are the same bank of computers and monitors she was using to watch the Lockheed job. All of them are hooked up and running, and what camera angles appear she can already tell are of the bunker they're all occupying.

A few folding chairs are set up in the room as well, and there's something close to Magus's desk that's been covered with a blue tarp. Beside the tarp stands another one of the Simonites…Leo, she thinks his name is.

"Thanks Mitch," Simon says. "Did she give you any trouble?"

"Other than a smart mouth, no," the man behind me replies.

"Would you mind leaving us for a minute?" Simon asks. He's noticeably calmer than the last time she saw him, when he was leaning over her with a gun in his hand.

"I'll be right outside if you need me." He turns and closes the door behind him. It doesn't escape Zara's notice that both Simon and Leo are wearing sidearms under their jackets.

There are a few ways she can play this. Obviously, Simon already knows her real name. But he might not know exactly *who* she is. Her best bet is to keep it that way, until she figures out *how much* he knows.

"So, here we are," Simon says, pinning his gaze on her.

"Yup."

"Anything you want to tell me?"

"Anything you want to tell *me?*" she shoots back. "One

minute we're finishing the op. The next you've hit me over the head."

"Because you weren't honest," Simon replies.

"Yeah? Is Simon Magus *your* real name? I don't think having a pseudonym is a crime."

Simon shoots a glance at Leo, who grabs the blue tarp and pulls it back. Zara does her best not to react, but she can't help it. In one of the folding chairs sits Agent Crowne, his face bloated and purple, with a single gunshot wound to the center of his forehead. He's shirtless, and she can tell he's been tortured by all the cuts, bruises, and marks on his body.

"I would have afforded you a little anonymity," Simon says, pushing himself off his makeshift desk and walking over to Crowne's body, circling it. "Who am I to judge, after all. But what I can't forgive, is the subterfuge. Care to tell me why you made a recording of our little operation the other night?" He holds up the data drive.

Shit. Obviously they got her real name from Crowne. But what else did he tell them before they killed him? Did he give her up completely? She decides not to answer, despite the danger.

Simon regards her a moment, then returns to his desk, pacing back and forth between it and the body. "See, I always thought it was odd someone like you had as many skills as you did. At first I was reluctant to look a gift horse in the mouth. It was only when things began going *too* well that I suspected I might have unknowingly opened myself up to Trojans."

He clasps his hands behind his back as he walks. "So I asked myself, who are my newest recruits? The ones whose background checks came back just a little too perfect. Run-ins with the law, but nothing serious. Skilled enough to get the job done, but hadn't been snatched up by anyone else yet. People who were professionals—just a little too good at the jobs I gave them." He turns to Leo. "Do you know what Leo here was doing before I found him?" He puts an arm around the man, who stiffens at Simon's touch. "He was living in the alleyways, eating out of garbage cans. Now look at him." He slaps a hand on Leo's chest, right over his heart. "It's a miracle."

"So you're saying you suspect me because I'm too good at my job?" Zara asks.

"Let's see," Simon says, approaching her. "You don't have any drug addictions, no other substance abuse problems—" He grabs her hand unexpectedly, inspecting her fingers. "Your nails are clean of dirt and grime, trimmed well." He runs his hand through her hair. "Unnatural hair colors aren't that uncommon, but you take *really* good care of your hair."

Zara pulls away from him. "What's your point?"

"Despite all the evidence to the contrary, you're no hacker for hire. And you didn't just fall in with our organization because you believed in our cause, or even because you needed the money. You're a plant."

She barks out a laugh, though even her own ears it sounds hollow.

Simon returns to his desk, then turns to face them again. "Tell her what happened today, Leo."

"Almost got pinched at the rally," he says. "Feds were waiting."

"The feds were waiting," Simon repeats, enunciating each word slowly enough that it makes Zara's skin crawl. "And what did our friend here tell us before he died?" He motions to Crowne's lifeless body.

"Something to the effect of we wouldn't get away with this," Leo replies.

"So let's recap," Simon says, still calm as a cucumber. "We get a couple of new recruits who seem too good at their jobs and whose histories seem…let's face it, manufactured, at best. We pull off the Lockheed job without a hitch, which, as you know Leo, nothing ever goes to plan. And finally, the feds start breathing down our neck as soon as we take Chloe—not her real name by the way—out of the picture. You know what that tells me?"

"We got spies," Leo replies.

Zara tries to keep breathing normally, but her eyes keep flicking to the weapons the men are still wearing.

"*Spies,*" Simon whispers again. "You know, I blame myself. This really is *my* fault. Had I been a little more careful, I think we could have avoided this. But then again, sometimes risks are necessary in this business." He turns to Zara, his face going still. "And you, little lady, were one hell of a risk." He returns back to Crowne again. "I have to give your partner here credit, though. He put up a good fight. And he wouldn't tell us exactly who you were with. I think it was in his final hours when he finally gave us your real names. But if I had to bet, I'd be willing to go with FBI." He turns to Leo, one arm outstretched. "I mean, it makes sense, right? The homegrown terrorist angle and everything."

"Makes sense to me," Leo replies.

Simon turns back to Zara. "And it's really hard to get anything done with the FBI on our backs. But now we have a secret weapon." He gives her a wink before heading back to his desk once more. "See, I know you're not a stupid person, Zara. You can't have made it into the FBI—trusted enough that they'd send you undercover for little ol' me. So I'm going to give you a choice: the same one I gave your buddy over there. Though, keep in mind, he'd been through the wringer, and I was hoping he'd have been a little more receptive to my offer. I don't have that kind of time, so if you refuse, I'll just shoot you right here and be done with it."

"What do you want?" Zara asks.

Simon puts his hands on his hips and looks down before catching her gaze again. "Well, simply, I want you to renounce your allegiance to the FBI and work for me instead. But you know, for real this time."

Before she can speak, he holds up a hand. "Now I know I

just threatened you with death if you refused, which would obviously prompt you to say whatever you needed to in order to keep yourself alive. Right now, you'll say just about anything to keep me for reaching for my sidearm. I could ask you to dive into a lake full of piranha and you'd do it because you'd think you had a better chance with killer fish than you would with a gun pointed at your head. So you're saying to yourself, Simon, how can you trust anyone if their only options are working for you or death? And to that I say it's all about proper motivation."

He returns to Crowne. "See, we didn't give your friend here the correct motivation. Either that or he was just stubborn. And he died for his stubbornness. It was an empty death —pointless, for him at least. He didn't help your cause, and all he ended up doing was giving us information about you. So he was pretty much a monumental failure.

"You can go that route, a meaningless death—and trust me, they'd never find your body. If you're thinking at least you'd die for your country, uh-uh. Nope, no one would ever know what happened to you. Your friends, your family would always be wondering if you were out there somewhere, perpetually in anguish over the thought of what might have happened to you. I might even sprinkle a few clues around that would hint you're still out there somewhere, just to keep that little spark of hope alive in their hearts." He comes close to her face. "Do you understand me, Zara? They would *never* know peace. *Never* have closure. It would be *torture*."

He steps away, spreading his arms wide. "Or, you can join us here and continue working for me, with the caveat that I assume you're always plotting or planning an escape or at the very least, hoping you can get word to your job or your friends or someone about what's really happening. I've gained new insight since you've arrived. And I have people who are true believers. And while they're not as good as you, they at least know enough that they can check your work and make sure you're not making secret recordings or something insipid like that." He forces a fake laugh and drops the jump drive, crushing it beneath his boot.

Zara watches him as he returns to her. Sweat runs down the side of her brow. It really does seem like she's out of options.

"So what do you say?" he asks. "Meaningless death, or jump into the piranha pit, and hope you make it out alive?"

Chapter Eight

AFTER A RESTLESS NIGHT I'm up early, making coffee before Liam is awake. Timber gets an early breakfast, which he's thrilled about, and I get to watch the sun light up the morning sky while I can practically *feel* my anxiety rise. All I can think about is where Zara might be and if she's still okay. I know I need to trust her decisions out there, but there are some things you just can't control. Sometimes shit just goes bad. I'm just hoping she's found a way to avoid most of it. But I have a bad feeling in the pit of my stomach, and I'm willing to do just about anything to make it go away.

"Morning," Liam says, plodding over to the coffee maker and waiting for it to deliver him a cup. "You didn't sleep well, did you?"

"Did I keep you awake?" I ask.

"Don't worry about it, I fall back asleep almost immediately. Comes from working all those night shifts back in Stillwater."

I don't see any need to rehash everything we talked about last night. I'd much rather just get to work and figure out how we can come back from yesterday's fuck-up. "I'm gonna grab a quick shower." I set my mug on the counter. "You've still got a spare set of clothes here, right?"

"In the guest room closet," he grins.

"Good, I want to be at the office early. See if we can't get a jump on Sandel."

"Em," he says, causing me to turn as I'm heading down the hallway. When I see his face I realize whatever it is, it's serious and I return to him.

"What's wrong?"

"It's nothing. Never mind."

I give him the glare. "No, tell me."

"I was going to…I was going to ask you something. But I realized it was…this isn't the time."

"Okay, well, now you have to tell me," I say, more than a little on edge by his tone.

"I was going to ask you to move in with me," he says, looking down. "But I was feeling impulsive, and maybe a little selfish. You've got so many other things going on that you don't need this right now."

I'm so caught off guard that I actually take a step back. Somewhere in the back of my mind I've considered that possibility a few times, it's never gone much beyond the conceptual stage because I've just had too much going on. "Recently I've realized that…life can be short sometimes, you know?" His tone is apologetic now, like he's sorry for even bringing it up.

"I'm not sure what to say," I reply, which is the honest truth. Is he asking me, or isn't he?

"You don't need to say anything. I shouldn't have even brought it up."

Still, this is a *big* decision. And now he's got me thinking about it. First a declaration of love and now this? "How about we table it for now. Circle back later?" I say, trying to keep my tone light. Last night we caught the end of a sitcom where the characters were making fun of office speak.

He picks up on it and gives me a nervous chuckle. "Yeah,

that sounds like good synergy." I laugh, genuinely this time and he wraps his arms around me. Within minutes we're back on the bed, tangled up in each other. Letting go with Liam feels safe, like I know he's not going to let me fall. And I allow myself to relax into that feeling when I'm with him. At the very least it provides a welcome distraction from everything we have to do today. But I make sure it's quick; I still want to get the jump on Sandel.

Finally, Liam flops over on the bed, heaving. "Man, if I'd known that would be your reaction maybe I should have brought it up sooner."

I get up and head for the shower. "And I'd have told you no," I call back, smiling to myself.

WHEN WE ARRIVE BACK AT THE OFFICE, THE ONLY ONE THERE is Agent Kane, who doesn't look like she's moved at all.

"Did you even go home?" I ask as Liam and I enter, both with fresh coffee and a box of bagels for the team.

She turns and her eyes go wide at seeing the box of bagels. "Oh, you're an angel," she says, going straight for the box. "I couldn't sleep. It felt like what happened yesterday was my fault."

"How could it have been your fault?" I ask, hanging my blazer on the back of my chair. "It was Cohen's guy who screwed up."

"Because we didn't ensure he'd given them proper instruction. It takes me back to what people say about the government—we really are inefficient. We need to make sure everyone is on the same page from here on out."

"Agreed," I say. "I don't guess anything happened while we were gone, did it?"

"Actually, I have made some progress," she replies, motioning for me to follow her back over to the computer.

Liam leans in and we go over everything Kane has pulled on Leo Bolton.

"This…this is a complete workup," I say, surprised. "This had to have taken what, four hours?"

"Three," she replies. "I'm quick when I'm motivated." She points to Leo's arrest history. "I think this might be something. When he was still homeless he frequented this soup kitchen a lot. There might be people there who know him personally—who might have some sort of access to him."

"He'll be on guard after yesterday," Liam says. "No way we'll be able to surprise him."

"Maybe not," she replies. "But if we can at least figure out his movements…maybe he's purchased a new home in the area recently? Or someone at least knows where he's staying now? Unfortunately, he hasn't posted any more on the sites since yesterday's…raid."

"You mean massive fuck-up." We turn to see Cohen enter the room, followed by one of his men. I catch Liam's eyes narrow. Cohen grabs the man by the arm and pushes him forward. "This is Agent Riggs. Riggs, go ahead."

The man has to be in his mid-thirties, at least. Square jaw, bulging biceps, he looks like a man who has tempered himself like a steel blade. And right now, Cohen is making him look like a third-grader. "I…wanted to apologize for my…mistake yesterday," he says. "I put the entire operation at risk."

I catch Sandel standing behind them, still outside the room. But the door is open, and he can hear everything. "It was stupid and won't happen again," Riggs says it through gritted teeth, and I'm sure it's taking a large amount of self-control to maintain his composure. In my experience, men like Riggs don't take well to being humiliated.

"We'll get him next time," I say, feeling for Riggs a bit.

Cohen nods, then turns to Riggs. "Go find Larson. Get the rest of the team squared away." Riggs leaves without another word, and without looking at Sandel as he passes him on the way out. "Did I hear you say something about a soup kitchen?"

"Agent Kane may have found a lead for us," I say as Sandel comes in, setting his own coffee down on his desk. Cohen crosses his arm, glaring at all of it. Like it was *our* fault his man screwed up.

"What lead?" Sandel asks, stepping around Cohen.

"Helping Hands," Nadia replies. "It's a kitchen Bolton used to frequent before he found the Simonists. He might still have a contact or two there."

Sandel nods. "It's worth checking out. I'll head down there."

"You mind if I tag along?" I ask. Sandel eyes me for a moment. "It's just that I've been going stir crazy lately, with my stay in the hospital and now being relegated to light duty. How much damage can I do in a soup kitchen?"

He considers it for a moment, then nods. "Very well. Nadia, good work. You and Coll keep looking for anything else that might help us track down Simon or any of his other followers."

"And what would you like me to do?" Cohen says, somewhat sullen.

"I need you and your men to start tracking that material from Lockheed. I doubt that Simon would attempt to sell any of it, but we have to cover all possibilities. He could be looking for additional funds and might only plan on using some of what he stole. We need to make sure it's not getting out there onto the open market."

Cohen nods. "Yeah, I can do that. I'll get my guys on it right away."

Sandel takes one more look around the room. "Good. Slate, you're with me."

~

I HAVEN'T HAD THE OPPORTUNITY TO SPEND MUCH TIME WITH Special Agent Elliott Sandel. But I wasn't about to pass this chance by. I wasn't lying when I told him I was going stir crazy, but I also want to get to know him a little bit better. If we're going to be working together, and my life is going to be in his hands, then I need to make sure he's the kind of agent I think he is. I hope Agent Kane is right about him, but I won't know for sure until I see it myself. Part of me still thinks that he and Agent Kane are working directly for Wallace in order to spy on me in some way, probably because I'm more paranoid than I need to be. I know that's ridiculous, and if I would ever say it out loud it would sound ridiculous, but then I remember my paranoia has served me well in the past. I probably wouldn't be alive today without it.

Sandel is quiet as we drive. I opted to take the passenger seat because I knew if I had tried to drive he would've made a big deal about it. I don't know how much longer I can deal with people driving me around all the time, but for now I don't see I have a choice. Seeing as he's obviously not going to make the first volley, I realize I have no choice but to try and be the chatty one.

"What's your read on this case?" I ask.

"What you mean?"

"I mean what's the deal with this Simon Magus guy? What do you think he's really after?"

He thinks for a minute before responding. "Recently I've stopped trying to get inside the heads of some of the people we chase. I find it a pointless exercise."

"Really? Because I find sometimes the only way to make sense of it all is to get inside their heads. To look at the world from their perspective."

"That may be, but you have to remember they don't always think logically. Sometimes they prefer chaos to order, just for the sake of chaos."

I glance over at him. "Is that what you think's happening here? He just wants to blow things up, no rhyme or reason?"

"His pattern of behavior so far indicates someone with an agenda. I don't quite know what that agenda is, I just know we need to find out before he decides to make a move."

Fair enough. I'm not surprised he thinks this way; many agents do. "How long have you been with the Bureau?"

"About four years now. I served two tours in Afghanistan before applying to Quantico." Now it makes a little bit more sense why he's so quiet all the time. I should have assumed from his behavior that he was a military man.

"Pretty rough over there?" I ask.

"I don't talk about it. It doesn't have anything to do in my current job." Wow, this guy is not giving me much to work with.

"What made you want to join the FBI?"

He gives me a sigh of frustration. "I saw how the CIA operated and I didn't like it. There are some shady individuals in that organization. I wanted to be part of something that did good in the world, something that made a positive influence."

"I can understand that. How long have you and Agent Kane been working together?"

He turns to me. "What's with the third degree, Agent Slate?"

Okay, time to lay it all out there. Better to get past it now, then have to deal with it later. "I don't know if you know this about me, but I don't trust people very easily."

"And you think I have some ulterior motive? Some nefarious goal I'm keeping close to the chest. Perhaps I'm only here to negatively impact your career prospects."

"No, I think you're going to get my friend killed if you're not careful. We can't afford to have another screw-up like we had yesterday. It might've been Cohen's men, but that was a result of bad leadership. Everyone should have been on the same page, and I need to make sure that you're going to be able to handle this."

"You don't like me very much, do you?" The man doesn't betray a hint of emotion as he says it. In some ways I feel like I'm talking to a computer.

"I don't need to like you; I just need to trust you."

"You just need to be able to follow orders," Sandal says. "As long as you can do that, we won't have a problem."

"So yesterday was just, what? A mix-up?" I can feel the heat rising in my cheeks. Does he really think that I'm just gonna sit by and follow orders like a good little soldier? That's not how I operate, and I think he already knows that.

"I will admit, yesterday happened because we rushed in too quickly. We needed more time to prepare, and mistakes were made. Next time, we won't be so quick to action."

"But being quick to action may be what we need to save our people," I protest.

"That's your problem, Slate. You're still focused on Foley. I understand, she's your friend and you don't want anything to happen to her. But we can't compromise the mission for one agent. There are too many lives at stake."

I turned to look out the passenger side window. "As long as we know where each other stands."

He doesn't respond and is quiet all the way to the soup kitchen. This little trip has told me at least one thing: Sandel doesn't like being put on the spot when he is wrong. I'll need to keep that in mind. If he's too proud to admit that he's made a mistake, he could put all of our lives in danger.

When we arrive, Sandel drives around the side of the building, off the main street. "We're here." He gets out of the car without another word, having parked us along the side of the building. I follow him at a close distance, realizing now I need a closer eye on Elliott Sandel.

The kitchen has been built into an old department store that runs along Connecticut Avenue. The windows have all been covered up so people can't gawk in from the outside and a bunch of tables and chairs have been set up in rows in the front. The kitchen itself is been set up in the back and is accessible through a couple of double doors. The place is quiet when we come in, only a few people sitting at the tables eating. A giant cross hangs on the wall to our left and below it is a banner with the words *Helping Hands of the Greater DC Area* written in a scripty font.

We make our way through the tables looking for anybody who might be in charge, until a man emerges from the kitchen dressed in sweats and jeans. He regards us for a minute then smiles approaching cautiously. "Officers? How can we help you?" I pull out my badge. "It's Special Agents actually," I say. "Are you with Helping Hands?"

He nods. "I'm Pastor Marks. Forgive me, agents. We get a fair number of cops in here, always looking for someone. You two have that look about you." He regards me for a moment. "Did you get into a fight?"

"I did," I say. I keep forgetting this damn thing is on my nose. It's probably the first thing anybody sees when they look at me. God, I can't wait until I get it off.

"Tell me who you're looking for and I'll do my best to help," Marks says.

"Leo Bolton," Sandel replies. "We know he used to be a regular here, but probably hasn't been around much lately."

The man gives us a resigned look. "I haven't seen Leo in at least six months. But I can ask around, he was a pretty popular guy when he was here. A lot of the regulars knew him. Is he in trouble?"

"We just need to ask him some questions," Sandal says. He hands the man one of his cards. "As soon as you hear something please give us a call, it's urgent."

The man takes the card, nodding. "I'll see what I can find out."

"That's all we ask." Sandel heads back out. For a moment

I'm thrown. Doesn't he want to speak to any of the other people here?

I follow him back outside to the car. "Is that it?"

"What else do you want to do, Agent Slate?" he asks, standing beside his vehicle.

"I don't know, speak to the other people there, find out if anyone knows anything maybe?"

"If any of those people had known Bolton, Pastor Marks would have pointed them out to us," he says. "There's nothing else for us here; we're wasting time."

God, I could throttle this man. "At least let me double check."

"You need to trust other people to get the job done. Your way isn't necessarily the only way."

"Because in my experience, other people suck at their jobs," I blurt out without actually meaning to.

Sandel slips on his sunglasses and gets into the car without another word, waiting for me.

"Great job, Emily. Just great," I mutter.

Chapter Nine

I GET the call in the middle of the night. It takes me a minute to wake up from the deep sleep, in which I'm dreaming I'm in an earthquake. As my eyes open and adjust to where I am, I realize it's just my phone buzzing on my bedside table.

I reach over and grab it, the bright light almost blinding me. I quickly hit the accept button. "Slate."

"It's Sandel. We just got a lead on Bolton. Pastor Marks called about fifteen minutes ago. One of the people from the soup kitchen spoke with Bolton just this evening."

I sit up in bed, shaking Liam awake. "Are you serious?"

"That's what the man said. I'm mobilizing a unit to tail Bolton."

"Wait, you have a location on him too?" I know I'm still groggy, but something about this doesn't seem right. We were just in the soup kitchen earlier today. And now Bolton shows up out of nowhere?

"We're still checking on the information. Kane is already back in the office. How soon can you and Coll get over here?"

Liam stares at me in the dark, his eyes wide. "Twenty-five minutes," I reply.

"Good, get moving. We don't want to lose this opportunity." He hangs up.

"Bolton, they found him?" Liam asks, getting out of bed and grabbing his pants.

"Guy at the soup kitchen said he just spoke to him this evening. Even gave a location. Does that seem strange to you?" Likewise, I'm already out of bed, having moved Timber over who just looks at me through a sleepy gaze and lays his head back down. It's not even one a.m. yet. I can't believe I was sleeping that soundly.

"Maybe, but then again Bolton could have been in contact with this guy from the soup kitchen all along. And now it's just coming up because you and Sandel went over there today."

"Yeah, maybe," I say, pulling on my bra, then my blouse, before grabbing my holster and slipping my arms through it as well. "Still, strikes me as convenient." I still feel like I'm only half awake. Maybe I'm overthinking this.

"Any idea of what Sandel is planning?" Liam asks, working on his shoes.

"Tail Bolton, just like we'd planned before. I'm assuming he's leaving Cohen and his men out of it this time."

"Not a bad call," Liam replies. Another fifteen minutes and we're out the door. Liam drives while I coordinate with Nadia back at HQ. She sends over all the information the informant provided to Marks, when he'd spoken with Bolton, where and what Bolton told him he'd be doing later this evening.

"I see why Sandel is so gung-ho," I say, reading over the information. "Bolton is heading to Baltimore tonight."

"Do you think that's where Magus moved his operation?" Liam asks.

"Could be. But remember how I told you Sandel made a big deal about not jumping into another situation without making the proper preparations? Doesn't this feel like we're doing exactly that?"

"Maybe they have more intel this time," Liam says.

"Maybe."

By the time we reach the office, Sandel is already at the door waiting, while Kane is back at her station, her face glued to one of the monitors.

"We have a good lead," Sandel says, motioning for us to turn around. "We think we spotted his van."

"Hang on," I say. "This is all moving a bit too fast. How did you guys find his vehicle already?"

"The informant from the soup kitchen gave us a description," Kane calls out from her station. "I ran it through the DMV and narrowed down all the potential license plates matching that vehicle description. We put out an APB with the local police on all potential matching license plates and we got a hit on three matches that are active right now."

"Still, that's—"

"Slate, we don't have time to explain to you exactly how we did everything," Sandel says. "You're going to have to trust me. Now come on, DC police are already tracking his vehicle and I want to get out there. I don't want to lose him again." He moves past me headed for the doors.

"I'll keep monitoring from here," Kane says. "We need someone to keep an eye on those other two vehicles in case this one doesn't pan out."

"Slate, Coll, either stay or come with me. Your call."

I exchange a glance with Liam, who only shrugs. "You said you wanted to be back out in the field right?" he says.

"Yeah, but something just doesn't seem right..." It feels a little too easy, but that could just be my paranoia again. If they really do have a bead on Bolton, I don't want to lose this opportunity either. Still, I can't get this weird feeling out of my stomach. "Lead the way."

Sandel drives while I take the passenger seat and Liam gets in the back. "Do you really think this is him? I mean, couldn't they be setting a trap of some sort? They already know we're onto them." I say as we hop on the beltway.

"Even if that's the case, letting this go because we suspect a trap would be irresponsible," Sandel says.

"Then wouldn't it be prudent to call in some backup?" I ask.

"It's one o'clock in the morning. I'm not going to disrupt another unit until we're sure," Sandel replies without looking at me. "DC police can help us for now. If we need someone else, Kane will call them in."

I turn in my seat and glance at Liam. His features are pinched, which tells me he doesn't like this anymore than I do. But Sandel is right, we can't just ignore this. We have to pursue any leads that present themselves. It could just be a case of incredible luck, but I doubt it. Especially if what we know about Magus is true. He's not stupid.

Sandel gets in contact with the DC cops, who alerted us to Bolton's current position. I must admit, Sandel is smooth with the car. We follow the beltway around until we get off on the BWI Parkway, heading away from the city. As soon as Bolton is in sight, he keeps us far enough back that we can't be spotted. He also keeps one of the DC cops close, in case we need reinforcements. We follow Bolton until there are no other lights around. If he suspects he's being tailed, he shows no sign of it. He keeps his driving regular, following all traffic laws and his speed never gets above forty-five. The further away from DC he draws us, the less I like how this is going.

"Where is he going?" I ask. The clock on the dash says one-forty-five.

"I can't say," Sandel replies. "But tailing him without looking suspicious will become difficult here in a moment. These rural roads don't have a lot of traffic on them during the daytime, much less this late at night. He'll realize someone is tailing him."

Just as he says it, Bolton pulls off the BWI parkway on an off-ramp, taking a right at the top. We follow at a good distance, only to realize he's made another right as soon as he got off the BWI. Sandel kills the lights, and turns onto the same road, continuing to follow him. "DC two-one-five, be advised, we have turned off BWI Parkway, onto Powder Mill, onto Soil Conservation. Going dark. Still in pursuit." He says over the radio.

Ahead of us, Bolton's car makes another turn, this time on to what looks like a dirt road. Because we don't have lights on, Sandel almost misses it. I grab my phone and call Kane back at the office. "Kane, it's Slate. Do you have a location on us?"

"Looks like you just turned off Soil Conservation Road onto a state maintenance road," Kane replies.

"What's out here?" I ask.

"Not much, it's government owned property. Borders up against nothing but woods."

"What the hell is he doing out here?" Liam asked.

Ahead of us, Bolton's taillights light up the woods around us as he slows his vehicle. "I want weapons ready," Sandel says. "Slate, you will stay in the car."

"But—"

"I need you to provide cover, no arguments."

I grit my teeth, unholster my weapon, but keeping the safety on. Bolton's vehicle slows to a stop, and Sandel stops our vehicle about a hundred yards back.

"Agent Coll, keep low and quiet," Sandel says as he opens the door.

I wonder if Sandel is getting to Liam as much as he's getting to me. Liam had five years experience on the police force before he joined the FBI, I think he knows how to approach a suspect without spooking them. But Sandel seems determined to control every aspect of this investigation.

The two of them creep forward, weapons drawn as they close in on Bolton's vehicle. I step out of the passenger side, doing my best to keep an eye on both of them in the darkness. Ahead of us, Bolton steps out of his car, seemingly oblivious to what's going on around him. He goes around the back and opens the back doors of the van, before reaching in and pulling something out that flops down on the ground. It's big and wrapped in a tarp. If I didn't know any better, I'd say it's about the size...of a human body.

Immediately, I'm sprinting for Bolton, passing both Sandel and Liam with my weapon raised. My body is flooded with adrenaline as I charge forward. I can hardly think straight; all I know is I need to get to him and find out who's in that bag.

"Hands up, FBI!" I yell.

Bolton turns toward me and in the reddish light of his tail-lights I see something pass over his face for a moment before he backs away from the tarp, holding both of his hands up.

"Slate," Sandel snaps as he and Liam catch up to me.

"It's a body," I say, pointing at the thing on the ground it's been wrapped in a tarp, and further tied off with ropes. Inside the back of the van are shovels and pickaxes. It looks like Bolton was out here to bury it. "Who is it?" I yell. I run up to Bolton, who backs away again but before he can I grab his collar, shaking him. "Who the fuck is it?"

"I want a lawyer," Bolton says. Liam walks around behind him and gets him in handcuffs. I stow my weapon and immediately bend down to the figure on the ground. It's definitely a body, it would be impossible for it not to be based on the shape. My heart feels like it's about to break out of my chest and my mind starts to go to all the worst scenarios that I can imagine. I don't want to open up that tarp, because I know if Zara is under there I'm not to be able to handle it. I will kill Bolton right here. But at the same time, I have to know.

I start yanking at the ropes, getting them loose enough that

I can start unwrapping the tarp. My hands feel like molasses, like I just can't move fast enough.

"Slate, leave it be, it's evidence," Sandel barks. "You'll contaminate it."

I don't look at him, all my attention is focused on the tarp. "I have to know." I continue to try and unwrap, tear, anything I can to get it off. Liam comes up beside me and I hear the click of a knife. He cuts through the ropes tearing them away and then carefully slices into the tarp, opening it up right down the middle.

As soon as I see who's inside, I lose it.

Chapter Ten

"EMILY," Liam says, shaking my shoulder. I'm down in the dirt, sitting across from the body with tears streaming down my eyes. "Emily!"

I don't respond until he positions himself directly in front of my face so all I can see is him. He holds my cheeks with both hands. "It's not her, okay? It's not Zara."

My entire world balances on the edge of a precipice right now and I'm dangerously close to falling off. "But it could have been," I whisper. "I thought...I thought she..."

"I know," he says, wrapping me in an embrace. "It's okay." He rubs the back of my hair, like someone might do to try and calm a child. In this moment I feel like one. I had convinced myself it was her already, and when he opened that tarp and I saw the purple face of Agent Crowne instead, I couldn't help but lose it. It made me realize just how close I am to losing her.

"We have to find her," I say softly into his shoulder. Even through watery eyes, I manage a glance over at Bolton, who Sandel is holding on the far side of the van while he speaks into his radio. In the reflection of the van itself, I see flashing blue and white lights growing stronger. "He *knows*. He knows where she is."

"Let's get him back to headquarters first," Liam says, pulling back. "Then we can interrogate him."

I don't know how long I sit there, watching Bolton, but it must be a while, because by the time I finally look around, there are multiple DC cops on the scene, and Cohen has shown up with some of his guys.

"What the fuck, Sandel?" Cohen says, stomping forward. He's in sweats, like he just got done at the gym. "Why'd I have to hear about this from your partner instead of you? We should have been called in on this."

"There wasn't time," Sandel says without breaking a sweat. "We barely had time to get on him ourselves."

"That's a convenient way of saying you didn't want us screwing up your op again." Cohen's face is full of fury until he looks down at me. "What's wrong with her?"

"*She's* fine, don't worry about it," I tell him. My tears have dried, but I'm sure my face is still flushed. Hopefully it's not as noticeable in the dark.

"We need to go over the van," Sandel says, interrupting. "I want to see if there's any residue from any of the weapons that they might have taken from Lockheed."

Cohen eyes him for a minute, then grumbles. "I'll get my guys on it."

"Good," Sandel replies. He grabs Bolton by the arm, leading him back to his SUV. "Slate, Coll, one of you want to stay on scene to coordinate this?"

"I'll stay," Liam says, shooting me a wink.

He nods. "Slate, we'll need to have a discussion about your behavior later." I grimace, *thrilled* that he said that right in front of our suspect. I don't know what it is, but Sandel really doesn't have much in the way of decorum. And so far pretty much every interaction with him has made me like him just a little bit less.

Though as he's passing, I catch Bolton shoot me a sneer and then a smile, like he already knows who I am. And if that's true, then there's only one person who could have told him. Before I can go after him to try and throttle him a second time, I feel a hand wrap around my arm.

"Don't," Liam says. "It's what he wants. Get him back to the office, everything by the book. We can't afford to screw this up. He's our only chance of finding her."

I hate that he's right. Why is he able to think about things so much more clearly than I am right now? I'm usually not this emotionally volatile. But I guess expecting to find your best friend dead and all the extra trauma has probably made things a little muddy for me.

"Thanks," I say. "For back there. I'll keep you updated if Bolton says anything."

He nods. "And I'll take care of everything here, including keeping a close eye on Cohen this time."

I want to give him a kiss, just to feel his warmth, but I know that would be unprofessional. Instead, I follow Sandel and Bolton. Sandel gets him in the back of the SUV and makes sure he's secure before leaving him back there. I climb back into the passenger seat and prepare myself for the long drive back to the office.

IT'S A QUIET RIDE BACK. IT SEEMS LIKE NEITHER SANDEL NOR Bolton wants to talk, and I am more than happy to sit in silence. Instead, I watch the lights outside the car become more and more numerous until we are back in the city proper. It's almost three-thirty by the time we reach head-quarters and get Bolton in and processed. Sandel suggests we wait until the morning to interrogate him, but I insist we do it as soon as possible. Zara might not have been in that bag, but that doesn't mean she's in the clear. She could be next on the chopping block, and we need to find Simon Magus right now.

"Hey," Nadia says, coming up beside me as I pour a cup of cold coffee from the machine. "I heard about Agent Crowne. I just wanted to say I'm glad it wasn't Zara."

"Thanks," I say, taking a sip before tossing the whole cup out. It's retched. Instead, I start a new pot.

"Did you know Crowne?" she asks.

"No, did you?"

"A little. Elliott and I worked with him on a few cases. He was a good agent. Smart." Funny, Sandel didn't show the slightest bit of remorse when we found out who was in that tarp. There's something not entirely right about that guy, and I don't like it.

"How long have you guys worked together?" I ask.

"About three years now, I think?" she says. "I know he can be a little brusque at first, but just give him a chance. I think you'll see he's a good agent. And he cares."

Definitely haven't seen that side of him yet, I think. As far as I can tell, he's about as cold and calculating as a computer.

"Agent Slate." I turn to see SSA Wallace come strolling in. His suit is pressed and immaculate just like any other day, despite still being the middle of the night. I give him a nod as the coffee machine heats up. "Sandel has the suspect in the interview room."

"Great," I say. "If anyone needs me—"

"Hang on," Wallace says. "Sandel and Watts are handling the interrogation. You can watch from the observation room. But I don't want you going in there."

"But he's *my* suspect," I shout. "I'm the one who apprehended him."

"Against Agent Sandel's orders," Wallace replies. "Look, I get you want to nail this guy, but you're too emotionally invested to be objective. Watch, listen and see if you can figure out what he's *not* saying. That's what you do best."

This is *maddening*. I swear, ever since Janice got promoted this place has gone to hell in a handbasket. She would have let me in there with him. Well…okay maybe she wouldn't, but at least she'd have given me some one-on-one time with the guy after it was all over. I'm pretty sure after tonight I'll never see Leo Bolton again, especially if they can connect him to the Lockheed raid. He'll be tried as a terrorist.

"Fine," I say under my breath. "Let me just get my coffee first."

BOLTON SITS IN THE INTERROGATION ROOM, HIS HANDS BOUND together with cuffs that have been attached to the metal table in front of him. He's leaning back, like he doesn't have a care in the world. I don't like how confident he is—it's like he knows this isn't going to stick. But he was found with a dead federal officer in the back of his van. There's no way it won't.

Sandel sits in front of him, flipping through a file folder, not looking up. Watts is in the corner, his arms crossed. Watts is a big guy, and his arms are like rolling mountains when his sleeves are pulled back. He's there purely for intimidation, even though he's one of the sweeter agents around here. But he can look as mean as a wolverine when he wants to.

I take a sip of my coffee as we watch. Wallace stands beside me, his arms crossed, while two other technicians in the room are making sure everything is being recorded through the two-way glass that looks into the other room.

"Is the sound working?" I finally ask.

"Yes, ma'am," the technician says. "They just aren't saying anything."

I figured as much, but Sandel's patience in there is scary. He hasn't so much as looked up in the past ten minutes. Only flipped back and forth through the file folder in front of him.

He must have read it at least five times by now; it's not that thick.

Finally, Bolton is the one to break first. "How much longer is this going to take? I'd like a glass of water, and to take a piss."

"It takes as long as it takes, Mr. Bolton," Sandel says without looking up.

"I already told you; I want to see a lawyer. You're not getting anything out of me."

Finally, Sandel closes the folder, glaring at him. "I heard you say that. But you're implicated in a domestic terrorist plot against this country. We don't have to give you a lawyer. In fact, we can lock you up right now, ship you off to some god-forsaken hellhole in the middle of Arizona where the after-noon heat will bake you alive. Whatever rights you think you have, think again."

Bolton shakes his head. "No, that's not right." Though immediately I see a crack in the strong exterior he'd been projecting. There's a hint of worry and terror in his voice. "I get to see my lawyer."

Sandel gives him a stern smile. "Maybe. Depends on how this goes. Right now you're looking at first-degree murder of a federal agent, as well as conspiracy to coverup a crime. Let's leave the terrorism off to the side for a moment. Tell me about Agent Crowne."

"Who?" Bolton says, but his eyes are already shifting, first to Watts, then to the window where we're looking in on him, and then back to Sandel.

"The body we found in the back of your van," Sandel replies.

"Oh, well, I mean first of all that's not my van. It belongs to—"

"Kyle Dearborn," Sandel says, opening the folder again. "Yes, we know. It was stolen from his property six days ago and has been missing ever since. And yet the preliminary autopsy on Agent Crowne says he hasn't been dead more than three days."

I know full well the autopsy on Crowne hasn't even begun yet, but Bolton doesn't know that. It's a good tactic to use.

"So don't sit there and try to tell me you stole the van with the body inside and you were just getting around to disposing of it."

Bolton swallows, his eyes shifting around the room some more. "No, I—well I mean I didn't steal…a friend of mine…" He's beginning to ramble, trying to find his footing. No doubt Simon coached him on how to respond if he was ever snatched, but he's not holding himself together very well. Despite his sharp new exterior, we have to remember Bolton was a transient for a long time. He's going to have mental scars from that.

"When did you kill Agent Crowne?" Sandel asks.

"I didn't kill him," Bolton insists.

"Then what were you doing with his body out in the middle of the woods?"

Bolton looks everywhere but at Sandel. "I…I want my lawyer."

Sandel shoots a glance at the window that Bolton misses. We can put off Bolton for a while, but if he's insisting on speaking to a lawyer, we can't really ignore that request. Sandel is pushing it as it is.

"Tell me about Simon Magus, Mr. Bolton," Sandel says. "And we'll get you your lawyer."

He opens his mouth, thinks better of it, then closes it again. "Simon who?"

"Don't play dumb with me," Sandel says, and I notice one of his hands is in a fist. I think Bolton notices it too, because all of a sudden that confidence is back. "We have you spouting the same ideology that Simon Magus ascribes to. Your records are online. How do you think we found you so quickly?"

Bolton leans back. At the mention of Simon's name he

knows better than to say anything. I could have told Sandel that. He should have kept pushing him on the dead agent angle. That's what we have him in here for, not his connection to Magus, despite that being the entire reason for this investigation.

"Dammit," I say, setting my mug down and heading out into the hallway.

"Slate," Wallace calls after me, but I don't bother stopping. I round the corner to the interrogation room, where Caruthers stands outside the door, waiting.

"Let me in there, Jim," I tell him.

"Whatever you say, Emily," he replies with a smile. He opens the door for me without even hesitating. Probably because he knows Zara as well as I do, and he knows I want answers.

Both Watts and Sandel turn as I enter the room and Bolton's eyes go wide. I make a bee-line for the man before Watts grabs me from behind. "Where's Zara, you little bastard! Where is she?" I yell. I manage to actually pull against some of Watts' strength and where Bolton was smiling before, he's not any longer, not when he sees there might be a chance I could get to him. He backs up a little in his chair, but can only go so far due to the handcuffs.

"Emily, don't," Watts says.

"*Where is she?*" I scream, breaking free of Watts and running for the table, grabbing Bolton by the collar again.

"Get this crazy bitch off me." He squeals.

Both Watts and Sandel grab me from behind has Wallace runs in and forcibly removes my hands from Bolton's collar. "You know where she is, fucking tell me!" I yell as they're dragging me back out of the room. At the very least Bolton looks rattled, but he doesn't break.

Finally, Watts and Sandel get me back out of the interrogation room, facing Wallace.

"In my office. Now," he says.

Chapter Eleven

I TAKE A DEEP BREATH. I hold, then let it back out again, taking another four seconds to fully exhale. Another breath in, four seconds of inhale, hold and repeat. I do this half a dozen times.

"Okay, you can open your eyes."

I'm lying on my back, looking up at the popcorn ceiling of Dr. Frost's office. The blinds are turned down so the light from the morning sun isn't blinding us in here. Soft music plays from somewhere in the corner and Frost has lit either a candle or incense which gives the room an earthy smell.

"Now what?" I ask.

"How do you feel?" Frost asks.

"Like wrapping my hands around that little twerp's neck and squeezing until he tells me where my friend is," I say.

Frost lets out a long sigh. I don't have to look over at him to know he's disappointed. But I don't care either.

"Emily, tell me why you're in here this morning, with me, before all my other patients?" Frost says. I can just picture him removing his glasses and wiping them with the edge of his shirt, but I just keep looking up at the ceiling.

"Because I assaulted a suspect two hours ago and my boss is 'concerned' about my behavior," I reply.

"Let me make that a bit clearer for you," Frost says. "If you don't get yourself under control, you will find yourself out of a job pending an official investigation."

"Is that what Wallace told you?"

"That's what I know. Do you think you're the only FBI agent I've ever seen?" he asks.

Finally, I turn to look at him. "I figured you'd counseled lots of agents."

He nods. "And I've seen what happens when people start putting their personal feelings over their better judgment. Let me ask you, what would you have done, if you had been in Wallace's position and you'd seen one of your agents run in and try to strangle a potential suspect?"

"Fired her," I say, flatly.

"Then you agree what you did was wrong?"

"The only wrong thing about it was I didn't get what I wanted. If he'd told me where Zara was and I'd been fired anyway, I would have considered that a win. But he's been coached—everyone could tell, even Sandel. His mistake was bringing up Magus. We had him. He was getting jumpy—like he didn't know what to do."

"So you're saying Agent Sandel made a mistake," Frost says.

I scoff. "Good luck getting him to admit it. Not to mention he might have cost us our only lead on Zara." I shift my eyes over to him and back. "And Simon Magus."

"Mm-hm," Frost says, taking a sip of water. "How has your sleep been lately?"

I shrug, even though I'm still lying down. "Weird. Some nights I sleep like death, others I'm tossing and turning all night. It's never consistent from one night to another."

"That suggests extreme exhaustion," Frost says.

"Does it? Great," I say, deadpan.

"Emily, do you honestly think you can continue to work on this case without allowing your emotions around Agent Foley to get in the way? Do you think it's wise for you to do so?" He seems like he's really asking my opinion. My go-to answer is obviously yes, but if I actually take a step back and look at the situation, I'm not sure I can say I should stay on it. I mean, obviously, they're going to have to drag me kicking and screaming, just like they did out of that interrogation room if they want to keep me away from the case. I would hope I'm not so compromised that I would put Zara in further danger.

"I don't know," I finally say.

"Listen, you've been under a lot of stress lately. Your trip back home, your time in the hospital, and now this. You need to give yourself some grace. Some downtime."

I sit up and narrow my gaze at him.

"I know, I know. Downtime is a four-letter word for you. But look me in the eye and tell me you wouldn't benefit."

"It doesn't matter if I'd benefit or not. The fact is, she's out there, and I can't relax until I have her back."

Frost gets up and walks over to his desk, taking a seat behind it. It's the first time he's done that since I've begun coming to sessions here. "If that's how you really feel," he says, pulling out a folder before opening it and making notes. "I'm going to recommend to Wallace that you no longer need therapy sessions. That way you no longer need to feel like you're wasting your time."

I furrow my brow. "Really?" I ask. "Don't I have to meet some sort of quota for these things? Or at least show some kind of measurable improvement?"

He looks up at me. "Sometimes, that's not how therapy works. Especially if the patient doesn't want to participate. I believe you being here is doing more harm than good, and that until you are willing to open up and be honest, there's very little I can do for you."

I work my jaw a minute. "Is this some kind of reverse

psychology trick? Pretend you don't want me here so I'll feel guilty enough to stay?"

He levels his gaze on me. "Emily, I don't want to make you feel guilty about anything. The truth is you have to want the help for me to be able to give it. And in most of these sessions we either end up going in circles or you just shut down. You're looking at these sessions like boxes you can mark off a list. And it just doesn't work like that."

"So you'd lie," I say. "Just to get me out of your hair."

"It's not a lie," he replies. "Being here is not conducive for you. It's not *helping* you. I will suggest to SSA Wallace that if you are ever interested in therapy again, that *you* need to be the one to seek out the help, and no one else."

"I appreciate that," I say, my voice a little softer. After all our sessions, this is the first time where I actually feel like he's been listening. "I don't want you to feel like I'm wasting your time."

"I don't and I don't want you to try and guilt trip yourself," he says, as he finishes scribbling in his file. "There are no hard feelings and no repercussions."

"But...what about what I just did? Wallace has every right to terminate my career."

"He does," Frost says. "You'll just have to convince him not to." The prospect of not needing to come to these sessions anymore is both a blessing and a curse. Because while it was maddening to sit here and try to figure out if Frost was on my side or not, at the same time it was somewhat cathartic. Even though we never really got into the deep stuff. I wouldn't let us.

"Emily?" he asks. "You're free to go. I'll send over my email to Wallace in a few minutes."

"I...I'm not sure that's the best idea," I finally say, hoping my breath doesn't catch as I say it.

"Why is that?"

"Because I'm not sure I can trust myself right now. You're

right, I'm hyper focused on Zara. Because focusing on her means I don't have to think about all the other stuff going on in my life." I lean forward, placing my forearms on my legs and lowering my head.

Frost removes himself from his desk and walks back over to his chair, crossing his legs as he sits. "What are you distracting yourself from?"

I can't believe I'm about to do this. But I don't think I've realized how much of a safety net I've begun to think of therapy. It's just that I was always thinking of it as a place where I could antagonize Frost, force my way through it. But the prospect of not having it to fall back on if I need it is…a lot.

"The anniversary of the day I lost my husband is coming up." I say. "Liam almost asked me to move in with him. And…" I hesitate. "…someone is sending me letters in my mother's handwriting."

Frost is quiet for a moment. "Which of those would you like to talk about first?"

"I mean, I know Liam means well. He loves me and has said as much. And I know from his perspective, moving in would solve a lot of our day-to-day problems. It would make a lot of things easier. But I've only lived on my own for less than a year now. I'm not sure I'm ready to move in with someone else."

"How did he take it when you told him?" Frost asks.

"I didn't," I say. "We agreed to come back to it. He actually…he kind of withdrew the question before he even asked it."

He nods. "Was that your idea or his?"

"Mine."

"And what do you think prompted that response?"

"So I wouldn't have to see the hurt in his eyes when I told him no. First, he hits me with the love thing, which…okay, yeah, I feel that way about him too, but feeling it and telling it are two different things. On top of all this is the thing with

Matt…I just feel like if I can get past this first year on my own, I'll be okay. But until then, I need to live just for myself. If Zara was here she would get it, but without her, I'm…"

"…lost," he finishes.

I nod, finally looking up. "Liam is an amazing man. He always has my back, never gets upset at stupid things, and is more supportive than I could ever ask for. And he recognizes when I need space, which is why I think he stopped himself from coming right out and asking. Matt and I…well, it's complicated. He wasn't the man I thought he was. But that doesn't mean my feelings for him weren't real. I can't just turn those off and pretend like they didn't exist because he lied to me."

"That's perfectly valid, Emily," Frost says. "I don't know all the circumstances, obviously, but—"

"He was a traitor," I blurt out before I can stop myself. "My husband was a traitor who was in league with an organization bent on undermining our government for their own benefit. He lied about his heritage, his job, and even his family. And the entire time we were together he was working to subvert everything I stood for." Tears begin to prickle at my eyes again, but this time they're fueled by anger, not by pain or sadness. "It was only in the last few months that he changed his mind and decided to try and disrupt the organization he'd dedicated his life to. And it was that decision that got him killed."

Frost is silent, taking it all in.

"And you know the worst part? Apparently, he was doing it all for *me*. His guilt about lying to me got so bad he couldn't live with it anymore. I guess somehow, I inspired him to try and take them down."

"And how does that make you feel?" Frost asks, softly.

"Shitty," I shout. "Really shitty. First for not seeing him for who he really was, and then for being…what…his princess on a pedestal? He couldn't figure out what he was doing was wrong on his own? It took someone like me before he finally saw the big picture? What kind of person is that? And what does it say about me that I chose a person like that to spend my life with?" I fall back into the couch, looking up at that damn ceiling again.

"You are carrying a lot of pain," Frost finally says after a few moments.

"Let me guess, now that you know all my secrets, you're going to suggest I not return to duty." I blow out a puff of air. Where had all that come from? I hadn't meant to just blurt it all out like that.

"On the contrary," Frost says. "I think your job keeps you focused. I'd hate to imagine what might happen if you didn't have it as a distraction."

I look over at him to find he's smiling. "Very funny."

"I'm only partially kidding. I really do believe you need your job to give you a kind of…center. To ground you in a way. At least until you have time to work through some of these issues. And I think with this anniversary coming up, it might be the perfect time to start." He glances up at the clock on the wall. "Unfortunately, I have another client coming in this morning."

"Right," I say, getting up. "I know you squeezed me in before your normal sessions. I appreciate it."

"And I appreciate you trusting me," Frost says, holding out his hand. "I look forward to working with you some more."

I give it a firm shake. "Me too. But what about Wallace?"

"Don't worry." He returns to his desk, opening his laptop. "I'm about to write you a glowing recommendation."

Chapter Twelve

BROOKE BEECH RODE the elevator down from the fourteenth floor to the lobby, rooting around in her purse for the gift card she'd stowed in there two months ago. It was a little past eleven-thirty and she was already starving. She'd missed breakfast this morning because of the corporate meeting with all the Baltimore branch heads, which of course, took place in her building. It wasn't the First National Bank of Baltimore for nothing.

The meeting had dragged on all morning, which meant she hadn't had a chance to even pop over to the small kitchen in their office which was usually stocked with at least some bagels or pastries. By the time the president finally adjourned the meeting, her stomach had been practically screaming— and she'd been sure everyone in the conference room had heard it. Which was exactly what she didn't need right now, more attention.

Finally, she found the gift card for the seafood place across the street and slipped it into her wallet. She withdrew her phone and dialed the first number she'd saved on speed-dial just as the elevator doors opened on the bank's lobby.

"Yeallo," the husky voice on the other side said.

"Hey you," she replied. "Wanna meet up for lunch? I just found that gift card your parents gave me for Christmas."

He chuckled. "Aw, no, every time you bring that up I feel bad. My parents are such cheapskates. Especially considering what your folks got me."

"It's fine, it's just what I needed actually," she said, her heels clicking on the marble floor as she made her way across the open expanse. The bank branch built into the ground floor of the building was off to her left; people were waiting in lines for the teller. "In fact, it's perfect because I'm starving, and this place is right beside my work."

"Well, Mom is nothing if not practical. When are you headed over there?"

"I'm on my way now," she said, pushing through the heavy glass door out into the morning sun. It glinted off the water of the inner harbor and she had to grab her sunglasses so she could see.

"Now? It'll take me at least thirty minutes to get over there. Not all of us work in fancy high rises, you know."

"Oh whatever," Brooke said, taking a few steps out, feeling the warmth on her skin. It was unseasonable for January in Baltimore, but she wasn't going to complain about a nice day outside. Especially when she had needed to wear her big overcoat to work all last week. Even though it probably wouldn't last, it would be a nice respite. "I've got an extra-long lunch. I can stretch it to an hour and a half if I need to."

Brooke was almost knocked off her feet as someone ran into her from behind. She stumbled but managed to catch herself without dropping her phone. For a second she thought they might be going for her purse, but the big man in the black hoodie muttered something under his breath and continued, trotting down the street. "Weirdo."

"You okay?" Jerome asked.

"Just some guy that didn't see where he was walking. Probably some drunk homeless person." Though he hadn't looked homeless. Nor had he looked drunk. He just seemed to be in a hurry. Though most people around this area of downtown wore business suits, like the kind Brooke was wearing. "Anyway, what do you think? Can you meet?"

There was hesitation on the other side. "Well, let me talk to Juan-Carlos. If he can take over for me here, I can be there by noon at the latest."

"Great," Brooke said, smiling as she turned toward the seafood restaurant. "I'll save you a—" Before she knew it, Brooke was in mid-air, the world twisting and tumbling around her. Everything disappeared in a blast of dirt and smoke, and she hit the ground, *hard*, rolling over and over again, her shoes lost in the chaos. For a few terrifying moments she couldn't even breathe, the air had been knocked out of her so hard. When she finally found a breath, it was like sucking in a mouthful of soot. She coughed, over and over, aware that something bad had happened, but also noticing the world was eerily quiet. She couldn't hear herself cough, much less anything else, all she could feel was the constricting of her throat and the vibrations that ran through her body as she tried to get a breath. Finally, she pulled her blouse up over her nose and tried breathing through that, which helped a little, and at least allowed her to expel some of the debris without drawing even more in.

She tried looking up, around, anything, but all she could see was smoke and ash. Terrified, she knew exactly what was going on. She had seen it on TV twenty years ago when she was still in kindergarten. People completely covered in white dust, looking like ghosts as they stumbled out from under the shadow where two tall towers once stood.

It had happened again, there was no doubt. She needed to get out of here, find safety, get as far away from the blast zone as she could. But where to go? She didn't even know where she was, and all she could see was the concrete ground underneath her hands. But there were lines on the concrete—she recognized them as traffic lines. She must have been blown out into the street beside the bank. Brooke began crawling on all fours, keeping her blouse in one hand over her mouth. She crawled as far as the other side of what she thought was Lombard Street. Yes, here was the parking lot across from the bank. The cars were all covered in the same dust, some of them with large pieces of concrete on them. Glass was everywhere, and it cut into her hands as she continued to move.

All she could think about was getting away. She crawled for what seemed like thirty minutes, hoping she was headed south toward the water. If she could just get to the harbor, she would be okay.

Another rumbling stopped her in her tracks and Brooke laid on the ground, covering her head. It was either another explosion, or some kind of aftershock. Whatever had happened, she still couldn't hear anything. And it was when she covered her head that she realized she was also covered in blood. When the shaking stopped, Brooke reached up to touch both of her ears, her hands coming away wet and sticky. Was she deaf? Had whatever happened to her permanently destroyed her hearing? She didn't know, but right now, survival was the main priority. The dust was beginning to clear the closer she got to the harbor; she could even see the sun trying to break through the dust cloud.

Finally, she reached the other end of the parking lot, only to find Pratt Street completely clogged with vehicles. Almost all of them were empty, having been abandoned in the middle of their commutes. Brooke managed to get up on shaky legs, noticing a few shadows running back and forth in the dust cloud. *Other people*, she thought. She weaved through the cars, the pavement hot on her bare feet, until she reached the Harborplace Mall. Right on the other side of the mall was the water. She just needed to get there.

She stumbled around the building, seeing more and more people now, some who were giving her strange looks, some who were running and others who looked like they were screaming, though she still couldn't hear them. Once she passed the Cheesecake Factory, Brooke finally turned around and gasped. Where the First National Bank of Baltimore had been there was nothing but a massive dust cloud. She couldn't even see the building anymore—was it still there? Or had they completely destroyed it?

She felt the ground vibrate again and when she saw other people look up, she did the same thing, in time to see a pair of fighter jets streak across the sky, heading north. They both split and went in opposite directions, and Brooke could feel the vibrations from them flying so low.

All around her people had panicked looks on their faces, some were curled up in balls on the ground, hugging themselves. A man ran up to her, saying something but she couldn't hear a word of it. And he was talking too fast for her to read his lips.

"I can't hear anything," she thought she said, but she wasn't sure. It was weird to talk and not hear your own voice. The man looked at one side of her head, then the other, then gently took her by the arm.

I'm going to get you some help, he mouthed, slowly.

"But I need to get to the water," Brooke replied, though she wasn't sure why. Her head was starting to feel fuzzy and white spots danced across her vision. She blinked a few times, only for her vision to become blurry. What was happening? Was she dying? She felt the strength go out of her legs just as the man helped her into the entrance of the Cheesecake Factory. The last thing she saw before she blacked out was the rows and rows of delicious-looking cakes, and all she could think about was that somehow, she was still hungry.

Chapter Thirteen

WE'RE BARRELING DOWN I-95, Sandel probably pushing the SUV close to a hundred miles per hour as he runs the flashers on top of the car. Behind us are two more SUV's, one with Agent Kane and two additional agents, and another with Cohen's men bringing up the rear. Cohen is already on site, having been closer to Baltimore when the blast happened. Liam, Sandel, and I are in the lead vehicle as we push as fast as we dare to reach what remains of the First National Bank.

The call came in a little after eleven-thirty. Some sort of bomb at the First National Bank of Baltimore. Given the proximity to how recently the explosives were stolen from Lockheed, Wallace decided it was prudent we be on the scene to determine if it had anything to do with Simon Magus. The local office already has agents on site, attempting to secure the scene and coordinate with emergency personnel. The news outlets are reporting a dozen dead already, and I'm sure that number is sure to rise.

Sandel's phone rings and he picks it up, keeping one hand on the wheel. "Sandel. Yes, tell him to hold anyone who might have seen anything. We're..." He glances at the GPS. "Ten minutes out." As he says it, I can already see the plume of smoke rising in the distance. From here it looks like it could be nothing more than a large fire, but the closer we get, the more apparent it becomes that it's something much, much worse.

"No one leaves the scene unless it's life-threatening," Sandel says. He seems on edge for the first time since I've met the man. We all are. After coming back from my meeting with Dr. Frost this morning I was feeling optimistic about today, hoping for a new break in the case or at least another run at Leo Bolton. I certainly didn't expect Magus to strike so soon.

"Well tell them to *wait*, we don't believe this is an isolated incident." Sandel hangs up. "Idiots," he mutters under his breath.

Liam and I exchange a glance. "How many wounded?" I ask.

"Not sure yet," Sandel turns onto I-395, bypassing all the traffic, which, thankfully, is getting out of the way of our convoy. "Probably hundreds. Emergency response is over-whelmed, they're bringing in additional resources from the surrounding areas, including DC."

The radio in the car crackles. "Hey guys," Nadia says. "I just got a visual on what's left of the building."

"How is that possible?" I ask.

"I have a local contact in Baltimore who sent in a drone, I'm looking at the feed now. The dust cloud is still thick—we're going to have a potential carcinogen issue to deal with and need to make sure everyone is out of the path of the wind. But the building is still there, mostly. Looks like the bomb went off at the base, but it wasn't enough to bring the entire building down, just the face of it."

"That means there are probably still people trapped in the building itself," I say.

"I've notified the emergency responders on the site; they're going to attempt to go in and clear the building. But there's no way of knowing if it's structurally sound or not."

"Christ," Liam says, rubbing his brow. "This is a nightmare."

"It's just another case," Sandel says, though he doesn't seem sure of his own words. "We work it like any other. Our first step will be to secure the premises and make sure everyone is out. I'll be coordinating with our teams already on the ground and the local authorities to take care of that. I want the two of you to begin interviewing any witnesses you can find."

"I just heard from Agent Black on ground there," Nadia says over the radio. "They've made a perimeter and only the emergency services are allowed in and out. They're holding all minor injuries until we arrive."

"You don't actually think Magus planted this bomb himself, do you?" I ask. "I'm sure they covered their tracks."

"Which is why I left Agent Watts back with Bolton, to see if he couldn't get anything else out of him while we tend to this," Sandel says.

The radio crackles again. "This is Riggs. If what Agent Kane says is true and the building is still standing, then it's unlikely Magus used the entire payload on this one job. Everything he stole is enough to bring down five city blocks, much less one building. If I had to guess, I'd say either he miscalculated how much he would need to bring the building down, or that was never his intention in the first place. Either way, he's still got plenty more explosives."

"As soon as we're on site, I need you to meet up with Cohen and verify if the compounds used match those that were stolen from Lockheed." Sandel gets off the interstate and winds through downtown Baltimore, weaving through the slow-moving traffic. Dozens of cars are pulled off to the side, their drivers out and looking at the plume of smoke that's growing ever closer.

"Copy that," Riggs says. We're silent the rest of the way. About five blocks out, fire trucks have blocked off the streets, helping to evacuate the civilians. The streets beyond are already empty which makes getting to ground zero much easier. Sandel takes us down close to the inner harbor about a block away from the site in the middle of McKeldin Plaza, where at least ten other ambulances have congregated.

When we step out of the SUV the air is thick and dirty, even though the wind is blowing the dust cloud in the opposite direction. I can practically taste it in the back of my throat. An agent comes running up, her dark hair pulled back and covered in what looks like a light dusting of ash.

"I'm Agent Black, Baltimore office," she yells over the din of emergency sirens, people barking orders and the wounded crying out.

"Agent Sandel." He shakes her hand. "Agents Coll, Slate, and..." he motions to the other SUV where Nadia has just gotten out, her laptop in hand. "Kane."

"Bomb squad is surveying the building now, making sure there are no additional explosives. We've already coordinated with Agent Cohen here. Did the rest of his team come in with you?"

Sandel nods, and motions for Riggs and the other men, all of whom have donned themselves in tac gear from their SUV and vests with their agency name on them. Sandel makes the introductions between Black and the ATF, and all of them head off in the direction of the building.

"Cohen is already getting a look at the building," Black says. "Come with me and I'll take you to him." Riggs and the rest of the ATF follow while I run back over to Nadia.

"Who is coordinating all the emergency services? I don't want to keep anyone here longer than they need to; if they need to go to the hospital then let's get them there."

"But Sandel said—"

"I know, but I'm not willing to risk someone's life for a witness statement. We can interview them in the hospital if necessary."

"I believe that is Agent Maldonado, though I don't know where——" She looks around until she finds a man under a makeshift command center that's been established under a few tents closer to the water. "Probably over there."

We trot over, weaving our way through some of the emergency vehicles. A constant stream of ambulances seem to be coming and going, picking people up for transport then coming back for more. I manage a look at one of the victims being treated in the back; thankfully his injuries don't look life-threatening.

"Maldonado!" I call out as soon as we're in the tent.

"Here," a man in his fifties replies. He's tall, with sharp features and deep blue eyes. Most of his hair is gray and he's removed his suit jacket and tie. Sweat stains mark around his armpits. He's a man who looks like he's been through a war.

"Slate, DC office," I say shaking his hand. "Agents Coll, and Kane. What can you tell us?"

He places his hands on his hips. "It's a clusterfuck, and that's about it. We're looking at seventeen casualties so far, at least fifty missing people and almost two-hundred wounded, some of them seriously. We set up a triage center in the next tent over to stabilize some of the wounded while they wait on transport."

"Anyone who saw what happened?" I ask.

"I haven't had time to interview them; we're still trying to make sure no one is left inside what remains of the building. Front of it's completely gone, and we suspect quite a few people are under the rubble."

"We're here as your backup," I say. "I'm happy to go with them to the hospital, take their statements there. Where are they taking everyone? Mercy?"

He nods. "But they're nearing capacity. We'll start sending overflow to UMMC."

"Okay, we'll start with the people that are still here—the

ones who aren't so injured they can't talk. Then we'll head over there."

"Do you have any idea who did this?" Maldonado asks.

"We think we do, but we have to be sure."

"Well, when you find him, make sure you send him straight to hell," the other man growls before turning back to the other people he was coordinating with when we came in.

I motion for Nadia and Liam to follow me over to the triage tent.

Inside the triage tent there are about a dozen people all in various states of distress. There are couple of serious-looking injuries, and emergency personnel are tending to those people trying to get them stabilized. There are a couple others lying on the cots, awake and alert.

"Okay, we'll split up. Start over there on the left, I will start over here on the right. Let's get through these people as fast as possible, talk to them about anything they might have seen, heard, or anything they might remember that could be important. But get their statements, their names, and if they have something crucial we can always follow up with them later."

"Got it," Liam says.

Nadia nods as well and they head off.

I bypass the first two people on my side, because it's obvious they are in a lot of pain and are still being tended to by the nurses on site. The third person is a man in his sixties who has a dazed look across his face.

"Sir? Can you hear me? My name is Agent Slate, I'm with the FBI."

He kind of stares at me with a blank look and I'm not quite sure if he heard me or not. "Sir?"

One of the nurses turns to me. "He can't hear you. A lot of these people have hearing damage. They were close to the blast when it happened."

"Is it permanent?" I ask.

"We won't know until we can do a full workup on them. It

depends on how close they were to the explosion when it happened."

"Have you given him anything yet?" I asked.

"Just something for the pain, he was complaining of a headache that wouldn't go away plus he's got a couple lacerations on his legs that we already bandaged. He'll be out of it for a while."

"Is there anyone in this tent who can still answer questions?" I ask.

The nurse nods to a young woman sitting on the very last bed in the tent. She's staring off into the distance, like she's looking through the tent itself. But she looks a little more lucid than the man I'm currently trying to talk to. "I would say she is your best bet. She's lucky, made it out of the blast zone with only damage to her hearing. You may be able to get something out of her."

I nod. "I'll make it as fast as possible." I head over to the young woman whose business suit is covered in dirt and has been ripped and torn. There are scratches and bruises along her exposed legs, and she keeps rubbing the side of her head.

"Ma'am, can you hear me?" I ask, gently.

She looks up. "What?"

I take out my badge and show it to her. "My name is Agent Slate, I'm with the FBI." I try to say it slowly so that if she can't hear me she can at least read my lips. "Can you tell me your name?"

"Brooke," she replies and her eyes tear up. "I'm sorry." Her words are slightly slurred, and I'm not sure if that's from some drugs they've given her or more because she's having a hard time hearing herself talk. "I've got this high-pitched whistle going off in my head, I can't really hear very much other than that."

I crouch down so she doesn't have to look up at me. "Did you see what happened?" Again my words are slow and intentional, and I notice her eyes keep going to my lips.

"I didn't see anything. I was on the phone with my boyfriend and the next thing I knew everything was cloudy and smoking I was on the ground." She swallows, hard.

"It's okay," I say. "We're going to take this slow." She nods, wiping away a few more tears. "What's your last name?"

"Beech."

"Okay, Brooke. Tell me everything you remember."

She takes a deep breath. I don't know how many times she's already gone over it in her head, but this is why we try to get to the witnesses as soon as possible. The passage of time, even a day can dull their memories and we need as much intel as possible about what happened.

"I…um…I was on the phone, inviting my boyfriend to have lunch with me. He works for Ladd and Company; they do a lot of the steelwork in the city."

"And what's his name?"

"Jerome. Baxter." Tears rush from her eyes again. "Oh, God, what if I can't ever hear again? I can barely even hear what I'm saying!" She covers her face with her hands and begins bawling.

I stroke her back as one of the nurses looks over at me, seeing if I need any help. Nadia isn't far away from me, trying to speak to someone else and she looks over, giving me a supportive smile.

"I'm sorry," Brooke says again. "I just…how could this happen?"

"That's what we want to find out. Do you remember anything strange before the explosion? Do you remember seeing anyone who might have been suspicious?"

She furrows her brow as she wipes her eyes again. "I…I don't think so." Then her eyes go wide. "Wait, there was one guy who ran into me right before it happened. I thought he was trying to rob me." I motion for her to continue, and a little bit of the strength in her voice comes back. "I was talking to Jerome, and he just…ran into me from behind, almost knocking me over. Then he muttered something and ran off."

"What did he look like?" I ask.

"Black sweats; I thought it was weird because it's so warm. I thought maybe he was a tourist or something."

"What about his face, did you see it?" She nods. "Would you be willing to sit down with one of our sketch artists? Once they check you out at the hospital?"

"S—sure, I guess," she says.

The flaps to the tent open and some EMTs come in, pulling a couple of stretchers. The nurses help the EMTs get the bad cases on to the stretchers, and they're gone in seconds, presumably to the ambulances waiting outside. The nurses move on to the next patients, one of them the man I tried to speak to earlier.

"Ma'am," one nurse says, coming over beside us. "Do you need anything?"

"Do I what?" Brooke asks.

"Need. Anything."

"Oh," she says, her voice smaller. "No, I'm fine." The nurse nods and heads over to the next bed.

I rub Brooke's shoulder, noting how the fabric of her suit is torn at the seam. "Don't worry, they'll fix you up. I'll be in touch soon, okay?" She nods again but doesn't reply. I have to imagine it's strange, not being able to hear your own words. On the few occasions when I've been incapacitated like that, I always get freaked out when I can't hear anything. Hopefully the doctors will be able to do something for her.

I head back over to meet up with Nadia and Liam who are both waiting for me. "Any luck?"

"A couple of eye-witness statements," Liam says. "Nothing concrete."

"I got one," Nadia says. "Man says he saw a guy in black sweats running out from the underground garage."

I make a motion to Brooke, who looks absolutely lost.

"That could have been the same guy who ran into Brooke over there. She's agreed to work with a sketch artist as soon as possible."

Nadia's phone rings and the three of us excuse ourselves back outside. "Ka—yeah, okay. I'll let them know." She hangs up. "That was Sandel. Cohen's guys just confirmed the residue matches what was stolen. It's him."

Chapter Fourteen

WE SPEND another three hours canvassing the area for witnesses. Navigating the chaos and trying not to step on anyone's toes or do work that's already been done proves to be a challenge. Every department from the Baltimore Police to the Environmental Protection Agency is all over this thing. I even get word that the Governor of Maryland will be coming to inspect the damage in the next couple of days, no doubt followed by the president next week.

Cohen and his men work hand-in-hand with the first responders and manage to clear the building, but by the time it's all said and done there are over sixty confirmed dead and another hundred people still missing. Out of everyone we interview, it turns out Brooke and the man Nadia spoke with are our best leads. They were both transferred to Mercy, where they'll receive good treatment until we can get them with some sketch artists. I speak to Maldonado, asking him to set that up which he says he will, if he remembers.

Seeing as this is their jurisdiction, Sandel decides to let the Baltimore office handle things and use us as needed. We've got what we came for: confirmation that the chemicals used to blow the face off the First National Bank were in fact the same ones stolen by the Simonites over a week ago. Once the scene has been fully evacuated and the engineering crews are on site inspecting what remains of the building, Sandel orders us back home.

It feels strange, leaving the scene like this, while everything is still so raw. But I don't have operational capacity here, and I'm already on thin ice with Wallace, so I don't fight it. Plus, I need to get back to Timber. Meanwhile, Nadia works on trying to collect all the camera data from both inside and out of the First National Bank.

"You okay?" Liam asks softly as Sandel drives us back to DC I didn't realize I'd fallen asleep on his shoulder. His question manages to wake me up without alerting Sandel up in the front seat that I was out.

"Yeah," I say, rubbing my eyes. "Just…going over all of it. I've never had to work a site like that before. So many people —so many agencies."

"What did you expect? This would involve the FBI only?" Sandel asks. He shoots me a look in the rearview mirror. I guess he caught me sleeping after all.

"No, but it's a lot different than the types of cases I normally work. At most I've only ever had to coordinate with one other agency at a time. Not *all* of them." He doesn't reply to this, only continues to drive as the sun sets off in the west. "Have you dealt with something like this before?"

"Other than a few encounters with the CIA overseas, no," he replies.

"What I can't figure out is how they got the explosive material under the building in the first place. I mean, this isn't the nineties, you can't just drive a white U-Haul van up to a building and leave it unattended without alarm bells going off all over the place."

"The footage will tell us more," Sandel says. "As soon as it's recovered."

"You mean as long as it wasn't destroyed along with half the building," I reply.

Sandel gets us back to the office in record time and I'm just about to call it a night and head back home, texting Tess as I go when Nadia comes rushing in. "They just sent over the links." She runs past us with her laptop in tow, setting back up in our makeshift command center.

"What links?" Liam asks.

"It turns out the First National Bank uses cloud storage for all their security camera footage," she says, booting up the computer. "Sixteen different camera angles and about forty-five hours of footage."

"Looks like we're going to be in for a long night," Sandel says. "Everyone take thirty then be back here ready to start analyzing."

"Ugh," I say, but don't elaborate. I need to get home to feed Timber and get him out of the house for a minute. Even though the sitter was there, he gets anxious without me and I don't like leaving him for that long. It's already been one hell of a day; I hadn't anticipated being here all night.

"Problem?" Sandel asks.

"Nope," I reply, grabbing my stuff. "Liam?"

"Right," he nods, following me out. "I almost think it would be better to bring on a fresh team for this," he says once we're down in the garage by his car. "You look as exhausted as I feel."

I wait for him to unlock the door before slipping in the passenger side. "No way. I'm not letting Sandel think I can't handle it. Because you know Wallace will hear about it one way or another."

"But Em, you need rest."

I stare straight ahead. "I'll rest when we find her."

∾

THIRTY MINUTES LATER WE PULL BACK IN THE SECURE GARAGE, three bags of fresh Chinese food in tow. Timber is in the back, practically drooling all over Liam's seats. He hops out once we've parked, following me and Liam to the security checkpoint.

"Agent Slate, there are no—" the officer begins to say as we check ourselves through.

"Jack, save it," I snap. "It's almost midnight, I have a hundred hours of footage to look through and I'm starving. I'm not leaving my dog at home after being gone all day."

"Okay, I might be able to look past it if it were a basset hound, but that's a pit bull," he says, staring at Timber, who just looks back up at him with big brown eyes and his tongue halfway out the side of his mouth.

"And he's not going to be a problem," I tell him. "This dog has never so much as growled at anyone. Much less hurt them."

He winces. "I wish I could, Agent Slate but—"

"Hey Jack," another officer calls from the security desk a couple of feet away. He's holding a phone receiver in his hand. "It's been cleared."

Jack looks at his partner, then back at me. "Really?"

"Yeah," the other officer says. "Let them through."

I look up to the security camera above the check-in station and smile. I have my suspicions about who just saved me a trip back home. I'll have to thank her later.

Jack puts his hands on his hips and releases a long breath. "Okay, go ahead." I grab the bags of food that have been scanned already and Timber trots through the security frame, the light going red when he passes due to the metal in his collar. "It's fine, go on," Jack waves.

Liam and I head down through the underground lobby until we hit the elevator bank. "Janice?" Liam asks once we're inside.

"That's my bet," I say. "I'm surprised she's working this late, though. I guess Wallace is keeping her up to date about the case."

As soon as we enter the office both Sandel and Nadia look up. Their reactions to Timber are the complete opposite though. Nadia practically rushes over, and introduces herself to him while Sandel seems to inch away.

"What is that doing here?" he asks.

"Do you have a problem with dogs, Agent?" I ask.

"No. But a command room is no place for a dog," he says, backing away even further.

"Hello there, hello," Nadia coos as Timber happily gives her a lick before rubbing his head into her open palm. "Oh, you're just a sweetie, aren't you?"

"He's not allowed in this office," Sandel says, his voice slightly higher.

"It's been cleared," I say.

"But—"

"Look, if you want me to work all night going through this footage, my dog is going to be right here beside me. It's quiet, the office is mostly empty, and he's not going to bother anyone. But I'm not leaving him alone all night, got me?"

"Very well. But keep him on your side of the room," Sandel says. He seems genuinely freaked out, kind of like how I get around kids. I neglected to anticipate that either he or Nadia might have had a bad experience with a dog in the past. I'm just tired of leaving him behind all the time. And seeing as I'm probably going to be sleeping here tonight, I might as well have him close by. Kind of like a security blanket.

"We brought dinner," Liam says, trying to break the tension by holding up the bags of food.

"Great," Nadia says, finally standing back up from giving Timber some love. "I'm starving."

"Thank you," Sandel adds, shooting Timber another cautious look. "That was very—thoughtful."

"Great," I say. "First we eat, then get to work."

WE END UP EATING *AS* WE WORK, SEEING AS THERE IS SO MUCH footage to go through. We split it equally, though Nadia already has a head start on us, having never gone back home after coming back from Baltimore. The footage shows angles from both inside the bank, around the lobby, and the outside cameras around the street level ATM. We begin with the footage right before the incident, but nothing stands out, so we wind it back, incrementally searching every fifteen minutes or so.

I'm going over the lobby footage, my eyelids already heavy when I see a young woman step off the elevator and cross the main lobby. She's on her phone, digging around in her purse. The footage isn't the clearest at this distance, but it's enough I can make out her blonde hair and business suit. It's Brooke, I'm sure of it. She leaves the lobby, and comes outside and I see a man approaching from the right who bumps into her. He seems to mutter something before trotting off. That was the guy she saw. A few minutes later, the cameras go dark when the explosion happens.

"Hey, Nadia?" I ask.

She turns to me. "Yeah?"

"Is there another camera angle on…" I double check the map of the building. "Uh, I guess this is the east side of the building? At street level?"

She takes a bite of lo mein, contemplating it. "I don't think so. There's a garage over there, but I don't think there's an exterior camera on it. But…" She sets the food down and begins typing something in the database we've been given access to. "Yep, there's security cameras in the underground garage."

"Look for a guy in a dark hoodie." I show her the picture of the guy bumping into Brooke outside the bank.

"He sure looks like he's in a hurry," she says before turning back to her monitor. "Hey El, help me comb through some of this footage," she says. "There are about eight different cameras down there."

"Sure," Sandel says as they start running through the footage. But as Liam and I watch over their shoulders, I don't see any guy in a dark hoodie anywhere. Plenty of vehicles come in and out of the garage itself, but none of their drivers look like the man who bumped into Brooke.

After about thirty minutes they've run through all the footage back almost two hours. Nadia looks up at me. "Sorry, Emily. It was a good thought."

I turn back to Sandel. "Has Cohen been in touch about where the explosion originated? It had to have been from here, right? The cameras don't show anything outside in front of the building." Plus, if that had been the case, Brooke probably wouldn't have survived.

"Haven't heard back from him yet. It's going to take them some time to figure out the blast point."

I sit back down in my chair. Timber, who had fallen asleep after a couple bites of sticky rice, looks up at the sudden movement, but then lays his head back down, probably trying to figure out why I'm disturbing his beauty rest.

Maybe the guy who ran into Brooke was nothing but a coincidence. Some jogger who was in a hurry, or a tourist who was late for something. "Damn."

"Don't worry," Liam says. "We can still take another run at Bolton. Now that we know the Simonites are responsible."

"I dunno," I say. "Something about him doesn't feel right."

"What do you mean?" Sandel asks.

"Things are just moving very...fast," I reply, but then shake my head in frustration. "I think I'm just tired and the lack of sleep is getting to me." Also my face still hurts, which only gets worse the longer I'm awake.

"The answers are out there," Sandel says before turning back to his console. "We just need to find them."

Chapter Fifteen

"EXCELLENT JOB, just excellent. I can't get over just how skilled you really are." Simon pulls back, having just spoken the words in Zara's ear. He's been doing that a lot lately, getting physically closer to her and it makes her skin crawl. But she knows she just has to endure it; he's in charge here, as if the handcuff around her wrist chaining her to the desk doesn't remind her of it every ten minutes. "Well? Don't you have anything to say for yourself?"

"I mean, yeah, it was fine, I guess," she finally replies, spinning back in the chair as far as the cuff will allow. "It got the job done."

Simon scoffs, turning to Omar who has posted himself at the other end of the cinder block office. He's scowling at Zara, which has been his default look ever since she agreed to renounce the FBI and work for Simon. Of course, he's not stupid. He doesn't think she's really renounced them; but he has her under his thumb for the moment and right now it doesn't matter where her allegiance lies. She has to do what he says—at least until she can figure a way out of this.

Simon holds out his hand to Omar. "You have to admit, it was good, right? The way she manipulated that footage?

Erased our man from leaving the building, seeing as *someone* was stupid enough to show his face to the camera." He turns back to her. "Is this the kind of work you did for the Bureau when you worked for them? Because you are scary good at it."

She quirks the edge of her mouth. "Not exactly."

Simon claps his hands together. "Well, I think this calls for a celebration." He heads over to his desk, opening one of the drawers. "You don't know it yet, Zara, but you've just taken the first step to being part of the new world order. When everything comes crumbling down around us, you will be one of the few spared and given the opportunity to begin a brand-new life, live it however you want." He rummages in his drawer for something.

"Great," Zara says. "Can't wait."

Simon pokes his head up over the table. "I know, I sound like a madman, right? Talking about totally upending the world and starting over—it sounded insane to me too when I first started thinking it. But you know what's even crazier? Less than five hundred people, making decisions for *five billion*. And maybe that wouldn't be so bad if the five hundred were the most altruistic, selfless people known to man. But unfortunately they are the complete opposite." He pulls out a small carton, placing it on his desk. He slides the top off, revealing a large bunch of maroon-colored grapes, nestled in a woven cradle.

"Do you know what these are, Zara? They're Ruby Roman Grapes, and they cost around two-hundred dollars per bunch." He picks one off, popping it in his mouth, then chews slowly. "That's because only twenty-four thousand bunches are harvested every year, making them extremely rare, in comparison to normal grapes, that is."

He picks another one, circles the desk and hands it to her. It's large—much larger than a normal grape. And it smells delicious. She holds it for a moment, contemplating how someone could have made a grape that costs this much. She's never been one for fancy foods; the most expensive thing she's ever consumed is the bottle of cheap champagne she and Emily normally share on New Year's.

Simon watches her a moment, smiling before handing another grape to Omar, who eats it unceremoniously. Simon smiles. "See, Omar here understands that it's just a grape. While you sit there, staring at it like it's going to disintegrate, thinking about all the other things I could have spent money on other than expensive grapes imported from Japan, Omar has taken the food, and nourished himself with it. Go ahead, try it."

Well, she's seen them both eat one. Odds are it isn't poisoned. Unless he just happened to poison *this* one. But before she can think about it too hard, Zara pops it in her mouth, biting down as an explosion of flavor extrudes from the soft fruit.

"There, was that so hard?" Simon asks. "See, it's just a grape. Like any other. But our society has conditioned us that we must revere it, *because* it is expensive. All hail the mighty dollar; money makes the world go round and all those other foolish colloquialisms. Don't you see? It's all nothing but a giant illusion. Money, like everything else, is a construct. And people have used that construct to become powerful and influential at the expense of the vast majority."

She's about to argue but before she can open her mouth, there's a knock on the door. Omar steps aside, opening it just a crack at first before finally opening it all the way. Three more of Simon's men stroll in, smiles on their faces. Zara knows two of them, but the third she never met, even though she's seen him around. The one in the lead goes by "Clint" but she's pretty sure that's not his real name. He's got brown hair down to his shoulders and a big grin on his face.

"Ah, back so soon? How did it go?"

"I think we got it," he replies. "Been doin' recon all day.

It's gonna take a little work, but we've got enough material to do it."

Simon smiles. "More good news." He turns to Zara. "You'll be especially helpful for a new upcoming project we're working on. Something that I feel will really test your skills. But you'll still have to keep the FBI off our backs. We want them to feel like they're making progress, but in reality they'll just be spinning their wheels." He removes a few more grapes from the bunch, handing each of the men one. "Enjoy."

"Thanks, boss," Clint says.

"Now, now, what have I said about that? I'm not your boss, I'm your..." He waits for one of them to finish for him.

"...friend," the mystery guy says.

"That's right, another for you." He tosses him a second grape before turning back to Zara. "We picked up Theodore here a few weeks before I found you and Agent Crowne. After Crowne exposed you, I thought he might be another agent trying to infiltrate our operation, but if so, he's pretty terrible at his job, aren't you, Theodore?"

The man locks eyes with Zara and she frowns. She feels like she knows him from somewhere—even the name Theodore seems somewhat familiar. "Sure am," he says. "Glad to be here."

"Theodore was the one who double-checked that you weren't trying to send a secret message in your work," Simon says. "Unbeknownst to you, of course. I'm happy to report you've passed your first test." A current of fear runs through Zara's chest. She had considered attempting a covert message of some kind, but couldn't figure out the best way to disguise it. Though it helps knowing *who* will be checking her work. She just wished she could have a better understanding of his capabilities. At least then she might have a chance of getting something past "Theodore".

"Excellent, excellent," Simon says, before turning back to

Clint. "How are things out there? Everyone happy? Do we need to make another grocery run?"

Clint shakes his head. "Nah, Geo took care of us. And the pantry is pretty well stocked. At least for a few days."

"Good," Simon replies. "Because we've got a busy schedule ahead of us. I want to make sure everyone is fueled up and ready to go." He turns back to Zara again, as if he's a teacher, explaining one difficult concept after another. "Once the world's economy collapses, there will be a lot of looting and fighting. The key will be to ride it out—let the weak eliminate themselves. Then it will be our time to rise up and take control. Show everyone there is another way. So in the meantime, we're stockpiling. The world will take a few months to sort itself out. Can't starve while that's happening, can we?"

Zara just smiles and nods, but she knows she's not fooling Simon. Likewise, she's sure he knows that she's only doing this because he's forcing her to. That if he gave her the chance, she'd run like hell. But they both keep doing this polite little dance anyway. All she wants is to get out of here and back to headquarters. Warn everyone of what's going on and find some way to nail this bastard to the wall.

"Here." Simon hands over the grapes to Clint. "Make sure anyone who wants one, gets one."

She doesn't miss the momentary flash of Clint's eyes as he takes the expensive grapes. Does he know exactly how much they're worth, and if so, is he considering selling them for a tiny profit?

"Wow, thanks, boss—I mean, Simon."

Simon smiles and places a reassuring hand on his shoulder. "You're welcome." Clint and the others head back out, and then it's just her, Simon and Omar again. "Now, I'd like to know the full extent of your capabilities. How far can you get us into the FBI database?"

"Well," she says, doing her best to stall. "They no doubt have wiped all of my access by now, so I don't think—"

"Now, Zara. I thought we had an understanding," Simon says, lowering his voice an octave, like he's verbally punishing her. "You can't avoid this forever. Sooner or later, you're going to have to prove your loyalty to me. Or, you know." He makes an imaginary gun with his hand and places it to the side of his head, pulling the trigger. He then makes an exaggerated move like he's blown his own brains out.

"I just altered evidence for you," she protests. "I've completely thrown them off your trail."

"And that might be all well and good," he replies. "But it's not enough. You know as well as I do that was nothing more than a softball to see if you could do even the most basic of tasks. Theodore could have done that for me. If you're really going to stay here, and be a part of our organization, you're going to have to commit. There's no getting around it."

She grimaces, wishing she could think of a way out of this. But for some reason her brain just doesn't seem to be working right. She's *smarter* than this. Why can't she see a way out? She doesn't believe it's completely hopeless, but at the same time, Simon is covering all his bases.

"Why don't we let you think about it some more?" Simon asks. "Your room is always ready and waiting for you." All the joviality and humor has drained out of Simon and he nods to Omar, who retrieves a key from his pocket as he approaches Zara.

"Finally," Omar growls.

"*Shit*," she says under her breath as he approaches. Omar hasn't been shy about how much he dislikes her—especially now that he knows she worked for the FBI. Before, when they had been on even footing, they'd done a lot of mental fencing, going back and forth, poking at each other. Zara always knew it was the only thing keeping Omar's desires at bay. Now that she's been outed as a traitor—even though she's "accepted" Simon's deal—it hasn't been hard to see that Omar has been itching to get at her. The only thing that's stopped him, until now, is that Simon has been around the entire time.

Zara steadies herself as Omar unlocks her cuff from the desk, then takes her by the arm, leading her back out of the office.

"Tomorrow we'll talk some more," Simon calls out, but she's not thinking about tomorrow. She's thinking about how the next fifteen minutes will go.

Omar takes her back through the main area where a few of the men are still working on their individual projects—no doubt getting themselves ready for the next stage of Simon's plan. Zara hadn't even known the exact target was the First National Bank in Baltimore until he brought her in and told her to alter the camera footage. It doesn't surprise her—he's going to keep her at arm's length for a while now, making sure that new guy double-checks everything she's doing.

When they finally get back to the same sparse room Zara originally woke up in, Omar pushes her forward, closing the door behind them. He's a big guy, and there's no mistaking the hunger in his eyes. The hunger and the *anger. He's going to take all his frustrations out on me, one way or another*, she thinks.

Omar snatches her arm with the cuff still attached and yanks it up, attempting to hook the other end on the chain that hangs about halfway down the wall. There's no doubt in her mind if he manages it, he's going to try and rape her at the very least, and she's going to be strung up like a turkey.

While he messes with the cuff, Zara uses all her force to drive her foot into his groin, which causes the man to release her and double over in pain. She scrambles away, going for the door only to realize there's no handle on this side. She can't open it.

"You're going to pay extra for that one," Omar says, wincing as he straightens back up. "What was it you said to me the other day? To go stick my dick in a tree? Let's see how you feel after I'm done with you."

Her pulse is racing, and she knows she has to stay as far away from him as possible. He's big, and not very quick. *C'mon Zara, it's time to put all those hours in the gym to good use. Emily would be disappointed in you if you can't even take down one assailant.*

Omar assumes a boxing stance, with both his hands out in front of him, approaching her slowly. She lets him make the first punch, if for no other reason than to try and learn his timing. She barely manages to duck it, but he slams into her with an unexpected uppercut that she didn't block in time. The hit sends her to the floor, and she scrambles back, the adrenaline coursing through her veins. She has to find a way to get him off-balance.

"Come here you little—" He lunges forward and this time she manages to slip out of the way, delivering a hard right to his unprotected kidneys. It's enough to cause him to grimace and Zara drops low, taking a cue from Emily's book and shoving the heel of her foot into the back of his knee, taking him down. Omar tries to recover, but she's smaller, and faster. Before he gets back up she grabs the other side of the open handcuffs and pulls the length of the chain across his throat, choking him. She's on his back like a spider monkey as he stands back up and he barrels back, slamming her into the cinder block wall in an attempt to get her off his back. Even though it feels like he's cracked her spine, she holds tight because she knows this is her only chance.

She pulls as tight as she can, the cuff still wrapped around her one wrist digging into the skin, feeling like she's going to rip her hand off. Omar grunts and struggles to draw in a breath, but it's no use; she's not letting go.

Finally, he falls to his knees, his arms going slack before toppling forward and smacking his face into the concrete. His nose makes a sickening crunch upon impact.

Zara takes a deep breath and extricates herself from him, her breath ragged and her body shaking. Did she really just do that? She doesn't want to check to see if he still has a pulse—all that matters right now is she's still alive.

As she's standing over him, trying to figure out what to do, the door to her cell opens again, causing her to gasp and take another step back. In the doorframe stands Theodore—the guy checking her work. He's holding a baseball bat in his right hand and his eyes go wide when he sees Omar on the ground.

Zara takes another step back. Theodore looks like he's in much better shape than Omar, and she's going to be pretty useless against that bat. But instead of coming after her, he sets the bat to the side and grabs Omar by the legs. "Here, help me flip him over."

Zara stands there, shocked for a moment. "What?"

"C'mon, c'mon," he insists. "Did you kill him?" He's got something of an English accent that isn't noticeable right away.

She's too stunned to move. "I—I don't know."

Theodore leans in, placing two fingers against Omar's large neck. "Shit," he says under his breath. "Okay, look. I'll take care of this. As far as you know, he brought you back to your room and left." He manages to flip Omar over on his own, but the dead man's nose is bleeding from where it hit the concrete. There's already a small stain on the floor. Though, unless you knew what you were looking for, you might not notice it.

"I don't understand," Zara says, rubbing her wrist where she almost pulled it apart. "Why are you doing this?"

"You don't need to know," he says, dragging Omar out of the room by his feet. She eyes the bat, but before she can get to it, he comes back in and grabs it.

"Wait, what were you coming in here for? Was that meant for me…or for him?" She nods to the metal bat in his hand.

"Don't worry about it," he says, grabbing the door. "Just keep doing what you're doing. And don't trust anyone. Got it?" He closes the door without another word, leaving Zara with only her thoughts.

She leans back up against the far wall, in something of a daze. What is Theodore's agenda? And was he coming to defend her? Who is this guy? As she slips to the floor she lets out a long breath.

Most importantly, does he know she already sent Emily a message?

Chapter Sixteen

I HEAD BACK into the office, coffee in hand. It's been, what, four whole hours since I was here last? We wrapped up going over the footage around three-thirty and called it, having not found anything useful. Liam drove me and Timber back home before heading back to his place for a set of clean clothes and a couple hours of shuteye. Instead of putting him out again, I had Uber pick me up and drive me to work this morning, promising Timber that Tess would be by later to take him on a walk.

Thankfully, he did great last night, which I knew he would. It was nice having him around; it gave me a sense of comfort while we worked, even if we didn't make much progress.

Even though I was exhausted, I didn't sleep very well. I can't quite figure out what Simon's agenda is. Despite having all this documentation about his supposed beliefs and these manifestos—which may or may not be directly from him—the man is an enigma. But I think it all comes back to his name in some way: Simon Magus. A man who wanted to *buy* religion. A self-proclaimed magician, or sorcerer.

Was he looking for access to an even higher source of power, and was willing to pay anything to get it? Or was he trying to corrupt the church by turning it into a financial transaction? So that only the rich and powerful could have access to God? From what research I've done, and it's open to interpretation, but the general consensus was the man was the impetus for keeping money out of Christianity, so that it would be accessible to all people.

And yet, *this* Simon's first target is a bank. What does that mean? Obviously, money is the common denominator here, so does that mean all of his targets will be financial in nature? And how many does he have planned?

"Morning," I say, taking a seat at my workstation in the makeshift command center. Sandel is already hard at work, but there's no sign of Nadia or Liam yet.

"Good morning," he says, though there's no warmth behind it. The man can be such a computer sometimes.

"Did you actually go home and sleep or do robots not need rest?" I ask, bringing my computer to life.

"I slept here," he says. Looking around my workstation, I now see that he's in the same clothes as yesterday.

"Sandel, go home. Get some real rest. Take a shower, change clothes. All of this will be here when you get back."

"Not all of us have that luxury," he replies.

"Why not? Because you're the case agent?" I ask. "You're allowed to take a break. In fact, you're compromising yourself and the rest of the team right now by not taking the appropriate time off. You're going to run yourself into the ground, then you're not going to be good to anyone."

He doesn't look up, only continues to study whatever is on his screen. "It's my responsibility to stay here and make sure things—"

"Everything will be fine without you for a few hours," I say. "I promise, if anything happens, we'll call you immediately."

I'm watching him carefully for a reaction. Finally he sits back in the chair and rubs his eyes. They're bloodshot and deep bags have formed under them. "Maybe you're right." He stands, stretching. "You'll call if anything happens?"

I put my hand over my heart. "Promise."

He glances around the room a moment, then finally nods and heads out. Just as he's leaving, Nadia and Liam come in, both with their own Grande Mochas. "Morning El," Nadia says.

"Goodnight," he replies without stopping.

Nadia furrows her brow and turns to me. "What was that about?"

"He hasn't been home yet. I convinced him to get some rest." Nadia shakes her head like she knows this routine all too well. Which tells me Sandel is even more of a workaholic than I am.

"Speaking of which," Liam comes over and plants a kiss on top of my head before sitting down. "Did you get any sleep?"

"Not really. I keep going back to Magus and his 'chosen' name. There had to be a reason he picked a two-thousand-year-old magician as his namesake. But I just can't figure out what the connection is yet. Other than the fact it has something to do with money."

"You think his motivations are financial?" Nadia asks. "The bank didn't report any missing funds."

"I'm not sure yet. We need more information on this guy. And seeing as we're not getting much from the site itself, I thought it would be a good idea to take another crack at Bolton. I doubt Wallace would let me in to see him again, but he might let one of you."

"Oh no," Nadia says. "I'm not an interrogator. I'm much better figuring things out behind the scenes."

I turn to Liam, expectant. "Maybe. But I had a thought while I was getting ready this morning. As I was headed out of my building, I caught sight of the guys polishing the floors. Did anyone look at the maintenance schedules for the

First National Bank on the days leading up to the explosion?"

I exchange a glance with Nadia. "I didn't. Did you?"

"No, I've been too focused on going over the footage. I didn't even think about the maintenance people."

"Maybe we've been looking at this thing from the wrong angle," Liam suggests.

"That's a really good point," Nadia says. "Give me one second—here." She grabs her phone and makes a call. "Hello, is this...yes, Mr. Sosa, this is Agent Nadia Kane over at the FBI. Thank you for the access to the footage. We have another request. Can you send us your maintenance schedule records for the past two weeks? Yes...we have reason—oh, okay absolutely. Thank you." She hangs up. "My contact at FNB who relinquished the footage for us. He's sending over the records here in just a second."

"Wow," I say. "Nice to have a responsive contact for once."

"Trust me," she replies. "They want whoever is responsible found as soon as possible too. Sosa has been coordinating with some of the other agencies as well, while his superiors deal with the collateral damage."

"Collateral damage?" I ask.

"Stock prices."

"Ah." That makes sense. I take a sip of my coffee, checking on FNB's stock. As expected, it's had a severe sell off since yesterday, halving its value. "Wow. I wonder if this plays into Simon's plans at all?"

"How so?" Liam asks.

"I'm not sure. Maybe the attack was a way to get the stock price to plummet so he could buy it up cheap. We should put an alert on anyone purchasing massive amounts of FNB's stock over the next few days. Who knows, this all might have been an elaborate scheme to get rich." And yet, sixteen people have paid for it with their lives so far.

"Here we go," Nadia says. "Maintenance schedules." She

sends us both copies and I scan down the lists of maintenance workers, when they were due to be on schedule, when they finished cleaning their sections and when they clocked out. Everything is normal up until the day before the explosion.

"You guys seeing this?" I ask.

"Yep," Liam says. "New guy. Jakob Fugger." He glances up. "That's an odd name."

I go a quick Google search. "That's because it's another pseudonym." I read off the page. "Jakob Fugger was a German merchant and Banker known as 'Fugger the Rich'. His total net worth was close to four hundred *billion* in today's dollars."

Nadia lets out a low whistle. "Whoa."

"It says here Fugger and his family had an almost monopolistic control of the European copper market at the time."

"That's our guy," Liam says.

"Has to be. Do you have an employment record on Fugger?" I ask Nadia. She searches through the FNB database, pulling up a record, but it's almost completely blank, and there's no picture attached.

"Looks like someone fudged their way in."

"Great," I say. "What about the cameras inside the building? Surely they were running the night Fugger was working, right?"

She snaps her fingers. "Should be. Let's see, his schedule has him working on the second, fifth and ninth floors, buffing and polishing. He started up on nine, then worked his way down. And it looks like he was alone."

"Which gave him plenty of time to plant any explosives," Liam starts looking through the footage on the ninth floor hallways. "I'll take the fifth floor; can you do the second floor?" I ask Nadia.

Together, we manage to get through all the footage in about thirty minutes. We find Fugger showing up in Liam's feed first. He starts out with a hat which covers most of his face, but by the time he gets down to the fifth floor, it's obvious he's sweating, because he's removed the hat and unzipped his workman's uniform to reveal a hoodie underneath. But we still don't have a good look at him.

"This might be our guy—the one that ran into Brooke," I say, studying the images on my screen. Infuriatingly, he seems to know exactly where the cameras are and never looks up. We don't even get a good look at his face looking down, only the back of his head. "C'mon you son of a bitch, turn around." But he doesn't, and then he's gone from my feeds.

"Guys, I might have something," Nadia says. We get up and watch her screen, where Fugger starts at the far end of the hallway before going into a few of the rooms, leaving his cleaning equipment out in the hall. He comes back out, making his way down the hall, only doing a half-ass job of cleaning the floors. He probably figures they won't be there in another twenty-four hours so why bother? Finally, just before he moves out of the frame, he glances up, though there's no indication why. But the camera catches his face.

"Can you run a facial recognition on him?" I ask. It's more than a little blurry, but I can make out a few details. Goatee, dark hair, medium build. And he's definitely wearing a hoodie under his workman's outfit. I check the timecode at the bottom corner. It's just before seven in the morning.

"So then I guess he spent the evening planting the bombs, then stuck around to detonate when he knew the building would be full of people." The timecode blips and I think I see a word, but it's gone faster than I can read it. "Wait, what was that?"

"What was what?" Nadia asks.

"Wind it back. The timecode did something funny." She winds back five seconds and the code at the bottom blips again, but it's so quick I can barely catch it. "Can you slow that down? I think there might be something wrong with the footage."

"Sure," Nadia replies. She winds it back and slows it to half speed this time. I catch the word in the middle of the timecode, which looks like it's been put there on purpose.

"*East.* That's odd. What does that mean?"

"I…I'm not sure," Nadia says. "Let me run the facial recognition on this Fugger guy and I'll get back to you."

I retreat to my desk, feeling slightly vindicated. We have a face now. At least that's something. I want to take that down to Brooke and see if she recognizes him. If we can get an eye-witness ID, that will go a long way to establishing this guy as our bomber. And I'm willing to bet this is the face of Simon himself. The only part I don't like is that he looked at the camera. Not directly, but almost like it was a mistake. Still, I'll take what I can get.

"Hey, Em, look at this." Liam shows me the time code on the footage from the ninth floor. He's slowed it down. "*Opened.* Not *Open*, but *Opened*. What does that mean?"

"Nadia," I call out. "Correct me if I'm wrong, but time codes don't normally have words inserted into the middle of them for no reason, do they?"

"No," she replies. "Did you find another one?"

"Liam did," I say, then turn back to my computer, going through the footage of Fugger again. I catch more blips this time. "*You. In. My. Room.* What the hell?" I've strung four different blips together. "Wait a second." I wind it back a little further and find three more. "*I want you in my room.*"

"That has to be a glitch, right?" Liam asks.

"It's a very specific glitch if so," I say. "Go back in yours, maybe there are more words in your footage." It takes us a moment to find them all and capture them. As soon as we do Liam reads it out loud.

"*I saw the sign, and it opened up my eyes.*"

"Oh, my God," I say. "It's Zara. She's sending a message."

"What?" he asks.

"The Sign! It's a song. Ace of Base, from the nineties!

How do you not know that?" I say, returning to the words on my footage. No, the *lyrics*. "*I want you in my room*. What…?" This has to be Zara; she's obsessed with nineties songs. The first one is self-explanatory. The sign, got it. Yes, we're looking for a sign. But I don't recognize what the line from my footage is from. I google *I want you in my room* and nineties lyrics.

"Shit," I say.

"What?" Liam and Nadia ask at the same time.

"The lyrics are from a song by the Vengaboys. *Boom, boom, boom.*"

"That's ominous," Liam says.

"Are we sure this is Zara?" Nadia asks. "What if it's someone taunting us?"

"No way, this is her. No one else would know to encode a message in something as silly as nineties pop song lyrics," I say. "But what does it mean? Pay attention to the sign, and obviously a bombing…right? Is she telling us to look for signs of another bombing?"

"Wait," Nadia says. "Give me one second. I'm looking for the rest of the words on my footage as well." It takes her a moment. "Okay, got it. *Doin' a little east coast swing.*"

"Motownphilly!" I yell, standing up. "By Boyz II Men!" I pause a moment. "Wait, Motownphilly…is she saying the next bombing is going to be in Philadelphia?"

Nadia's computer beeps a second later. "Oh, the facial recognition came back. It got a hit."

As soon as Liam and I lay eyes on the profile that comes up, I swallow. Hard. "Well, someone call Sandel back. He needs to see this immediately."

Chapter Seventeen

"So you believe that Agent Foley has sent secret messages through the time codes of the First National Bank's security tapes, to warn us of another impending attack?" Wallace glares at the four of us with his arms spread across the desk. To say that he's skeptical would be an understatement.

Agent Sandel came back in less than thirty minutes after he left, having gotten home with just enough time to change his clothes and turn right around and come back to the office. But there was no avoiding it. I wasn't going to keep him out of the loop, especially after we found out about both Zara's message and the facial recognition match.

"That seems to be Agent Slate's assessment, sir," Sandel says. "I reviewed the time codes myself, that's what they say, though I'm a little more dubious on if they actually refer to songs from the nineties."

"Before you write this off," I blurt out. "You have to know Zara like I do. She loves this stuff, and she knows I would've caught it. Which means it was a message directly for me. No one else would've known to send that and no one else would've recognized it for what it was."

Wallace glares at me. "That may be, Agent Slate, but

you're putting a lot of faith in someone who may have been compromised." I move to object, but he holds up his hand. "We know Agent Foley is highly capable. There's a very good chance she could've altered that footage, and obviously she could've put this message in here as a way to throw us off the trail."

"She wouldn't do that." I want to scream it, but I manage to restrain myself as my voice comes across slightly elevated instead. I've got half a mind to go to Janice right now. She knows Zara like I do; she knows this is something she would do.

"We can't afford to be that cavalier. We have to take every possibility into account. It is very possible Agent Foley is under duress, and is being forced to do things that she doesn't want to do. We don't know what her circumstances are, but we can assume they are probably not good, if Agent Crowne's condition is any indication."

"But, sir—"

He grits his teeth. "Agent, I have heard your argument, and I'm taking it into consideration." He turns to Agent Kane. "Tell me about this facial recognition. What are the odds it could be faulty?"

"I mean, there's a possibility someone could have altered the images. If they had enough skill."

"Someone like Agent Foley."

Nadia shoots a look at me, sympathy in her eyes. "Yes, sir."

Wallace blows out a breath of frustration. In front of him on his desk, is the facial recognition match that came up when Nadia did the search. It shows that the person who had signed in as Jakob Fugger is in fact Special Agent Cohen. At first I didn't believe it, until I recalled he was already close to the bombing when it happened.

"It's right there in black and white," I say. "That's why Zara inserted the words in the time codes over his images.

She's telling us that he's the threat and she's also telling us where the next attack is going to be."

"There are an awful lot of targets within the city limits of Philadelphia," Wallace says. "How are we supposed to know which one it is?"

"It will be a financial institution," I say. "Something that has to deal with money."

"Well, I appreciate your confidence." He takes a moment to go over the information again. I don't know why he's just sitting here wasting time, when we could be starting to narrow down potential attack locations in Philadelphia. Instead, we're here, arguing over the possibility that Zara even sent these messages, or that she did it at the direction of Simon. Which is ludicrous.

Wallace's phone rings before he can say anything else. It looks like he might ignore it, but instead he picks up the receiver. "Wallace." His face grows even sterner as he listens to the person on the other side. "I understand. I'll let them know." He hangs up. "That was Cohen. He said intel just came across his desk indicating the next bombing will be in the Capital One Arena here in Washington."

"Well, obviously you can't trust that," I say.

"I can't ignore it either, agent." Wallace stands up. "Is there any way to verify that this footage has not been doctored in some way?" he asks Nadia.

"I mean, maybe? But it's going to take some time."

I can't contain my frustration any longer. "I don't understand why you're not arresting Cohen right now. It's his *face* on the camera. That's it, done. He should not be working on this investigation anymore."

"Except, by your own admission, Agent Foley has doctored this footage. You say that all she's done is add words to the timecode, but how do I know that she hasn't doctored the face of the person who's looking up at the camera?" He shakes his head. "I'm sorry, but until we have some independent verification that Agent Cohen is dirty, I'm not going to go to the ATF and falsely accuse a man of treason." Wallace turns back to Sandel. "Do you have any reason to believe that Magus wouldn't want as high of a body count as possible?"

Sandel shoots to glance at me, before turning back to Wallace. "The first bomb went off in the middle the day, when the building was as full as possible. I don't know if he's going for body count or not, but his first hit would seem to suggest that."

"And there is a basketball game at the arena tonight," Wallace says, blowing out a long breath. "We may have to evacuate. Even if this isn't accurate intel, we can't take the chance. There'll be twenty thousand people packed in there."

"So what we do, just ignore Zara's message?"

"I think our priority needs to be the arena. At least until we can get independent verification on some of these other factors." Wallace removes his glasses and rubs one of his temples. "Get in contact with Cohen, coordinate with his team and make sure the arena is evacuated for this evening. I hope you're right, Agent Slate. I really do. But I can't afford to be optimistic here, I have to plan for the worst. We have no clue what this man is doing, or why he's doing it. And until we do, we have to be running defense."

God, I hate sports metaphors.

"Sandel, get on it. If there's anything you can do to verify any of this information from the First National Bank, do it. But your priority is the arena."

"Yes, sir," Sandel says.

And that's it, no further discussion, no further consideration. Wallace dismisses us and Sandel leads us back to our command center.

"I can't believe how hardheaded he's being," I say. "How can he be so blind as to not see this is clearly a message from Zara?"

"Because if he makes the wrong call, a lot of people can die," Liam says.

"That's true either way. Simon could be in Philadelphia setting up for another bank right now."

Sandel approaches me. "It's admirable how much trust you put into Agent Foley," he says. "But right now we can't let our hearts lead us. We have to follow the facts."

"The *facts* show the man that just told us about the next bombing is in fact, the bomber himself," I say, flatly. "Have any of you considered the reason Simon is so good at this is because he's had experience? As in, he's a member of a federal agency with, I dunno, access to all data available on firearms and explosives?"

"Not to mention it was his man that spooked Bolton," Liam says, backing me up. "Maybe the footage is accurate."

"How long will it take to find out?" Sandel asks Nadia.

"I can run it through a few rudimentary detection programs," she says. "But an in-depth analysis would take a few days, probably. And more manpower than we have right now, especially if I know anything about Agent Foley. If she did alter that footage, she's wouldn't have been sloppy about it, right?" She's looking at me as she asks the question.

"No, she wouldn't have," I admit. "At least let me and Liam coordinate with the Philadelphia office. Give them a heads-up."

Sandel nods. "I think that's prudent. But make it quick, I want to meet up with Cohen and look the man in the eye."

"Yeah," I say. "Me too."

∾

After placing a call to the Philadelphia office alerting an Agent Rockefeller of our suspicions and telling them to at least be on guard, the four of us head over to the arena to meet up with Cohen and his team. It turns out they got back from Baltimore this morning as well, which was convenient timing, I have to admit.

Liam seems to be the only one who understands that Zara's message isn't a ruse of some sort. She wouldn't have done that. If Simon had forced her to send us a clandestine message, she would have made it clearer; she wouldn't have gone to the extreme lengths she did to hide it. I mean, had I not seen the timecode flip, we never even would have known the message was in there. And if anyone else would have decoded it, they probably would have passed it off as gibberish.

But I *know* my friend. If all those times up at karaoke has taught me anything, it's that Zara is obsessed with stuff like that. She's not going to use it flippantly or unintentionally. A bomb is coming to Philadelphia, I'm sure of it.

By the time we arrive at the arena, Cohen is already there, with one of his lackeys in tow. It's not the guy who jumped on Bolton too early, instead it's one of the guys who first came to the FBI that day: Larson.

"Good timing," Cohen says, shaking Sandel's hand as we arrive. "We just got this tip as soon as we got into the office this morning. Most of us spent half the night going over that clusterfuck up in Baltimore."

"Yeah, about that," I say. "Where did you get this intel?"

"Anonymous tip to our line," Cohen says without missing a beat. "But given the proximity of the Baltimore event, we thought it was prudent to get on it."

"Have you already evacuated the building?" Liam asks.

Cohen shakes his head. "Not yet. I have my guys in there going over the sensitive areas first before beginning a full sweep of the building. I even had to call in another team. But I didn't want to cause a panic. Not until we're sure."

"Uh-huh," I say. As best I can tell, he's either a phenomenal liar or he really believes what he's saying. But I've met people in the past who could pass a hundred lie detector tests and yet they were fibbing through their teeth. Some people are exceptionally good at it. I know from experience.

I turn away in disgust and head off through the open lobby of the arena, unable to stomach this any longer.

Liam catches up to me a minute later. "You need to cool it, Em. If he really is a traitor, your behavior is only going to make him more suspicious."

"I just...doesn't this feel wrong to you?" I ask.

"Well, who's to say there won't be two attacks at once?" he asks. "And Wallace does have a point. We can't ignore a tip like this, even if it turns out to be bogus."

"Do you buy that crap about it being anonymous?" I ask. "We should check with other members of his team, see if they —" I look around for anyone else who might belong to the search team.

"Em, if you make the wrong call and it goes back to Cohen, he'll know you're on to him," Liam warns.

"I can't just stand here and wait for them to clear the building," I say.

He pulls me into a hug. "I know. This isn't ideal. I've got an idea." He lets go of me. "We stay here for an hour or so just to make it look like we're on board, then we head out. If we stay off 95 we can probably be in Philly in under three hours."

I smile up at him. "Now that sounds like a plan. I want to swing by Baltimore on the way. We can show Brooke the picture of 'Fugger' to see if it jogs her memory." I'm even more glad now that I brought Timber to the office last night. I'll have to arrange something with Tess. She's really working double duty lately, but she's the best solution I've found so far. Still, our non-discussion about our living conditions looms over both of us.

I notice Cohen perk up as we approach everyone. "Slate," Sandel says. "Nadia is going to take over from Cohen's men on notifying the arena about the threat. I want you and Coll to help manage any crowds. There are sure to be a lot of disappointed people that will be showing up here not too long from now."

"Got it, boss," I say a little too enthusiastic, which earns me another warning look from Liam. *What?* My return look says. If I'm going to be playing the part of good little agent, I might as well put my all into it.

Chapter Eighteen

ZARA SITS with her back against the cinder block wall, her forearms on her knees as the empty handcuff hangs from one arm, swinging back and forth with the smallest motion. Omar's bloodstain on the ground only a few feet away has dried and serves as a stark reminder of what happened in here. She's been alone for what feels like days now with no word about what's going on out there. Did Simon find out she killed Omar and this is her punishment? Or has Theodore done something? He said he would take care of it, but what did that mean, exactly? She knows for a fact she can't trust him and the entire time she's been alone she's been trying to figure out where she knows his face from. She's seen him before; she just can't remember where.

The bigger question is what is his agenda? Is he working for another agency, infiltrating as well? Or is it something else? She has to believe if he was a true Simonist, he would have killed her the moment he saw Omar's body. But he seemed more concerned with covering it up. Not to mention he came in here ready for a fight. And as best as she can tell, she *wasn't* his target.

Then again, he could be nothing more than a trick from

Simon—someone she's supposed to confide in, who will then report back to Simon. She can't discount that very real possibility.

Em, if you were here, you'd never believe this, she thinks.

She isn't sure how much time passes but eventually she hears the telltale throwing of the door bolt before it opens. And sure enough, Theodore appears again. He peeks in at first, as if he's not sure where she'll be and is on guard. As soon as he spots her up against the wall, he comes fully into the room, leaving the door open. She could try to take him out, get through the door, but then where would she go? As far as she can tell, this area only leads in one direction: up to the main bunker area. She just wishes she knew *where* they were.

"Here," Theodore says, tossing her a small package wrapped in foil.

"What's this?" she asks.

"Dinner."

She unwraps it to find a burrito, and her mouth waters in response. Theodore bends down and rolls a bottle of water over to her. "Thanks," she says. She hasn't had anything to eat since yesterday, so she's more than grateful. But the question remains, did Theodore get this for her himself, or did Simon order him to do it? In an attempt to get closer to her?

"So are you my guard now?" she asks.

"Just making sure you don't die in here," he grumbles.

"Why do you care?" she asks. "Or did Magus hire you to do more than just check to make sure I was doing my job properly?"

Theodore glances around the door, past where she can't see. He then closes it almost all the way, leaving just enough space where he can still get the door open. "You mean like those messages you built into the timecodes?"

Her heart practically stops in her chest. So he *does* know. He must be pretty good then. She's not about to deny it. Even if Theodore showed him how she did it, she doubted Simon would understand. He'd just have to take Theodore's word for it. Which means it could come down to nothing but a he said/she said. "Why didn't you tell Simon?"

"Because I didn't want to see you shot," he replies.

Hmm. Interesting. "What's it to you? Aren't you a true believer?"

"No," he whispers. "This is just——" he stops before saying anything else, but now her curiosity is piqued.

"Just what?"

"Nothing, I need to go," he says, grabbing the door.

"What about Omar?" she asks. "What'd you do with him?"

"Had to cut across the neck to hide the chain marks," he replies, nodding to my cuffs. "But lucky for you, he wasn't a popular guy around here. The rumor is that Clint had something to do with it. He's not the first follower Simon has lost and I doubt he'll be the last. Simon barely even acknowledged it."

"Does he suspect me?" she asks.

"I don't know. But don't give him any reason to," Theodore growls.

Damn, who *is* this guy? She gets up and he takes a step back. "What's your deal?" she asks. "Are you the good cop in this situation? Being all nice to me so I'll open up to you?"

"I don't think I would have staged a body if I were," he hisses, looking at the door again.

"Then what? What's your agenda here?"

"It's none of your business, love," he says. "Can't you just be grateful and move on?"

She cocks her head at him. "Unfortunately my brain doesn't work that way. I'm an investigator. I have to know why people do the things they do."

"Maybe some people don't have reasons. Maybe they just…do, and that's it."

"No way. You're talking to a seasoned professional here."

Well, seasoned may be laying it on a little thick. She's only been in the field for about a year. Still, she's seen a lot. *Everyone* is motivated by something.

"Then you'll just have to wonder that pretty little head of yours." He moves back around the door, pulling it closed.

"Billy boy!"

The voice causes Zara to recoil and head back to the wall. She hides the bottle of water and burrito behind her as she sits back down on the ground. "Checking on our resident?"

"Just making sure she wasn't about to die of thirst," Theodore says.

Zara fumbles pulling the bottle of water back out and makes a big show of making sure it's open and she's drinking it when Simon bursts into the room, Theodore not far behind.

"Well, that was awfully nice, wasn't it, Chl—sorry, Zara. I still can't help but think of you as a Chloe." He's got a gleam in his eye, like he knows something is up.

"I *was* getting pretty thirsty," she says, but remains seated.

"Oh, don't you worry. We're not about to let you waste away here. Now, I have to ask, have you had a chance to consider all your options?"

She nods. "I have."

"And?"

"Seeing as my only path forward is with you, then I guess you have yourself a new follower."

"No tricks, no hesitations," Simon says.

"Nope. I'm all in."

A wicked smile comes across his lips. "Excellent. Then come with me. I have another little job for you. Make sure you bring your water. This one might take a while." He turns to leave but stops short right at the blood stain that's soaked into the concrete.

Zara finds she's having a hard time catching her breath. "I guess we need to make sure you have all the products you need for your—needs," Simon says, though he says it like she has a disease. Clearly a man who has been around a lot of women in his life.

"Yeah...sorry about that," she says. "Biological functions and all that."

"Yes," Simon says, a bit more subdued now. "Billy, make a run for us, would you? Get her whatever...things...she needs."

"Playtex," Zara says. "Regular size."

"Got it," Theodore says.

"Very good. But first, come along Chlo—*dammit*, ZARA," Simon says, correcting himself halfway. "Improvise, adapt, overcome."

She gets up to follow along, though she doesn't like the look on Theodore's face. She still doesn't know what to think of him, but she doesn't think he's a threat right now. At the very least, if he and Simon are in league together, they're doing a fantastic job of disguising it.

"Did I ever tell you about my time in the Marines?" he asks. But before she can answer that he's never been shy about letting people know he used to be a marine pilot, he goes on. "I can't tell you how many times we were faced with a series of difficult situations, much like you are right now. And I had to push through. Find the best way forward and move on. There was this one time, I was flying training runs out of Norfolk and one of my engines died mid-flight. Now, I could have panicked, but I kept a clear head, assessed the situation, and was eventually able to restart the engine before my other one flared out.

"Now you, you have a similar decision ahead of you. One engine is gone, and you've only got one left. Do you let it flare out and crash into the ocean, or do you keep a calm head, and do what you know you need to do to survive."

"You tell me," Zara says.

Simon laughs, though it's mirthless. "You know, it's taken

me some time, and more resources than I'd care to admit, but I finally got a bead on you."

"A bead?"

"Oh yes, Special Agent Zara Foley, with the FBI for what, four years now? But last year you transferred out of intelligence into field work, where you regularly work with your friend and partner, Special Agent Emily Slate."

Oh, no. If he knows about Em, he probably knows just about everything.

"I'm so glad you've decided that this will be your new home and family, because I'm sorry to say that your old one will not make the transition into the new world."

"That's too bad," she says.

"It is! But don't worry. Anyone who doesn't come along to rebuild a better world for all of humanity will be giving us a wonderful gift: freedom. Without all these institutions to impose restrictions, create insane laws, or restrict the will of the diligent and the noble, then we will be free to obtain our true potential as people. It's going to be glorious. I know that right now you're just saving your own skin—taking the path of least resistance, working on that one engine. And I can respect that. But trust me, one day soon you'll see that staying in the air is the better option. And you'll be grateful I spared your life."

He leads them back up the staircase to the main bunker which is mostly empty. A few of his followers are sitting at tables, conversing, or going over plans she can't make out. But it's a lot quieter than before.

"Everyone is out on assignment," Simon says. "Today is a big day. What am I saying? *Every* day from here on is a big day! With our last opportunity, we had a little bit more prep time. But I was counting on you coming around, and this time I think we can make an even bigger splash." Simon clasps his hands together like an overexcited clown.

Zara already knows what's coming, she's seen the plans.

When Simon's back was turned, and he had her working on the footage for the Baltimore job, she was able to open up a small subroutine that ran a quick search in his own systems. Simon has some big plans, and she sure she's sitting here again because of what he wants to do in Philadelphia.

Zara holds her hands out. "Whatever I can do."

Simon motions to Theodore, who has followed them in. "Now this is going to be important, so I want you to keep an eye on her. If she so much as deviates one inch from what she supposed to be doing—" He reaches behind him and pulls out a Glock nine, cocking it. He turns it around and hands it handle first to Theodore. "I hope I've made myself clear." All the humor is gone from his voice.

"Perfectly." One thing she can say for Theodore is that he is succinct.

"Excellent. Now, our next opportunity is at the Philadelphia Federal Reserve. Clint and the other teams are already prepping on site. But I need you, Special Agent, to make sure they can get through security without an issue."

"That's a big ask," Zara says. "There's going to be multiple levels of security, especially in a government building. They're going to have metal detectors possibly even bomb-sniffing dogs. I can work with computers, but I can't do anything about animals on site."

"Don't worry about that," Simon says. "It's just computers today. We've already taken precautions. But we need someone with enough skill that can make sure the systems don't sound alarms when the boys take those bombs through." He leans down close so his face is only inches from hers. "I want to be very clear here, if every single one of those men does not make it through not only will I have Theodore here shoot you in the head, but I will have him go out and find all of your friends, family, co-workers, and anyone else that you ever cared about, and I will have him shoot them in the head as well. I will find your kindergarten teacher if I have to. Do I make myself clear?"

She swallows, hard. "Very clear."

"Great. Then I look forward to seeing a master at work. Now you should have access to all the necessary systems you need, and I trust that if you don't, you can find your way in. I'll leave Theodore here to keep an eye on you as I have somewhere I need to be." He turns and heads back over to his desk, rummaging around it for a few minutes before extracting a couple of folders, and a small leather pouch.

"Theodore, keep your phone close. I'll be coordinating with you and Clint once they're past security." He pauses for a moment looking at Theodore as if he's evaluating him for the first time. Does he suspect that Theodore might not be entirely loyal? She's not sure, but she knows she has little choice right now.

Eventually, Simon just shakes his head and leaves them alone.

"So what are you going to do?" Theodore asks as soon as they're alone. It doesn't escape her that he hasn't put down the gun yet. It seems like he might be Simon's inside man after all.

"I'm going to do what I have to," she replies.

Theodore takes a step back, raising the gun, and for a moment she thinks he might have already made a decision about her and knows she can't be trusted. But he doesn't level the gun on her, instead drops the clip out of the handle and pulls back on the hammer, ejecting the chambered cartridge, before placing the empty weapon right beside her.

"I'm not about to do this with a gun to your head," he says.

"Do what, exactly?" she asks, surprise in her voice.

"Help you stop a lot of people from dying."

Chapter Nineteen

AFTER SPENDING a couple of hours placating Agent Sandel and Agent Cohen, Liam and I manage to sneak off and head out of town, going north. We get to Baltimore in just over an hour, getting lucky with the traffic. On the way I had the local office create a lineup for me with "Fugger's" picture mixed in to see if Brooke can give us a positive ID. We meet the agent at Mercy, who hands over the mockup after informing us the Baltimore division is keeping a close eye on the witnesses, just in case. I'm glad they're being proactive.

We get off on the sixth floor and head to Brooke's room. Even though the sun is up the shades are drawn and the TV is on, but the sound is off. I knock softly, motioning for Liam to stay outside a second. There's no response so I poke my head in to find Brooke sound asleep. I hate to wake her, but we need an ID if we'll be going after Cohen. Maybe more than that *I* need it so I can rub it in Wallace's face.

"Brooke?" I say softly. And then I remember.

I approach and touch her on the shoulder, and she jerks, coming out of the sleep like she's been electrocuted. "Oh! Agent…"

"Slate," I say. "How are you feeling?" I make sure to speak slowly so she can read my lips if she needs to.

She reaches over on the table and grabs what looks like a hearing aid before inserting it in her ear. She messes with it a second before wincing. "There. Sorry, I'm still getting used to it."

"Hearing aid?" I ask.

She nods. "At least until some of the damage heals on its own. Both my eardrums burst. When I finally could start hearing again it was like everything was muffled. Even my own voice."

"I hope you make a quick recovery," I say.

"Thanks."

"I was hoping you could help me identify the man who ran into you," I say. "If I show you a few pictures, do you think you might be able to pick him out?"

"I'm not sure…it's still a little fuzzy. But I'll be happy to look," she says.

I hand her the lineup, which has been printed on a small cardboard card, and each of the six faces on the card are about two inches by three inches. Cohen's picture is on the bottom right.

She stares at it a minute which is never good. Usually, we like to see an identification immediately. "I think it was the guy on the bottom right," she finally says.

"Are you sure?" I ask, keeping any emotion out of my voice.

"I think so, he's the only one who looks familiar."

I take the lineup back. "Okay, thanks for all your help."

"Did I pick the right one?" she asks.

"Sorry, I can't comment on it," I tell her. "But you have definitely been a big help with our investigation."

"That's good," she says. "At least all of this isn't for nothing." She motions to her ears. I look around the room and see a large bouquet of red roses.

"Jerome?" I ask.

She smiles. "Yeah, he was by earlier today. If everything goes okay tonight, he'll take me home in the morning. Work is a mess, though. I'm not sure I can ever go back there."

"Do yourself a favor, and find a good therapist to help you with this," I tell her, feeling like a huge hypocrite. "Don't wait. The sooner you can get in, the better."

Brooke gives me a sad sort of smile. "I will. Thanks, Agent Slate."

I leave her to rest and rejoin Liam back in the hallway.

"So?" he asks. "Any luck."

"Oh yeah," I say, making a little victory fist as we make our way down the hallway. "Plenty."

LIAM WAS RIGHT, WE MANAGE TO MAKE IT TO PHILADELPHIA IN another hour and a half, right when the sun is headed back down toward the horizon. It's a clear day, in a couple of hours the entire sky will be lit up in pinks and oranges, a beautiful winter evening. Hopefully by then we'll have this situation under control.

Once we make our way inside the Philadelphia field office, we ask to speak with the Special Agent in charge of counterterrorism. After waiting a few minutes, we spot a man in his mid-forties approaching. He has kind eyes, but he also has a nasty scar that runs along the bottom of his jaw. It old but still visible, and I can't help but wonder if it happened while he was on the job.

"Agents," he says, holding out a hand as he approaches us. "I'm SSA Rockefeller. Welcome to Philly."

The man we spoke to earlier. I take his hand first. "Agent Emily Slate, this is Agent Liam Coll. Thank you for taking the time to meet with us."

"Well, when you described what you folks are dealing

with, it was kind of hard not to. How soon do you expect the attack?"

"Imminently," I say. "We have intel from someone on the inside who has pointed to Philadelphia as being the next target of a man who we know to be something of a fanatic."

"Philadelphia is a big city. Is there any chance of narrowing that down?" he asks.

"It's going to be a financial institution, or something that has to do with money," I say. "And I think it's going to be somewhat symbolic. But that's just a hunch."

"You're obviously not thinking about bank branches out in the suburbs," Rockefeller says.

"No. This is going to be something big, something substantial. You know how these kinds of people work; they want to make a splash. Can you give us a list of all of the buildings in downtown that have some sort of financial connection? Or even history?"

Rockefeller smiles, but he doesn't outright laugh, which I appreciate. I know it's something of a ludicrous ask, but at this point we have to look at all the possibilities.

"Come with me," he says. "We can get you set up. I expect you two will have a long night ahead of you."

As Rockefeller takes his back through the large and airy lobby he takes a quick glance back at me. "That from being on the job?" He asks. I reach up and feel my nose; I had almost forgotten the splint was still there.

"You could say that. I was acting in an official capacity, unofficially."

He responds with a belly laugh, which makes me smile. "That's how I know you're the real deal. Always on the job, even when you're off."

He takes us through a couple of security checkpoints, into a larger bullpen-like area that's somewhat reminiscent of our own back at the home office. A gigantic screen dominates one side of the room, while a couple of rows of desks and computers sit in front of it, most of them full.

"Do I need talk with your SSA? I want to make sure we're coordinating on this," he asks as he indicates the stations where we can get set up.

I exchange a quick glance with Liam. "Let us—"

Before I can say anything else one of the agents calls out. "Sir?" Rockefeller turns his attention away from us and heads over to the agent who got his attention.

"What's going on?"

"We're getting reports of alarms from the Federal Reserve, they could be nothing, but it looks like preliminary fire suppression alarms?"

My heart jumps up into my throat. The Federal Reserve building. I trot over to the desk, looking at what the agent has on their screen. "You need to mobilize all emergency responders over there immediately," I say.

Rockefeller looks at me. "You think this is the target? That building sits right beside ours here."

"If what we saw in Baltimore was just a preview, I don't want to find out. Make sure that building is evacuated immediately. And you need to make sure emergency response teams are standing by and ready." I turn back to Liam. "It makes sense, doesn't it?"

Liam is bent over one of the empty stations, typing something furiously on the keyboard. "I'm trying to get a good look at what's around the building."

"It's literally the building next to us," Rockefeller says, pointing behind us. "Right over there. All the federal buildings are clustered here together. And we're close to the National Constitution Center, the Liberty Bell, Independence Hall... the list goes on. Any of which could be high-value targets."

I furrow my brow. "I don't think he's going for landmarks, as such. But the collateral damage from the building could be enough to—"

"Sir!"

There's a massive rumble through the room and for a second I think I might have called it wrong, and Simon has hit the FBI building instead of some financial institution. Someone has thrown up a satellite picture of the Federal Reserve in downtown Philadelphia on the large digital wall. As we watch in horror, explosions rip their way through the building creating a black plume of smoke, until that's all that's visible. The explosions are enough to shake the desks in this building, knocking over anything that isn't nailed down. Somewhere I hear windows shatter and people screaming.

"Dammit!" I yell as Liam grabs on to me and people begin hitting the floor. Behind us the entire wall of windows rattle in unison as another explosion rips through the building across the street, and I expect them to shatter at any second. The sound is terrible, like a giant monster screaming and groaning all at once. But somehow the windows hold, which is good because the smoke billowing out of the building across the street is all we can see when we get up.

"Everyone okay?" Rockefeller calls out. No one calls out in pain or distress. "Okay, let's start working the problem here. To your stations. I want a full sitrep on this right—"

He's cut off as the entire room is engulfed in organized chaos, the agents fielding calls from emergency personnel, and coordinating with anyone else on the ground. Rockefeller is doing his best to contain the chaos, but there are a lot of moving parts. Liam and I get up, taking another look at the smoke roiling against the windows. I turn and watch in horror as the building on the satellite view goes up just like the First National Bank in Baltimore did. Zara was right, I *knew* she wasn't compromised. She was trying to tell us, and Wallace wouldn't listen. Which means Cohen is definitely a double agent. Of course he would've diverted the ATF to another site, to throw the rest of us off the trail.

"You okay?" Liam asks.

"Yeah, you?"

"Just a little spooked," he says. "I thought those windows weren't going to hold."

As we watch the destruction unfold in front of us, and the agents in the room are attempting to coordinate with all the personnel that are headed to the site, I feel Liam's hand on my shoulder. "She tried to warn us," I say.

"I know. You were right."

"We need to get in contact with Wallace. We need to warn him and Sandel that they need to arrest Cohen."

Liam shakes his head. "You do that, and Cohen gets suspicious. Right now, he has no idea we're here, and no idea that we knew this was coming."

"So what you want to do? Keep pretending like he's on our side?"

"I'm just saying confronting him head-on may not be the best strategy. Let's get in contact with Sandel and Wallace, and get them on board. We have to make it look like we didn't know about this to the ATF. No doubt Cohen and his men want to come up here and inspect the building once the fires are out."

I nod. "He wants to plant any evidence that would point the finger in another direction, or remove anything that could be incriminating." I should've seen it before, that's why he was so anxious to get into the building in Baltimore. There are dozens of ATF departments all around the country, but he insisted that it was his team to go in there and look. Now I know why.

The next fifteen minutes are a blur while everyone tries to get a handle on the situation. Rockefeller does a good job managing his team and making sure the appropriate emergency personnel reach the building in time. Part of me wants to go out there on site, but I know I'll just be in the way. This time I'm going to let the Philadelphia office do their jobs, and we can interview any other witnesses later. Out of the corner of my eye I see Rockefeller approaching. He looks like he's been put through the wringer. His tie is a little bit looser and his hair is messed up, but his eyes are still bright.

"Well, there's good news. Apparently the fire alarms that we were notified about started going off almost an hour ago. Which means the entire building was already almost empty before the explosion happened."

I swallow out a lump in my throat because I know that's not a coincidence. "That was our person on the inside, I'm sure of it. She's doing everything that she can to help prevent loss of life."

"Then she did a damn fine job of it," Rockefeller says. "So far we're looking at less than a dozen people still in the building when the bomb went off."

"That's great news," I say.

"We're still trying to find any witnesses who might've seen something around the building before it exploded. But that's going to take a while. It's a busy area, with a lot of tourists. Most of the injuries being tended to are superficial from flying glass or other bits of shrapnel. But still it's going to be a lot of wounded people to talk to."

"I think it's about time I gave my SSA a call," I say. "If he doesn't know about this already, he'll need to."

Rockefeller nods. "I just wish you folks would've made it here little earlier, maybe we could've prevented the whole thing from happening." He gives us a small little wave of his hand before heading back to his team.

"I'm not quite sure how to take that," I say.

"I think he's just frustrated, like we were in Baltimore. Simon taking down the Federal Reserve is no small deal. That will cripple financial institutions all around this area for months," Liam says.

"I can't wait to see the look on Wallace's face when I tell him I told you so," I say, heading for one of the workstations. I plan on making the call from right from here.

"Em, there's something else," Liam says. "What happens when Simon finds out that Zara evacuated the building early?"

That pit in the bottom of my stomach returns with a vengeance. He's right. Zara is on the front lines. She's doing her best to help us, and now she might be compromised. She won't be able to hold out for much longer.

We have to find her, and we have to do it now.

Chapter Twenty

THE FIRST CALL we make is to Elliott and Nadia, informing them of what's going on. Surprisingly, Sandel sounds more contrite than usual on the phone. I wonder if acting as the lead agent is beginning to get to him, especially since he agreed with Wallace and ended up making the wrong call. Both let me know they're headed up to Philadelphia immediately. We've already discussed not informing Cohen that we knew about Philadelphia ahead of time, which they agree is the best plan. Cohen and his men are headed up as well, and Nadia has assured me they'll play nice like we're all one big happy family. I think in this instance, Liam is right. We can't let Cohen and his men know we saw this coming. There's no telling how many of his people could be involved.

The call with Wallace though, isn't going as smooth.

"Yes, sir, I understand that." I say, trying to restrain my frustration. "But you have to understand—"

"Slate, don't argue with me," Wallace says.

I glance over Liam and just roll my eyes. For as much as Wallace says he wants to help me, he sure likes to fight me on everything I try to tell him.

"But this not only proves that she was right, but that she's not compromised."

"I don't think we can make that assumption yet; we don't know what Agent Foley is thinking."

"*I know* what she's thinking, sir." This man. I swear, if there is anyone who will drive me into an early grave... "I've known her a long time, I know how she thinks. She may not have been able to stop the bombings, but she emptied that building before the bombs went off. And now her life is in danger."

I can practically hear him sighing on the other side. "Let's say you're right, and it's best to err on the side of caution. We operate like Agent Foley's life is in imminent danger. I don't suppose she left any clues about *where* she might be being held?"

"Not that we've found yet, but Liam is searching back through everything we have from Baltimore as well as the preliminary information coming in from the blast here in Philly."

"That's another thing, Slate. You abandoned your assignment. *Again.* Do we need to revisit the talk we had on unapproved travel?"

"I tried to tell you the arena was not under threat. *You* were the one who insisted we focus on that location first and we'd follow up here later. Well, guess what? It was the wrong call, and you know it. You keep saying you want to be able to work with me, but if that's the case, you're going to need to actually *trust me* when I tell you something. Zara obviously sent me a message. The lead agent here even said if we'd arrived earlier we might have been able to stop it from happening at all. We could have caught them in the process."

He's quiet on the other end for a moment and I'm afraid I may have overstepped. "You're right. I should have trusted you. I'm not used to my agents going off half-cocked because nine times out of ten, it turns out they're wrong."

"I wouldn't have even suggested it if there was that much of a possibility of it not panning out. But I know my friend. And right now, she's in imminent danger."

"Sandel and Kane are on their way to you right now, with Cohen and his group in tow?" he asks.

"Yes, sir."

He's quiet for another minute. "How do you want to proceed?"

"Agent Coll reminded me that Cohen and his men have no idea about the message from Zara. I want to keep it that way. Lull them into a false sense of security. But it's still his face on that tape. I think it's best we keep up the ruse until the opportune time comes to arrest Agent Cohen."

I can practically hear him opening the bottle of Tums on his desk. "I think at this point we don't have much of a choice. If you're right, and Cohen is involved, we can't allow him to continue operating as part of the team hunting Simon."

"Other members of his team may be involved as well," I say.

"I'm aware. If you can get Cohen alone, you have my permission to arrest and interrogate him. See if you can get anything out of him before he lawyers up. Show him the tape if you need to. But I don't want to alert anyone else in the event they could compromise anything. Let's get our facts straight before we go off half-cocked up against the entire ATF." He pauses. "Did Agent Foley indicate anything about another attack?"

"Still working on that one, sir," I say. "But if there's a way, she'll have found it. Given the quantity of explosives stolen from Lockheed, I don't think Simon is done yet."

"Neither do I," he says. "Keep me updated, and Slate— when you go after Cohen, be careful. If he has infiltrated the government this far, he's obviously a dangerous and well-connected person."

"I understand," I say. Wallace hangs up without another word.

"Sounds like that went well," Liam says, offhandedly as he scrolls through rows and rows of data on his screen. The energy in the room has died out a bit, especially after it was discovered that the building had been virtually empty. But we're still working out of the field office's bullpen.

"About as well as I could expect. He gave us the green light to arrest Cohen."

He arches an eyebrow. "Seriously?"

"I think he's finally taking Zara's warning to heart. He's going to have a hell of a time explaining to Janice why he authorized an operation at the arena when we had intel about this attack."

"To be fair," he says. "Even if we'd had another day, we might not have found it. It's not like we knew it was going to be the Federal Reserve building specifically. Also, there are two Federal Reserves here, did you know that? The old one, which is part of the college now, and the one that was destroyed."

"It's like I said," I say. "He's not going for symbolism. Otherwise he would have taken out the original. He's trying to have a real-world effect on financial markets. First with the largest bank in Baltimore, now with the Federal Reserve. He's escalating. I don't guess you've made any progress on any hidden messages."

"If she's left something about another attack, I haven't found it yet," he says. "But we haven't received the footage from inside the Federal Reserve yet. Rockefeller is still working on clearing it. Want to help me look?"

I check the time on my phone. It'll be a couple more hours before everyone else arrives and I can't think of anything better to do. The minute we find Zara, I'm going in to pull her out of whatever hole Simon has stuffed her in, damn the consequences.

"I'd like nothing better," I say.

∽

By the time Kane and Sandel arrive, the smoke from the building has cleared enough so that we can look out on the destruction ourselves. Kane and Sandel join us in the bullpen just before the sun dips below the horizon and we get our first good look at the destruction in the nation's third-largest Federal Reserve.

"Agent Slate," Sandel says, approaching from behind. "I just wanted to say I'm sorry for not backing you up, earlier. I should have trusted your instincts. It's not something I'm very good at." He holds out his hand for me and I hesitate.

"What's that? Trusting people?" I ask.

"Instincts," he says. "I've always been a facts kind of person. It's hard for me to just trust a gut feeling."

I give him a nod, taking his hand. This is a rare moment for him, and his face is strained, like he's the most uncomfortable I've ever seen him. "That's okay. It's not always easy to put your faith in something you don't believe in."

"I'm just glad you two are okay," Nadia says, looking around us. "How are those windows intact?"

"SSA Rockefeller informed us they're the same kinds of windows they use in the White House, apparently," Liam says. "Double reinforced so in the event someone decides to start shooting at the FBI—"

"Nothing gets through, got it," she says, impressed. "Did you manage to find any more clues from Agent Foley?"

"Nothing yet. Unfortunately, the servers that held the camera data from the Federal Reserve were *in* the building when it blew," I say. "They never used offsite or cloud storage. Which means we have no chance of seeing who planted the bombs or when. And we also lose any opportunity for another message from Zara."

"I wonder if Simon expected that this time," Nadia says.

"Maybe that factored into why he chose the Reserve. He knew there wouldn't be any evidence left behind."

"That's possible I say. Of course, there's always someone we can ask in person." I look around them. "Speaking of which, where are they?"

Elliott shakes his head. "They didn't come up with us. Cohen said he wanted to get his guys on site as soon as possible. They brought all their equipment up with them."

"What did he say when you told him about the attack?" I ask.

Elliott and Nadia exchange looks. "He seemed surprised, shocked really. Insisted the intel they had was for the arena."

"We need to get him isolated, away from his men and into an interrogation room. Wallace has given us the authority to arrest him, based on the video images."

"But—I haven't finished running my analysis yet," Nadia says. "What if it's been doctored?"

"I think we can safely say at this point that's unlikely," I reply. "Zara was trying to tell us the whole time. We need Cohen off the case and for him to start talking. And we need to do it quietly. If he has other people on his team involved with the Simonites as well, I don't want to alert them."

"Do you think his entire team might be compromised?" Elliott asks.

"I don't know. Did he say how long their investigation would take?" I ask.

"If it's anything like Baltimore, they'll be here all night," he replies.

"We need to get him off that site," I tell Liam. "He's going to see the body count is much lower this time. He could report that back to Simon. And if that happens, we can kiss Zara goodbye." I head out of the bullpen back down to the elevator banks.

"Won't the media report that anyway?" Nadia asks, following along.

"I'm hoping we can get a lid on that, at least for a little while. We need as much time as possible." I hit the down button on the elevator.

"Where are you going?" Sandel asks.

"To find Cohen. Cell service is spotty at best, and I want to get to him before he has a chance to look too closely at the building."

"But, Emily, it's like a warzone out there. The National Guard has the area locked down. No one will be allowed out there without proper clearance," he replies.

"Yeah, I'm willing to bet that building was probably built back when asbestos wasn't a known carcinogen," Nadia says. "You'll at least need protective gear."

"Uh-huh," I say as the doors open. "I'm sure I'll manage. Trust me."

"Don't forget what your doctor said—" Sandel begins but the doors close on him. I know full well what the doctor said. But at this point if it comes down to my *condition* or getting to Zara in time, there's no question which one I'm going to prioritize.

Just hang on, I think, hoping that somehow she can hear me, wherever she is. *I'm coming.*

Chapter Twenty-One

SANDEL WAS RIGHT, the place is an absolute warzone. Debris made up of metal, glass, concrete, and everything in between litters the streets between the FBI building and what remains of the Federal Reserve. Unlike the First National Bank in Baltimore, the face of the building itself is still intact, though all of the windows have been blown out. Most of the destruction seemed to come from the middle of the building.

Emergency personnel swarm the area, with fire departments providing cover as the police keep civilians back and the rescue squads tend to the wounded. As I make my way across the street I note just how fewer casualties there are. Zara really did it; she probably saved hundreds of lives with that evacuation trick. The National Guard has deployed and is providing a perimeter around both buildings, so I don't have to cross any lines to get over to the site of the destruction, though I do have to show my badge to a few well-meaning soldiers.

Once I've reached the front of the Federal Reserve, I get my first good look at the level of carnage Simon's bombs created. There seems to be a makeshift command tent set up right in the middle of the street in front of the building, which is where I head first to try and find Cohen.

Much like in Baltimore, representatives from different agencies are all working to try and contain the situation. Just as I'm entering the tent, I hear the telltale sound of jet engines overhead. I step back out and look up as a pair of F-18's streak across the sky. No doubt with the incident yesterday in Baltimore and now this, air traffic has had to close airspace over a couple of cities.

"I'm looking for Agent Cohen with the ATF," I say, stepping into the tent and holding up my badge at the same time.

A couple of people look over, but only one speaks. "Is that the guy from DC?" he asks. I nod. "Then maybe you can tell me why he's insisted his team has jurisdiction in Philadelphia?" He rounds one of the tables and I catch that the patch on the side of his jacket sports the letters ATF as well.

"You're from the local division," I say.

"Hank Barger," he says, and I shake his hand quickly. "We were on response when I get a call from this Cohen character telling me they're taking over the investigation for the department. Can you explain that to me?"

"Not right off the top of my head, I can't," I lie. No need to bring in more people on this. "But I do need to find him. It's of some urgency."

Hank throws a hand in the direction of the building. "He's at the base of the first floor, with the rest of his team. Insisted on being in there even before the bomb squad finished its search. He's one reckless son of a bitch, I can tell you that."

"Don't I know it," I say under my breath as I leave the tent, headed for the front of the building. Fortunately, the wind is taking most of the smoke and dust away from the scene, but it's still thick in the air. I'm about to head back and grab some protective equipment when I spot Cohen speaking with Larson at the front of the building, just up the steps. Above them the face of the building looms large, almost like it's looking down on them, waiting to collapse. He spots me before I can say anything to him.

Surprisingly, he trots over to meet me. "Slate? What are you doing out here?"

"We've got a problem we need your assistance with," I say. "And cell service isn't exactly reliable right now."

"You need to be wearing protective equipment if you're going to be out in this," he says.

"No need, I'm headed right back. But this is urgent, Cohen. It concerns the next attack."

"The *next*…" He says it like he can't believe it. "But this is already…fine. Lead the way."

We trudge back through the debris field and head back into the FBI office, though we have to go through security again. Once we're back in the elevators, heading up to the main floor, I notice he has a fine powder of dust on him.

"Kinda bad in there, huh?"

"It's like hell, only worse," he replies.

"Why not just wait until the building has been cleared before going in? Aren't you putting your team at risk by charging in without knowing if there are any other explosives in there?" I ask.

"That's exactly why, and we expect there to be more. Often times not every unit ignites like it's supposed to, so you have live explosives just sitting there, waiting. I see part of our responsibility as finding and disarming those as soon as possible, to prevent any further destruction."

"But aren't you placing everyone's lives at risk when you do that?"

He turns to me. "How is that different than what you do? Or are you saying the FBI doesn't put its agents' lives on the line every day?"

"No, but we have safety protocol we follow." The doors open on our floor. "Even Hank, the guy running the local branch thinks you're too brash."

"That's because I get results," Cohen says.

"And the arena?" I ask.

"That…was unavoidable," he says. "We had good intel. And seeing as we didn't have any other leads, I thought it was worth exploring. I just wish it had been more accurate information."

"Where did that come from, anyway?" I ask.

"I told you, random tip on our lines." He doesn't look at me when he says it, which means there's a good chance he's lying.

I catch sight of Liam down one of the adjacent hallways. He's motioning for us to follow him to what I hope will be a secure room.

"You said you have information on another attack?" he asks. "How many places is this guy going to hit?"

"I guess as many as he thinks is necessary to get his point across," I say, keeping a close eye on Cohen. But he's not betraying anything. Liam holds the door open for him, bringing him into a room with a couch and a couple of chairs. Agents Kane and Sandel are already inside, sitting at the only desk.

Liam closes the door behind us and Cohen looks back. "What is this, some kind of secret meeting?" Some of his brashness has melted away, replaced by suspicion.

"We think we have a leak," I say. "So we don't want any of this intel leaving this room. Right now, we're the only people we can all trust."

"Okay," Cohen says, though he doesn't sound completely convinced. Instead, he sits on the couch. "Want to tell me what's really going on?"

He's already suspicious; I'm not going to get anything from him until I answer his question. But what matters is we have him in custody—more or less. He can't notify Simon of anything while he's in here. "How about you tell us how long you've been working for Simon Magus."

He blurts out a half laugh, but his face turns into a scowl.

"You must have broken more than your nose if you think I'm working for that psycho."

I nod, pretending like I believe him. "Okay. So then why were you down at the Baltimore Inner Harbor the morning of the bombing?"

"What?" he asks.

"We have a positive ID on you, from one of the victims. A young woman named Brooke. She says you ran into her right before the building exploded."

"That's ridiculous!" he yells, standing back up. "I was *helping* people down there, at least as many as I could until reinforcements arrived. I was trying to get people away from the blast."

"That's awfully nice of you," I say. "But there's one other little wrinkle in that story." I nod to Liam who pulls out his phone and plays the video of Cohen inside the building that morning, looking up at the camera.

"What the hell?" he says. "That's not me! Is that supposed to be inside the building?"

"You would know," I say.

"No, I wouldn't," he emphasizes. "Because the only time I've ever been in that building was yesterday, after the explosion. I don't know where you got that footage, but it's obviously fake."

"That's really unfortunate," I say. "Because this footage came along with an encoded message from our operative on the inside. A message that named Philadelphia as the next target."

"Wait," he says, his face growing red. "You knew? You knew about this attack ahead of time?"

I nod. "And while you were trying to throw us off the trail by focusing on the arena, Liam and I came up here to see if we couldn't stop something terrible from happening. Obviously, we failed."

"Now, wait just a second," Cohen says, his eyes going

wide. "I told you; we didn't have any reason not to believe that intel that came in. It looked like a solid lead. Why didn't you tell me you had conflicting information? We could have been here hours sooner!"

I screw up my features. "I would think that's obvious. We didn't want you to know we were on to you."

"There's nothing to be on to!" he yells, his face going even a deeper shade of crimson.

"Whoa there, calm down," Liam says. "You're not going to make us cuff you, are you?"

Cohen takes a breath. "This is ridiculous. You've gone too far this time, Slate. Wallace will have your head for this."

"Wallace authorized your arrest," I tell him.

Cohen sits back down and puts his head in his hands. Funny, I had pegged him as a fighter; I thought we'd have to restrain him before he broke down. "This is all wrong," he says.

"Let's say you're right," I say. "Let's say you weren't in that building. You already admitted to being down at the inner harbor when the explosion happened. And I know you were already on site because you called in your team from there. So why were you there if not making sure the explosion went according to plan?"

He drops his hands and glares up at me with more hatred than I've seen from a person in a long time. "I was down there because that was one of the places my daughter loved when we still lived in Baltimore. Yesterday would have been her nineteenth birthday. I've been to the inner harbor every January twenty-sixth for the past three years. For her."

As I stare at him, I feel that pit growing in my stomach again. Either Cohen is an exceptional liar, or this is the truth. For the first time since we saw his face on that camera I'm not sure we have the right person. But Brooke identified him… though, I have to admit, it wasn't a home run. She hesitated and was having trouble remembering the events of the day.

"You said you helped people when the bomb went off," I say. "Who did you help?"

"There was a young couple with a baby that I got indoors to safety," he says. "An elderly woman who was having trouble walking, a small tourist group from Sweden—at least I think they were Swedish and probably a dozen other people," he says. "Why? Gonna tell me I didn't and killed them instead?"

"What about anyone that was close to the blast?" I prompt.

From the way his head is moving I can tell he's exasperated with me. "Yeah, a few covered in dust. Some suffering from smoke inhalation."

"Anyone bleeding from the ears?"

"One or two. This one blonde lady collapsed in my arms as soon as she saw the building going up in smoke."

Shit. I glance over at Liam and he's staring right back at me. Brooke must have gotten Cohen confused with the man who ran into her. Then again there's nothing to say they aren't one and the same, but I wouldn't expect her to run to him for help if he'd just almost knocked her down moments earlier. I don't think we can rely on Brooke's memory.

"Nadia," I say quietly. "Where are we on your analysis?"

"Still running," she says. "I told you it would take a while."

"Analysis, what analysis?" Cohen asks.

"The analysis on the footage with your face on it," Sandel says. "In an attempt to determine if it's genuine or not."

"So you don't have any proof," Cohen says, sounding vindicated.

"We have a lot of information at this point, and all of it points to you being implicated in this bombing," I tell him. "If you weren't, care to tell us why someone would go to the trouble of putting *your* face on that camera? Why you specifically?"

"How am I supposed to know?" he asks. "Maybe I'm an easy

target. I've been on the job a long time, maybe someone thinks it's easy to frame a guy who lost everything a few years ago. Maybe they think that will make it seem like I have an ulterior motive."

I hadn't known about Cohen's daughter until now, but that doesn't mean someone else didn't already. If the footage has been doctored, then I'm fairly sure it was Zara who did it. Maybe she didn't have a choice in the matter—and she sent the encoded message as a warning; the only one she could get to us.

Unfortunately, Cohen is right. All the evidence we have against him is circumstantial, except for the footage, which may or may not be doctored.

"Can you tell us where you were in the early hours yesterday? Before the explosion?"

"I woke up, about four a.m. Went to the gym early, worked out. Took a shower and headed to the harbor. My plan was to leave after lunch to come back and continue working on the case with you." He pauses for a moment, looking me dead in the eye. "You can check with my gym, and my EZ pass on the Baltimore tunnel. Both will show me exactly as I'm telling you."

I don't need the evidence. This man isn't lying, not about this. But we're going to check it anyway. "Can you check with his gym for me?" I ask Liam.

"Planet Fitness," Cohen says, deadpan. "Off eighth."

"I've got him on the tunnel cameras," Nadia says, staring at her computer. "He crossed the tunnel heading into the city at nine-forty-five a.m."

That was fast. "The gym will take me a minute," Liam says, holding his phone up to his ear. I was so convinced Cohen was our man. That Zara was trying to point us to him. I should have considered that she might not have as much control in her situation as I'd hoped.

"You know," Cohen says, leaning forward and dropping

his voice. "It's customary to apologize to someone when you wrongfully accuse them of treason, murder and terrorism."

I shoot a furtive glance to Sandel, who only gives me the *briefest* of smiles. I'm big enough to admit when I'm wrong. "You're right," I say. "I should have checked your whereabouts first. I'm sorry. But when you receive intel with a face on it, you tend to think that's your suspect."

He nods. "I can't blame you there." Liam is speaking with someone on the phone, but he throws me a thumbs up. Which means if Cohen was at his gym yesterday morning, there's no way he could be on the footage as well.

"Nadia, since now we know the footage has been faked, is there any way to reconstruct the original image? Show us who was really on there?"

"Unfortunately, no. It's not like there's a skin sitting on top of the original image that we can 'erase'. It's already been done at the source and re-encoded."

"But you could tell if it wasn't him—"

"That's because of image fragmentation, or pixelation where it shouldn't be. The evidence would show us that the image wasn't original, but reconstructing it is impossible without the source file, which has already been overwritten. I've been through all the servers."

That sounds like Zara all right. I wonder why she was so thorough with it. She could have made it more obvious the culprit wasn't Cohen, but she took the time to cover her tracks. Why?

Until I find out, I can't let Wallace know. He'll assume she really has been compromised.

Back to square one.

Chapter Twenty-Two

"CAN I GO NOW, or are you trying to manufacture more evidence to charge me with?" Cohen asks.

I've been conferring with the rest of the team on how we should proceed from here. Obviously, Cohen isn't our man and right now we have no new suspects. And given that the Federal Reserve's servers were destroyed in the blast we have no way of knowing if Zara tried to send us another message about another attack. But given how quickly Simon has ramped up his plans, he could hit a third location as soon as tomorrow.

I check my phone. It's already almost midnight. We just don't have the time we need to get ahead of him. And now we're out of leads.

I glance over at Cohen who is still sitting on the couch, waiting for a decision. I have to assume Zara intentionally used his face to cover the real bomber's identity. The question is, why? Why go with Cohen at all? She could have picked any random person in the entire world, and she chooses to use the head of the ATF unit we're working with? That doesn't make any sense. Unless she was *forced* to use Cohen's face.

"No, you can't," I say. "We need to figure out who would

want to frame you. Do you have any enemies? Anyone who might be harboring a grudge against you?"

"Wouldn't I have already told you if I did?"

I cock my head at him. "C'mon. You can't tell me in the twenty-five years you've worked for the agency you haven't pissed *someone* off."

"More than my fair share, probably," he replies. "But not enough that someone would want to frame me for all this."

"And you don't know Special Agent Zara Foley, correct?"

"Never met her in my life," he says, though he's already answered this question after I showed him a picture of her.

"Em, c'mon, it's late," Liam says. "I think we all need some rest. We'll have to pick this back up in the morning."

Cohen scoffs. "Yeah. Rest for you. I still need to get back out to the blast site with my team."

I turn to him. "Why are you so insistent on being out there right now? It's not like it's going anywhere. You've been adamant about getting on site as soon as possible at both locations. Why?"

"Because in my business, the sooner we can get a look at the damage, the better. You'd be surprised how quickly evidence can disappear from a scene, either from carelessness, weather or something totally unrelated. The way I operate may be a little unorthodox, but you can't argue with the results. I'm not one of these guys who's willing to sit around and wait until everything is deemed 'safe'. The important thing is to get in, secure the scene, record the evidence and find the culprit."

"So you think by getting into the sites sooner it will give you a better chance of finding Simon," I say.

"That's the idea. It doesn't always work like that. Take this Magus guy, for example," he says, spreading his hands wide. "He's meticulous and has orchestrated his bombs in a way that they leave very little behind, which tells us he's a pro. He's been in the business a while and knows what he's doing."

"Like you," I say.

He concedes the point. "True. Ideally, someone who wanted to cover their tracks would be intimately familiar with all of our procedures as well as many different types of explosives."

"Would being part of the ATF also give them access to explosives stockpiles?" I ask.

He's still for a moment. "It would."

"Is there anyone on your team—anyone new?"

He screws up his features. "Now wait a second, why are you zeroing in on my team? I've known most of those guys for years. We've been to each other's weddings, kids birthday parties. They wouldn't—"

"Because someone chose *you* to take the fall for this," I say. "More than likely that's someone who knows you. Maybe even knows your schedule." My mind begins racing with all the possibilities. "How many people on your team know about your daughter?"

"Maybe five or six," he says. "But—"

"And the other times you've come into Baltimore for her birthday, did you always take the tunnel?" I ask.

"No…I had to take a detour around. There was a big wreck on I-95 that morning and it was easier to take the bypass. I didn't want to be stuck in traffic for two hours."

"Which agents would have known you'd be in Baltimore yesterday?" I ask. Liam and the others look on expectantly.

"Um…let's see." He counts off on his fingers, seeing where I'm going with this. "Dobson, Larson, Riggs, and maybe O'Reilly. But you have to understand, I *know* these guys. They wouldn't—"

"One of them might," I say, turning to Nadia. "See if you can't get an alibi on any of them."

"I'll take Dobson," Liam says.

"I've got Larson," Sandel replies.

"Wait," Cohen says. "This is crazy. These are my guys.

They're down there, right now, digging through rubble trying to find anything they can to help us track this monster down. You don't seriously think one of them is involved with him, do you?"

"One of them might be," I say. Even when I still suspected Cohen, I was wary of his team, not knowing how deep the corruption ran. Now I realize that one of his own guys might have been undermining him this entire time.

"Dobson is clear," Liam says.

"So are Riggs and O'Reilly," Nadia says. "ATF records show them in the building yesterday morning at the time of the recording." That's funny, I was already starting to suspect Riggs since he was the one who almost cost us Leo Bolton.

"I've got nothing on Larson," Sandel replies. "No alibi."

"Get him up here," I tell Cohen.

"What? You mean, *now?*"

"Do you see that we have time to waste?"

He pinches his features, then I hand him his two-way, watching him switch it on. "I can't believe I'm about to do this," he says. "*Cooper, come back,*" he says into the unit.

"Yeah, boss?" Cooper responds almost immediately. "Some of the guys been looking for you."

"Do you see Larson anywhere?" Cohen asks.

"He was with Sweeney is over by the south entrance," he replies. "But I don't see him now. One sec." The radio goes silent before coming back on about twenty seconds later. "No one has eyes on Larson. Hasn't seen him since you left the site. We thought he was with you."

Cohen exchanges looks with all of us. "Coop, you need to find him, right now."

"Why, what's going on?" the man asks. "He's probably just over on the other part of the site. It's not exactly the picture of calm down here. Plus it's dark and—"

"Cooper, listen to me," Cohen says, his voice stronger now. "Confirm Larson is no longer on site. Top priority."

"Yes, sir." The radio clicks off.

"How much do you know about Larson?" I ask.

"I mean, I've known the man for years. No family, but he's always been a friendly-enough guy. Always willing to do anything to help out. He helped me and Ronaldo build a shed for their ATV. And he was one of the groomsmen in O'Reilly's wedding. Hell, we all were."

The radio clicks back on. "No sign of him boss. He must have split."

"Ten-four," Cohen says, resigned as he stows the radio on his belt.

"Do you have a way to contact Larson?" I ask.

"Sure, I've got his cell, his home address, his email. What do you want?"

I turn to the rest of the group. "Are you thinking what I'm thinking?"

"That Larson orchestrated this thing with a hand on the inside the entire time," Liam says. "Yeah, I think we're all on the same page."

I turn back to Cohen. "You're officially off the hook." I head to the door. "We need to track him down. Put an APB out on his vehicle. If he is working for Simon, he'll already know the body count wasn't as high as it should have been. And then Simon will know Zara double-crossed him." We all file out, heading back for the bullpen. I turn back to Cohen as we walk. "What does he drive?"

"A twenty-fifteen Honda. A CR-V, I think."

"I need you to pull his record. Get a plate number and get all local PD on lookout for the car. From here back to DC." When we reach Rockefeller and his agents, everyone scrambles into action. All of a sudden I begin to see how the pieces fit together. Simon has been manipulating this thing from the inside this entire time. Just as we've had a man on this inside of his organization, he's done the exact same with us.

The question is, how did he turn a dedicated ATF agent and how long has Larson been working for him?

I grab my phone and call Wallace while everyone else works on putting out alerts on Larson's car and tracking his cell phone. Did he know we were close, and that's why he decided to leave the site? Or is he headed to report back to Simon about Zara's betrayal? God, we have to hurry.

"Wallace," the man says, picking up. I have to hand it to him, despite it being midnight, he still sounds as fresh as if it were nine in the morning.

I give him the rundown of what we've discovered, as well as what we think Larson might be doing. The odds are he's heading back to Simon. If we can find a way to track him, we can locate Simon's base of operations and rescue Zara before it's too late.

"I need to FaceTime with Bolton," I tell Wallace after informing him of everything that's happened.

"Bolton, why?" he asks.

Now that we know Larson may have been working on the inside this whole time, I have to re-evaluate everything. The rally, arresting Bolton, and even the "anonymous" call to the ATF, telling them the arena was the next target. "Because I'm not so sure his arrest wasn't on purpose," I reply.

Wallace seems flabbergasted, at least, that's what I'm inferring from the sputtering I'm catching on the other side. "Wait, on *purpose*? What are you saying? He wanted us to catch him and bring him in?"

"I think it might have been a delay tactic, sir," I say, thinking back to when we picked up Bolton. I always thought it was a little too easy to find him, especially the *day* after we put out word about him. It seemed too easy in my mind, even though I really had no reason to think that at the time.

"If that's the case, I doubt he's going to confirm it for you. He's been tight-lipped ever since your...outburst. If what you're saying is true, then his devotion to Simon and his followers goes deeper than we thought. You're not going to break him, not tonight. Focus on finding Larson."

I sigh. He's right. But some part of me needs confirmation. I need to *understand* these people and right now I just don't. What kind of person sacrifices themselves for a cause like this? And if that's what Bolton was willing to do, how far will Simon's other followers go?

And most importantly, what are they planning next?

Chapter Twenty-Three

ZARA WRINGS HER HANDS. She's trying to act casual, but she's having a difficult time of it. Even though it's after midnight, there's an electricity in the air among the remaining Simonites. She's been given more freedom to move around, but has stayed mostly in the office, with Theodore keeping a close eye.

True to his word, he managed to help her trip the fire alarm systems in the Federal Reserve building in Philly, giving the people enough time to evacuate before Simon's bombs were due to go off. He was the one who worked on that while she was clearing Simon's men through security. It turned out to be easier than she'd thought; all she'd needed to do was fool the scanners into thinking the bags with the explosives were empty which required a little skill, but it was nothing she couldn't handle. At the same time, Theodore had been setting up early-warning alarms to make the entire building's fire system go off at once. They had to wait until Simon's men were out of the building so as not to give them early warning, but they also couldn't wait too close to the detonation.

It had been a tightrope, and Zara thought they'd done the best they could. She's been peppering Theodore with questions ever since he emptied the gun, making sure she knew he wasn't a threat, but he's given up very little about who he really is or what he's doing here. All she knows is he's not a true Simonite. None of them would have gone against Simon like this guy has, that much she's sure about. Everything else, from his demeanor to the hint of a British accent is something of a mystery about the man.

"What's going on?" Zara asks when Theodore returns from the main chamber. He makes sure to shut the door behind him.

"Clint and his team are back. No sign of Simon yet. Everyone is celebrating the successful destruction of yet another financial landmark."

"Then they don't know yet," she says.

"And hopefully it stays that way. Do you think your friends will be able to cover up the fact we emptied the building before it blew?" He sits down beside her, a can of soda in his hand. He pops the top and drinks greedily. It's the first time she's seen him nervous.

"I hope so." She can only imagine what Emily is thinking right now. Zara knows she's probably not getting out of this alive; she just hopes she can do as much damage as possible while she's still here. There's at least one more job scheduled. She knows it's for New York, but she isn't sure exactly where. The files she managed to sneak a peek at weren't as descriptive as the Philly job. Obviously, Em missed her warning about the Federal Reserve. Or, at least, she didn't get the message in time. Back when she thought Theodore was watching her every move for Simon, she hadn't dared do anything more. But now that she knows he's "on her side", provisionally, she can take more of a risk. Simon will never know.

"We need to get word to them," she says. "But I need to know what to tell them first. I don't suppose he told you what he was planning."

Theodore takes another sip, staring at the far wall. "Nah.

His only directive to me was to watch you. Make sure you're doing the job he 'hired' you for."

She blows a breath up, which ruffles some of the hair off her forehead. "Maybe the next one we can actually stop. Do you have access to the explosives cache?"

He shakes his head. "It's under guard by a couple of the bigger guys. They won't let me get close to it."

"Then what about the detonators?" she asks. "Those are smaller, right? They would just need a little tampering—"

Before she can finish the door bursts open, smacking into the cinder block wall. Simon stands in the doorway, staring at us as he removes a pair of black gloves, one finger at a time. "Quite the night, isn't it?" he asks. It doesn't escape her notice that two more of his followers are positioned behind him.

Theodore stands, setting his soda on the desk. The gun Simon gave him is still at the command center, and still unloaded. They thought they'd have more warning before Simon returned.

"Yes, it has been an educational evening." Simon is wearing different clothes than he was when he left. In fact, he's got on what looks like ATF tactical gear. As Zara sits up straight, she can even see the ATF logo on his shoulder. And the name *Larson* in bold letters on his lapel. She looks up to see Simon has followed her gaze and is smiling at her. "I had really hoped you'd come around," he says. "But it's clear to me that your loyalties lie elsewhere and there's little I can do to change that."

He knows. Somehow he found out. Has he always been a part of the ATF team? Is that why he forced her to use that other ATF officer's face to cover up Clint on the Baltimore video? She wants to protest. To pretend like she's really been working for him all this time. Maybe that would buy her a couple of extra minutes of life. But Zara Foley is no coward. She stands. "I guess your ego got in the way of your better judgment, huh?"

He cracks another smile. "You've got a mouth on you. Some might consider that a bonus." He pulls out another handgun and before she knows it he's pulled the trigger. Beside her Theodore staggers back, a clot of crimson forming across the middle of his shirt where he's now holding himself. He falls to the ground, his hand on wound. "But I just consider it noise."

Zara bends down to help Theodore, who is looking at his wound with large, round eyes. But before she can get to him, the two other Simonites rush into the room, each grabbing one of her arms and wrenching them behind her back. This is it, and she knows it. She does her best to fight them off, stomping on the toes of the first one, causing him to let her go before shoving her palm up into the nose of the other man, shattering his nose and driving some of that bone in the direction of his brain.

He cries out and falls to the ground as she scrambles to the command table for the unattended gun, though the clip is still in Theodore's pocket. But the first acolyte grabs her again, this time by the cuff still dangling around her wrist. He wrenches it back, pulling her off her feet and she yells out in pain at the strain in her wrist. Before she can recover, he flips her over and attaches the open end of the cuff to her other arm. She tries her best to wriggle out of them, but they are attached tight, and there's nothing she can do to free herself.

Simon approaches, his gun still in hand. He doesn't even glance over at Theodore who seems to be bleeding out on the floor next to her. "You must be one hell of a lay if you got him to go along with you. Seems like my safeguards weren't quite enough."

She almost laughs. "You think I have to sleep with someone to make them do what I want?" Her true fury is coming out now. "I didn't even have to *say* anything. He just went right along with it. He was never with you. And I'd be willing to bet he wasn't the only one."

Simon's eyes flash and his grip tightens on the gun before he stows it back in its holster again. "I can't wait until this little arrangement of ours comes to an end. I am really tired of fighting you, Zara. I feel like we've been doing that since day one."

"You're a regular Sherlock Holmes, you know that?"

He grimaces before standing. The men who attacked her are back up as well, though the second one is holding his bloody nose. "Bag her. I want her transported and ready."

"What about him?" the first one asks, motioning to Theodore.

"Leave him, let him bleed out all over the floor. He can think about his life choices while he slowly succumbs to death." Simon reaches into his belt and pulls out another set of cuffs, tossing them to the second man who cuffs Theodore to the desk.

Simon turns back to Zara. "It was *you* who killed Omar, wasn't it?" He laughs, like he can't believe it. "I should have seen it earlier. Then again, I have been a little busy." The first man gets Zara up on two feet, facing Simon.

"You infiltrated them, didn't you? The ATF?" she asks.

Simon runs his hand down her cheek and she flinches away. "Sadly, that's where you're wrong. I've always been part of the organization. Ever since day one. My father always said if something was worth doing, it was worth doing right." He looks past her and nods, and the next thing Zara knows, a strip of tape is slapped over her mouth and a black bag comes over her head, blocking out all light.

Now she's really screwed.

Chapter Twenty-Four

"WE'VE GOT a location on Larson's vehicle!" Nadia says, looking up. We've been working through the night, each of us taking twenty-minute breaks to sleep while the others continued coordinating the search for Larson. Considering the rest of the Philadelphia office is preoccupied with the destruction of the Federal Reserve, it's just the four of us, but Wallace has tasked additional resources in the DC office.

Cohen and two of his guys sit nearby, still trying to pinpoint any known associates or maybe distant family members for Larson.

"Where?" I ask.

"Local PD spotted it on Wyneva Street, off Stenton Ave," Nadia says. "In Germantown."

"How far?" I ask.

"Maybe twenty minutes? Give or take," she says.

"Don't let the unit leave," I say, heading for the doors, motioning for Liam to follow. "Tell them we'll be there as soon as we can. You stay here in case we need to—"

"Agent Slate," Sandel says, standing from his own station. "May I have a word?"

"Can't it wait?" I ask. But the look on his face tells me it can't. I point back to Nadia. "Tell them I'll be there as soon as I can."

Sandel motions for me to join him on the far side of the room, away from most of the activity. Before I can ask what this is about he crosses his arms, and pins me with his gaze. "Remind me, at what point did you become the case agent on this investigation?" he asks.

I'm taken aback. I hadn't even considered who was in charge here, especially not after Cohen's bombshell. "Well, I mean I just assumed—"

"You assumed because you determined Larson was our suspect that it was your investigation now, am I wrong?

"Well, I mean I didn't even really think about it," I admit. Though I realize now, looking back, how it could look like I was trying to take over. "I wasn't trying to step on your authority. I just…I need to find Agent Foley. That may have made me more…headstrong than usual."

"I've noticed that about you," Sandel says. "You're the kind of agent to jump into things, no matter the consequences, feet first. Sometimes without even looking. But that's not how I operate. And that's not how this investigation will operate, do you understand?"

"Are you telling me not to investigate Larson's vehicle?" I ask, unsure where this is coming from all of a sudden. I thought Sandel and I had gotten past our differences.

"No. I just want to you to keep in mind that this is not your case. You came up here on your own accord, not informing me or Agent Kane. I just want to make sure we all stay in contact through this entire process. We're all on the same side here, and we will work best together if we *trust* each other."

"You're right," I say. "I haven't trusted you. Because I don't do so well with people. This…working in an environment where I have to interact with so many different people all the time, it's difficult. I'm not used to it. I'm used to—"

"Doing what you want, when you want," he finishes for me.

I can't help but smile. "Yeah. I guess so." Maybe I need to cut Agent Sandel some slack. Zara trusted him; that should be good enough for me. And while we might have gotten off on a rocky start, I believe Agent Sandel to be a good person. A good *agent*. "I won't jump ship again. And I'll be sure to report anything we find. We'll need to coordinate with Nadia anyway, I'm sure."

"Good, glad we have an understanding." He puts his hand out and I give it a shake. "Now get moving. He's already got a head start on us."

I meet Liam at the door, and we head down to the requisition office. "What was that about?" he asks.

"He's just making sure I'm not going to run off with the leash again," I say.

"Em, you're not a dog," Liam says.

I laugh. "No, I know. But he's right. I've been too impulsive. It hasn't been fair to them."

"Wow," he says. "Where did this come from?"

"I think when I realized just how wrong I'd been about Cohen," I say. "I guess sometimes I need a reminder that I'm not infallible."

He gives the splint on my nose a light tap. "I would think that would be reminder enough."

"Ugh, this stupid thing," I say, taking a minute to pull the tape back and remove the white covering from my nose. As soon as it's off I feel like I can breathe deeply for the first time in a week, though it's still a little sore. "How does it look? Is it covered in bruises?"

"Actually, it's just a little pink. That's it. But aren't you supposed to—"

"One limit at a time," I tell him as we find the requisitions officer for the building. Surprisingly, the lights in the office are still on. I push through and find the place to be a buzz of activity. An agent behind the desk looks up.

"Yes?" he asks.

"We weren't sure you'd even be open this late," I say. "We need a vehicle. For a few hours." I show him my badge.

"DC huh? Yeah, they called everyone in after the explosion. Here, fill this out." He hands me a short form which I fill out quickly, handing it back to him. He grabs a key fob, tossing it to me without another word.

"That was easy," I say as we make our way to the parking garage.

Fifteen minutes later we're on I-76, which runs parallel to the Schuylkill River, headed for Germantown. There's virtually no traffic as I'm sure people are on edge. Two large-scale attacks in as many days will do that. But I have a feeling Simon is done in Philly. He didn't stay in Baltimore and I don't expect him to stay here. He's no doubt moving on to bigger and flashier targets. The only question is: which ones?

We get off on Roberts Avenue and follow it as it winds through an industrial section of town. Philadelphia is such an old city, it's interesting to see how things are mashed together. Large warehouses dominate the right side of the road, while row houses dominate the left. All are in a sorry state, most in various states of disrepair, though some have been well kept. But it's definitely not the nicest part of town. A gigantic brick factory of some kind appears on the right side of the street, taking up most of the sky. Smokestacks with lights on them twinkle in the darkness, but above them I can't see any stars. There's too much light pollution.

We pull up to a Philly PD patrol car sitting on the side of the road at the intersection of Stenton and Wyneva, the latter of which is nothing more than an outcropping of a street that dead ends into some trees. But there is a parking area for what looks like one of the factories just off the road. And in the third spot, beside a beat-up Toyota, is a blue Honda CR-V. I hop out of the car and get a look at the plates. They match the ones Cohen provided from Larson's personal file.

"Have you seen anyone since you arrived?" I ask the officers, who are both standing outside their patrol car now, watching us.

"No one in or out. Haven't even seen a pedestrian," one of them says.

"What about the building? Any evidence of a break-in?"

They both shake their heads. "Already checked all the doors and windows. Building is sealed up tight. He didn't go in there."

I glance up, looking for anything that might help us. Across the street I see a security camera that's pointing right into this alleyway. "Then let's find out where he *did* go," I say. "What building is that right there?"

"Uh," the officer checks something on his phone. "Paper Resource Products Inc."

"We need to get in touch with them, get hold of their footage."

"Lady, it's two in the morning," one of the officers says. "Can't this wait until daylight?"

I throw him a stern look. "Did you happen to *see* the Federal Reserve this evening?"

He groans, heading back to his patrol car. "Fine. I'll call it in."

BY THE TIME SOMEONE FROM PAPER RESOURCE PRODUCTS, Inc arrives, it's almost four. The man is wearing a full set of sweats, like he's about to go running, though his eyes are bloodshot. He reminds me of Rocky, which is funny, considering. I'm sure Zara would have a choice joke or two for the man, but I have nothing other than an impending sense of foreboding.

"Here," the man says, leading us up the stairs and into his office. "Here's the footage you so desperately need."

Liam and I left the patrol officers outside, so it's just the two of us who sit down in front of the single computer showing the various camera angles. All the footage is live right now and I see both of them leaning up against their car at the mouth to Wyneva Street.

But sitting here also reminds me how this is usually Zara's department. She always handles viewing the security footage. God, I hope she's okay. Larson already has a five-hour head start on us.

"Em, what are you doing?" Liam asks. "Wind the footage back."

"Right," I say, getting to work. We rewind to midnight, then move forward at four times normal speed until we see the Honda pull into the road-slash-alleyway. As soon as I see it, I play it at normal speed.

"There's Larson." He gets out of the car, but he's taking his time, wiping it down. Why would he do that? If he thinks we're on to him, it's not like we're not going to know he was in the car. Did he not see the security camera? Maybe he was in too much of a rush. When he gets out I get a better look at the man. Yep, it's the same guy that came in that first day with Cohen, no doubt about it.

"Okay, so he wipes down the vehicle, and then…" Liam says, watching the footage. We watch as Larson jogs in the direction of the camera, toward Stenton Avenue. He then takes a left and runs off-screen.

"Where is he going?" I ask. I turn back to the Rocky impersonator. "Do you have any other angles, maybe one that looks down Stenton?"

He shuffles over and taps a few keys. "We don't use these cameras as much because it's nothing but an empty parking lot over there half the time," he says. "But they record anyway."

When he switches it over, we get a good view down Stenton and of the parking lot that sits on the other side of Paper Resources. I wind the footage back again until we see Larson jogging away from us this time, headed for the parking lot. There are a handful of vehicles parked there.

"Do people normally keep their vehicles there overnight?" I ask.

"It's sort of like an overflow," he says. "No one owns the lot, so people just leave their cars there sometimes. That Jeep in the corner has been there for at least six months."

We watch as Larson heads for a sedan, unlocks it and gets in before driving off. Unfortunately, he's too far away for us to make out a license plate. "We're going to need to update the APB," I tell Liam. "Get in touch with Nadia. Tell her we're looking for a dark gray or maybe even black Subaru Impreza."

"On it," Liam says.

I turn to the man. "How long was that Impreza there?"

"I really don't know," he replies, holding himself like he's cold. "Maybe a week or two?"

"Do me a favor, go back in your footage and look to see when that vehicle was parked there. And let me know if the same man who just drove off in it parked it." I hand him my card as Liam and I make our way back out of the office and down the steps.

"Hey, wait, no I'm going for a run this morning. This isn't my job."

I stop. "Sir, did you hear about the Federal Reserve building yesterday?"

"Well, yeah, of course. It was all over the news—"

"And the explosion in Baltimore the day before?"

"Yeah..."

"We're trying to stop number three. And that man is the key. Wind it back. If you can find out when someone parked it there, it would be helpful."

"Yeah," the man says, less sullen and more reproachful now. "Sure, I can do that."

"Thanks. And you can call, anytime. That's my cell."

Once we're back outside I call Sandel who informs me the forensic team is already on the way to inspect the vehicle. Since Larson wiped it down, I'm not sure we're going to get much from it, but it's worth looking. He might have been in a hurry and missed something.

When they arrive the very first rays of light begin penetrating the night sky.

It's going to be another long day.

Chapter Twenty-Five

WE GET BACK to the office around six. As best I can tell, Rockefeller and his team have switched out with the morning shift, who have taken over the damage control from the attack on the Federal Reserve. Additional reinforcements came in overnight and all high-value targets in Philadelphia have been closed and secured.

Meanwhile, the forensics team found very little in Larson's car, other than a couple of stray hairs which may or may not belong to him. Regardless, they're being tested anyway.

All I know is I'm about to collapse. I can't even remember when the last time I slept more than thirty minutes straight was. Seeing as I'm *still* not allowed to drive, Liam takes over the duty of getting us back and I fall asleep for what seems like less than five seconds but is really twenty-seven minutes. I don't wake until we pull back into the building's underground parking lot.

"I'm sure they'll be glad we returned the car in one piece," he says as we get out.

I give him a sleepy smile and head back into the building. I'm going to need someone to shoot caffeine directly into my veins if I'm going to make it through today.

When we get back to the main floor, Elliott and Nadia are still at their desks, but Nadia has her head on her arms and is snoring softly. Elliott looks up as we enter, giving us a nod hello.

"No progress?" he asks.

I yawn. "We have the new vehicle's description, but he switched out vehicles around one a.m. He was long gone by the time we got there and by the time we figured out he'd changed over into a Subaru he has over four hours on us. He could be anywhere. It looks like he was planning for this possibility."

"Like a backup plan?" he asks.

"Like an escape route," Liam says, slumping down in one of the chairs. One look at the circles under his eyes tells me he's as exhausted as I am.

"I wonder what set him off?" Elliott asks.

"Probably when he figured out Zara betrayed them," I say. I know it's probably wishful thinking at this point, but I'm just hoping by some miracle she's still alive.

"Oh, that reminds me," he says, turning back to his computer. Nadia snorts once and wakes herself up. She sits up like she wasn't sleeping and wipes her eyes a few times before getting back to work. Sandel doesn't seem to notice. "I got a call from Wallace while you were gone."

"Doesn't that man ever go home?" I ask, grabbing my own chair. It's not comfortable at all, but I know if I close my eyes I'll probably sleep for four good hours sitting straight up.

"He said due to the fact Larson has been with the ATF so long, he's spoken with the ATF director, and they've agreed that it significantly raises his threat level."

"Great," I say. "Now he's even more dangerous."

"He indicated that if we locate Larson, we are not to engage. Instead, he's sending in SWAT."

My eyes pop open. "A kill squad? Is he insane?"

"They're not a kill squad. He's probably thinking one

wrong move and Larson could level an entire city with the amount of explosives he stole. Better to stop them all before they have a chance to use it."

"Okay, but Zara is still in there with him, presumably. What is she, collateral damage?"

He winces while I shoot a *can you believe this* look at Liam. "Slate, I think even you have to face the facts at this point. More than likely Agent Foley is dead."

"*No goddammit!*" I yell, catching the attention of most of the people in the room. "She's not dead until I see her lifeless body!" I get up and storm out of the room. Liam calls after me, but wisely he doesn't follow.

SWAT. I can't believe it. Wallace has gone too far. I need to call Janice, though something like this wouldn't have been approved without her say so. And while I can't believe she would ever intentionally put Zara in the crosshairs, she's probably come to the same conclusion as Sandel, Nadia, Wallace, and every fucking person but me.

God, I want to kick something I'm so mad, but there's nothing out there, so I just utter a guttural yell until it becomes a scream in the middle of the hallway, running both of my hands through my hair. People who are just coming to work give me a wide berth, but I barely notice. There *has* to be something I can do. Talking to Wallace won't get me anywhere. Even talking to Janice will be pointless by now. She's not the kind of person to make decisions on a whim, nor is she likely to change her mind once it's made up. The gears are already in motion. I've been trying so hard to find Zara's location and now, as soon as I do, it will become a target. I know they say SWAT makes every effort not to harm any friendlies, but their track record isn't exactly stellar.

Think, Emily, think. There has to be some way to find her before everyone else does.

"Hey."

I look up to see Liam heading my way. He's got something

of a reproachful look on his face and he holds his hands up, that easy smile spreading across his face. "I come in peace."

"What?" I ask, perhaps too harshly.

"I heard the guttural scream from down there," he says. "I thought maybe I could help."

"If she's not dead already, they'll finish the job when they breach Simon's location," I say.

"You're trying to figure out how to get to her first," he replies.

"Am I that transparent?" I ask.

"No. I just know you. And I know you'll throw yourself head-first into whatever dangerous situation is out there to beat everyone else to the punch."

"If she's even still alive." There's a bench in the hallway and I gravitate toward it, sitting down and leaning back against the wall. It's cold and it feels good against my head.

"Cohen says Larson has turned his phone off, all his calls are going straight to voicemail. So we can't even ping it."

"Of course he did," I say. "He probably removed the SIM card and smashed all of it or tossed it in a fire. He's been planning this for a long time. I just can't figure out how Simon got someone like Larson to go along with this. From what I can tell, he's a career agent. That would be like someone infiltrating—" I sit up.

"What?" he asks.

"Like someone infiltrating the FBI," I say. "Something you and I happen to know about."

"You think this is connected to the Organization?" he asks.

"No," I say, leaning forward again. "But we know Hunter was able to infiltrate the FBI by inserting himself into the Bureau when he was young. He played the long game. Kept his head down, biding his time. If it weren't for us, he could have gone another few years before being detected, if ever. His plan was to always remain in the background, waiting for his opportunity to strike."

"What does that have to do with Larson?" he asks.

"What if...what if Larson and Simon are the same person?" I ask, thinking it through. It would make sense. "That way he'd be able to monitor the situation from our end, while orchestrating his people on his. He could have learned about the stockpile from his contacts at the ATF and decided now was his time to strike. Zara and Crowne being in his organization at the same time could have been nothing but bad timing. No wonder he's been able to stay one step ahead of us this entire time."

"You really think he would do that?" Liam asks. "Why not just get one of his followers to take the risk."

"Because it would have been impossible to plant a mole in the ATF without looking suspicious. Whoever it was would have been the first person we pointed the finger at on day one of the bombing."

"It seems like a huge risk."

"And a huge rush. What do we know about this so-called Simon? He's a narcissist, obviously. He's got a god-complex. He enjoys manipulating people for his own needs. And he gets off on being the smartest and most powerful man around. Imagine what a rush that would have been for him, to work right beside the people working on his own case, all the time knowing that he was the one everyone was chasing? No wonder he never let anyone take his picture—if Zara or Agent Crowne had gotten that to us, we would have known immediately."

Liam rubs his temples. "If you're right, it makes things extremely complicated. How does that help us find him?"

"We need to check back with Cohen. Go over every part of Larson's history with a fine-tooth comb. Something has to stand out. At some point he'll have used something familiar to him. We just have to track it down."

"But...that could be anything," Liam says.

"You're right, it could. And that's why we need backup.

We'll need all of Cohen's men working on this." I stand and head back to the office.

"But what about the explosion?" Liam asks, coming after me.

"What about it? We already know it was the Simonists. There's not going to be anything in there left to find. Larson…or Simon would have made sure of that."

"Em," Liam says, stopping me with a hand on my shoulder. "Are you sure about this? Because last time——"

"Last time I accused an innocent man, I know," I say. "But this is different. It *has* to be. Tell me it doesn't make sense."

He looks like he's about to say something, but then he stops short. I know I'm trying his patience; we're both exhausted and so far, we've made very little progress. And the next bomb could come at any minute. But I can feel this in my gut. I know I'm right. Everyone has a history—everyone leaves a mark. We just have to find every piece of information about Larson that we can.

Finally, Liam smiles. "Okay. But good luck convincing Sandel to trust *your* gut."

"Leave that to me," I say.

Chapter Twenty-Six

It took a good bit of convincing, but I was finally able to get everyone on the team on board about my Larson/Simon theory. Now, all we have to do is dissect a man's entire life as fast as we possibly can.

Jeffrey Larson was born August fourth, nineteen-eighty. Which puts him at just over forty years old. Nadia has agreed to take his early years, while Elliott is working on high school. Cohen is deep on his entire work history and has assigned Sweeney Larson's military history, while Riggs tackles any overseas relationships he may have had. Meanwhile, Liam is going after any adult friends outside the ATF. Finally, I have assigned myself the most difficult category: family.

When Cohen said Larson had no living family, he wasn't kidding. It only took about thirty minutes to find out that both his parents were killed in a mudslide in California back in two-thousand-seven. He's an only child, though he had one uncle and one aunt, both of them with kids of their own. His aunt is deceased, but she had a daughter, Olivia, who lives in Houston. His uncle, however, is still living in New Jersey, and of his two sons, one works in Manhattan and the other moved out to Iowa to wrangle cattle. Talk about polar opposites.

There is no evidence I can find that leads me to believe Larson has spoken to his uncle or his cousins in years. But I call them up anyway.

"Yes, hello," I say. "I'm a Special Agent with the FBI, am I speaking with Mark Larson?"

The man on the other end of the phone is gruff, like an unpolished rock. "FBI? What the hell do you want?"

"Sir, I'm looking for information on Jeffrey Larson. I believe he's your nephew."

There's something of a grunt on the other side of the phone. "I guess."

"Have you spoken to him recently? In say the last six months or so?"

"I haven't talked to Jeff in almost ten years," he replies. "Why would he be calling me now?"

"We're trying to locate him," I say, losing hope that Mr. Larson will be able to give us any useful information. "I don't suppose you know him very well if you haven't spoken in so long."

"I couldn't even tell you what state he was living in," the other man replies. "Saw him at the funeral, and a few times after that. Then he just…disappeared."

"Your brother's funeral?" I ask. He grunts in response. "Did you know he was working as part of the ATF?"

"No, but doesn't surprise me. Jeff always did have a thing for guns."

That piques my interest. "How so?"

"Kid was obsessed with firecrackers, cherry bombs, anything that could explode. Bullets explode, just in a different way. I took 'em shooting a few times when he was young. He had a natural talent for it."

"Where was this?" I ask.

"Oh, different places. There's an old farm about an hour outside the city, used to be owned by my grandfather. Nothing but space out there. I'd take him shooting with his cousins."

I perk up. "Where was this farm, exactly?" I ask. He gives me the address and I scribble it down, waving for Liam to come grab it. "What's on this property? Anything?"

"Just a busted-down old barn," he replies. "Used to use it for target practice. But other than a bunch of woods, there's not much else around. That's kinda the point. Don't need to go shootin' where there are people."

"That's great, Mr. Larson, thank you. Can you tell me if Jeff had any property down in DC?" I'm thinking back to the original location of the Simonites; the one they abandoned right when Zara went dark. It had been an abandoned building, though I was hoping we could tie it back to his past in some way.

"*Washington* DC?" he asks. "No, why on Earth would he have property down there?"

"Well, he works out of DC with the ATF," I say. "I just thought—"

"Naw," the gruff man replies. "Jeff was never into owning property. He didn't believe in it. Thought landlords were the devil incarnate. I remember him going off on Mark Jr. about renting out his apartment in the city. Said he was being nothing more than a soul-sucking greedy corporate something-or-other. I don't really remember. That was after the funeral. Like I said, we didn't see much of him after that."

"If he didn't believe in owning a home, then where did he live?" I ask.

"Who knows," the man replies. "Wasn't my business and I didn't care to engage. The boy always seemed a little off to me, even when he was young. To be honest, Agent, I've been glad not to have to deal with him these past few years and I'd prefer to keep it that way."

"Of course," I say. "Well, thank you for your time. I appreciate all the—" He hangs up before I can even finish. "—information." I hang the phone up and head over to

Liam's desk. He has the property Larson gave me pulled up on the satellite image.

"Looks like empty farmland," he says. "It's about an hour north of here, outside of New Brunswick, New Jersey."

"How old is the satellite image?"

"About four years," he says.

"Larson's uncle said they used to go shooting there. We know Simon—I mean Jeff, has been planning this for a long time. Maybe he built himself a backup hideaway in the event his first one got burned. Just like the car."

"You think he's out in the middle of some field in New Jersey?" Sandel asks, coming over to see what we're talking about.

"I'm saying it's not out of the realm of possibility. Has anyone else had any luck tracking him down?"

"Consensus seems to be he was a weird kid, a weird adult and not a lot of people wanted to be around him. At least, until he cleaned up his act and joined the military."

Cohen comes over, handing me a printout. "His military record. Joined at age eighteen, stayed in for six years before retiring as a Staff Sergeant in the Marine Corps."

"It says here he excelled at leadership duties, but clashed with his own superiors," I say, scanning over the documentation. "This didn't come up when he applied for the ATF?"

"We're not as stringent as the military, as I'm sure the FBI isn't. I wasn't the one who hired him, but I reviewed his record when he joined my team. He'd been in the agency for almost two years by then and hadn't caused a single problem. I figured it was something he grew out of."

"And you never saw any signs that made you think he had a problem with authority?" I ask.

Cohen shakes his head. "None."

"He learned something in the military," I say. "He learned how to act around people so as not to get their suspicions up. But the structure was too rigid. So when he joined the ATF, he managed to keep his head down. He learned how to pretend to fit in."

"Or he just fit in," Cohen says, a little heat in his voice.

"Look, I'm not blaming you. People like Larson are often chameleons. He obviously learned from each of his experiences about how to blend in better. About how not to make waves. His entire personality was probably tailored specifically for you and your team so you wouldn't notice anything was wrong."

Cohen looks up, shaking his head. "How can anyone live like that?"

"These guys do, and they get good at it," I say. "But when he's not in normal society, when he's filling the role as the leader of his acolytes, he becomes an entirely different person. He becomes the leader the military taught him to be, with a dash of narcissism and a whole lot of dangerous thoughts. If he wasn't any good at it, people wouldn't follow him. They wouldn't sacrifice themselves for him, like Leo Bolton."

"How does any of this help us?" Nadia asks. "Knowing he's a sociopath doesn't tell us where to find him."

"It might." I take another look at Liam's computer. "I think we need to mobilize a unit to go out there. His uncle said they used to go shooting on that property when Larson was young. It's still owned by the family, but apparently no one pays it any attention. It would be the perfect place for him to set up shop if he needed a backup."

"Who's to say he's not in fucking Alabama or Texas by now," Cohen replies.

"Because all of his targets so far have been on the east coast. First Baltimore, then Philly. If we follow the line, then New Jersey or New York makes the most sense. If he knew he'd be operating in this area, it would make sense to have a place to work from if he needed it."

"So the Washington location was what? Just a decoy?" Liam asks.

"Maybe. He could have always been planning on abandoning it. Or maybe he'd just been using it as a recruiting center. We know from Zara that was where most of the Simonites joined the cause. DC is a politically charged city. Where better to recruit if you're looking for people to follow you to paradise?"

"If we notify Wallace, he'll send in SWAT," Sandel says. "And if Larson really is there, it will be a massacre."

"Which is why we need to go first," I say, grabbing my blazer and slipping it back on. "You said it's an hour out?"

"More or less," Liam replies.

Elliott steps forward. "Slate, I don't think this is what your doctor was talking about when she said light duty. As the case agent I—"

"You're not pulling me from this, not when Zara's life is involved," I tell him. "I'll stay back if I have to, but I'm going."

He glares at me, but I don't see the same hardness I saw when we first scoped out that soup kitchen together. "Okay. But you'll stay back. I don't need you as a potential casualty out there." He motions to the rest of them. "Everyone else I want you with vests, no exceptions. If Slate is right, this could be a very dangerous situation. Full precautions."

"I want in," Cohen says. "This guy pulled the wool over us for years. My guys deserve to help bring him in. And it sounds like you're going to need some extra backup."

"We'd appreciate any assistance you can offer," Sandel replies.

It takes us less than ten minutes to get suited up and in vehicles headed northeast. The entire time I'm sitting in the back of one of the SUVs watching the road ahead of us like I can force it to go by faster. It's another clear day, and thankfully the traffic is light. We reach New Brunswick within an hour. The closer we get to the location, the more rural things become. When we're less than a mile away, the double yellows on the roads disappear and the pavement itself is barely one lane wide. We pass the sign for a rural airport which I'm sure is little more than a dirt runway.

"Any sign of countermeasures?" Sandel asks as we approach. "Any early-warning systems?"

"Nothing that's showing up on infrared," Nadia replies. She's in the SUV behind us, with Cohen and half of his team. Eight agents in total. If we can surprise them, we may be able to retain the advantage. At last report, Agent Crowne had reported over twenty Simonites. There's no telling if the numbers have increased or dwindled since then, but we're going in no matter what. And I don't care what Sandel says, I'm not staying behind. I have to see this through myself.

"Coming up on the property," Sandel says, slowing the vehicle. Liam pulls out his firearm and I do the same, taking a quick glance at the assault rifles that are stored in the back of the SUV. I really have to appreciate how off-book Elliott is going here. We should call Wallace, get operational approval. But we all know what that will lead to, and if there's even a chance Zara is still alive, we have to do this ourselves.

Sandel makes the turn off onto a dirt road that's barely visible through the high grass.

"This is it," Nadia says. "We're on the property."

"Anyone see anything?" Liam asks. But all I see are grass and trees. Then, in the distance, I make out what looks like a structure.

"There," I point. "Is that the barn?" Something isn't right. If Larson had been using this property anytime recently, the dirt road wouldn't be so overgrown. There would be something here, but as far as I can tell, there's nothing. It's just like Larson's uncle said. It's an empty bit of property, with an old collapsing barn on one end.

Sandel pulls the vehicle to a stop and I open the door, standing on the sideboard so I can get a good view of the property. "Nothing." I say. "There's nothing here." I was wrong.

"Let me send up a drone to make sure," Nadia replies on the radio.

"No, I think she's right," Sandel says. "We'd be seeing activity if someone were here. We should be right on top of them. This is just an empty field."

Damn. I can't believe it. Everything fit. He should be here. I want to scream in frustration, but instead I get out, and begin walking in the field.

"Em!" Liam calls out, coming after me.

"She's not here," I say.

"No, but we will find her. I promise," he says.

"You can't promise something like—" before I can finish, I feel my phone vibrate in my pocket. When I pull it out, it's coming from a blocked number. "Hello?"

"Em?" her voice comes through as clear as a bell, sending a shiver down my spine.

"Zara! Where are you? What's going on?"

"Em, I think I'm about to die."

Chapter Twenty-Seven

MY HEART IS in my throat as Sandel pushes the accelerator to the floor. We're back on the 95, heading north to New York.

"Em, I don't know what to do," Zara says. "He said if I try to leave, it will go off. If I hang up, it will go off. If I do anything he doesn't like—"

"He has a camera on you," I say, trying to coordinate with both Liam and Wallace back at the home office. We've already been able to pinpoint the cellphone Zara is using. She's just outside Manhattan, across the Hudson at the NY5 data center. And she has a bomb strapped to her chest.

"I—I guess," she replies. "Em, it all went wrong so fast. I was trying to warn you, to let you know and somehow he figured out—"

"No, no, it's okay," I say. "Don't worry about that right now. The important part is you're still alive. And we're coming. We're only thirty minutes from your location."

"He told me to call you," she says. "Before they left me here, when we were bouncing along the road and they were strapping this thing to my chest, he said that if I didn't call you specifically, that he would start detonating bombs he has planted in locations all over the city."

I've got her on speaker so everyone can hear. Liam holds up a handwritten note: *Can she speak with anyone else?*

"Z, can you speak with anyone else, or just me?"

"He just said to talk to you. Em, it's a trap. It has to be. He knows everything about us. He knows how long I've been with the Bureau, who I've worked with...I just..." She trails off.

"Zara, I need you to maintain your focus," I say. "Stay with me. It's a normal day, we're just talking okay? Just keep talking."

"Em, it is *not* a normal day." The stress in her voice is palpable, but finally I get a little of that Zara snark I've been missing.

"I know. But we need to keep you calm until we can get there. We're going to figure this out. Now, tell me again what happened."

She takes a deep breath. "I was trying to figure out how to get a message to you after the Federal Reserve blew up," she says. "But when Simon came back, he knew I'd betrayed him. He had his guys restrain me and they covered my head with a bag before moving me. I don't know how long they had that bag on me, but it felt like they put me in one of their vans shortly after that. And then we drove for a while. I must have fallen asleep sitting up, because I remember not feeling the van moving anymore for a bit. And then he came back in with us."

"Simon," I say.

"Right. He started talking to me about how I'd disappointed him and all that bullshit, and then began telling me again about their new world that I would help usher in. Thanks to my help, they'd been able to circumvent the security measures at a highly secured facility. And that I would be instrumental in changing things forever."

"But you still didn't know where you were?" I ask. Part of me is just thankful to hear her voice again because I was sure she was already dead. I hadn't given her enough credit, or

Jeffrey Larson either, apparently. He wants to make an example out of Zara.

"No, and I didn't until they brought me in here and removed the black bag on my head. By then I already had the unit strapped to my chest. That was the first thing I saw. The second were all the servers in this warehouse. Em, I've got enough C4 on this vest to level the entire building."

"I know, and reinforcements are on the way," I say. "We're evacuating the nearby buildings and the National Guard is setting up a perimeter."

"That's not going to help," she says. "Not when this thing goes off."

"I know," I say, but I'm not about to let that happen. I glance up to see Sandel is pushing the SUV past a hundred as we scream down the highway, lights flashing. In the distance, I see the skyscrapers of Manhattan rising up like new plants sprouting from the ground.

According to the GPS data on the phone she's using, Larson left her in the NY5 warehouse, which carries all the financial data and handles all the transactions for the New York Stock Exchange. Most people don't realize that the stock exchange works too fast these days for human traders to stay down on the trading floor, yelling numbers at each other. Today, millions of those transactions are handled every second through the servers in that building and four others like it. My bet is Larson had wired them all to blow, though Zara is the lynchpin.

"We've also already evacuated the other data centers," I tell her. "From what little Nadia has found, it looks like new maintenance crews came to work at each building during the night."

"Em, when this thing goes off, it will cripple the economy. The stock market will cease to exist. All the records, all the transactions, everything Wall Street is based on will go up in an instant."

She's right. Which will cause economic chaos. International markets will more than likely follow as people try to figure out how much money they have. It could absolutely destabilize the global economy in one fell swoop. It could even ignite conflicts between nations. Other countries are heavily invested in ours and vice versa. If all that disappears, there's no telling how some of our less friendly neighbors might respond.

Larson is certifiably insane. And the worst part is, we still have no idea where he is.

"Let's not focus on any of that right now. All that matters is that we're on our way and we're going to figure a way out of this," I say, trying my best to sound reassuring. It's crossed my mind about a thousand times already that at any second the phone could cut off and that would be the last time I ever spoke to my best friend.

"Em, I'm really scared," she says. "I know I shouldn't be, that I should be stronger about something like this but—"

"No," I say, interrupting. "Don't do that to yourself. You have every right to be scared. I'd be worried if you *weren't* scared. Did Larson say anything else? Did he tell you when he would detonate the bomb?"

"He just said he would wait until the time was right," she says. I wish I could get an eye on the camera he has on her. But I also have to assume he's monitoring this phone call, though I'm not about to communicate with him through it.

"How far?" I ask Sandel.

"Another ten minutes out," he replies.

"We're coming," I tell her. "Just hang on."

"Em, just in case—"

"Stop," I say, a little harsher than I mean. "You just focus on the now. Look at the device you're wearing, try to figure out how it works. Nothing else matters, okay?"

"But—"

"You don't have to say anything," I say. "I already know. And you already know too, don't you?"

Her voice is a little quieter. "I do."

"Good. Now just take deep breaths, and try to figure the device out." It's not that I don't want her to say it, what I don't want is for Larson to be waiting on the other end, waiting until the most heart-wrenching time to kill her. I can just imagine the sadistic fuck sitting there, waiting for Zara to try and tell me she loves me as he presses some goddamn button, laughing like a psychopath. I can't let that happen. First order of business is to secure Zara. Then I go after Larson, no more restrictions.

Liam holds up another note that says *mute.*

"Zara, hang on, okay, just hang on." I mute the call. "What?"

"Wallace has informed us the National Guard has been mobilized. They're not about to let those buildings go up in smoke," he says. "FBI from the New York office are already on site. No sign of Larson or any of his men anywhere."

"Why would there be?" I ask. "The man isn't going to stick around, he's got a camera on her, watching her every move. We have to find that camera, trace the signal. It's our only chance of finding him and stopping him."

"But we have no idea what will cause Larson to push the trigger. It could be anything."

"He's waiting for us," I say. "Or...maybe just me. Because he knows I'm important to Zara. She betrayed him, and he wants to hurt her in the worst way possible. If he could have strapped that bomb to my chest instead, I'm sure he would have done it. My bet is the minute he sees me on that camera he does it, blows the whole thing."

"Then I suggest you not go in the building," Sandel says.

"Wrong. I'm going in. It's up to the three of you to find the camera and trace the signal before it's too late. I'm going to try and help Zara disarm the vest."

"Em?" Zara says over the phone. I unmute it.

"What? What's wrong?"

"I—I was just checking to make sure you were still there," she says. I hate how scared she sounds. I've never heard Zara sound this scared in her life. I think had Simon tried to end her life quickly, either in a fight or with a gun, she would have endured it because it would have been quick. But this slow death, not knowing when or if something is going to blow and kill you, it's another form of torture.

Another form of control.

"I'm not going anywhere. We're almost there. I'm going to stay on the phone with you until I see you in person, okay?"

"No, Em, you can't come in here. You have to find a way to disarm the other explosives. He's never going to let me go. Not after what I did to betray his trust. I—I'm just glad I got to talk to you one more time before the end."

"Wait a second, Zara, don't do—"

"Em, you've been the best friend anyone could ever ask for." Before I can say another word, she ends the call.

"Zara!" I yell, but it's too late, she's already cut the line. I look up in the distance, expecting any second to see a small mushroom cloud rise over the industrial buildings that sit along this side of the Hudson River. But there's nothing. "Get an eye on that camera, right now," I yell at Nadia.

"I'm looking!" she yells back. "There should be an errant signal transmitting from somewhere, but I just can't find it."

Every second we're not there is another second when Larson could hit the button. It's perpetual torture, even as we move through the National Guard who have set up the perimeter two blocks out from the building.

"C'mon, c'mon," I say.

"Are you sure we should still go in there?" Liam asks. "She obviously cut the line because she doesn't want any of us getting hurt."

"I don't *care* what she wants, I can't lose her," I yell at him, not caring how I look right now. I can already feel the tears welling in my eyes and all I can focus on is getting to the building ahead of us. It's like time has slowed down and everything is taking much longer than it should. I feel the SUV slow, and I'm out the door before it has come to a complete stop. Liam yells something after me, but I don't hear it. All I'm focused on is the main doors to the three-story warehouse building. An entire platoon of soldiers stands on guard, their weapons pointed right at the front doors.

I rush past them, pushing my way through, entirely sure one of them is going to shoot me in the back, until I hear someone barking out orders for them to stand down. I reach the glass doors of the building and pull open the main one.

Inside is a small lobby with a desk, though it's been abandoned. Another set of doors sits beyond the lobby, which no doubt lead to the massive server room which takes up a majority of the building.

I've just walked into a building wired to explode at any second. I know it's reckless, but I'm not going to let her die alone. I push through the second set of doors, noting that the magnetic lock beside them is showing green without needing a keycard for access.

When I see her, I gasp. She's standing in the middle of the room, a bulky vest wrapped around her, throwing her proportions off. Her back is to me, and her platinum-blonde hair reflects the blinking lights from all the servers. I look above me, searching for a camera, but don't see one anywhere. It must be well-hidden.

"Zara?"

She turns and I see the tears streaming down her cheeks. I look at the vest. There's a small light on it shining bright green. And the minute she sees me, it switches to red with an audible *beep*.

Followed by a second beep.

Followed by—

Chapter Twenty-Eight

—I SLAM INTO ZARA, wrapping her in a hug, squeezing the device between the two of us.

"Em," she says, her voice shaky. "You—"

"I'm not leaving you here to die alone," I say. The device between us beeped a third time and the red light is still on, but it hasn't gone off.

"I was sure the second you arrived he'd blow it," she says, holding on tight to me.

"He did," a voice calls out.

I begin to release my hold on Zara to look to my left where the voice came from. "No, no, no, stay right where you are," he adds. He's got a slight English accent, but not enough that it makes me think he's a current resident. It sounds more like an accent that's waned over time.

Out of the corner of my eye I see a man in a blue suit approaching. He's got a trim beard and distinctive features. He almost looks like a model, though I can't quite see the color of his eyes.

"Theodore?" Zara asks, her voice a little muffled as her face is up against my blazer. "What the holy crap? I saw you get shot."

"Are you sure about that?" he asks, his voice playful. "Maybe what you saw was a possum playing dead. You have those animals here, am I right? Regardless, let's not worry about it for the moment." His voice is cool and calm. "The important thing to keep in mind here, is that device has a pressure sensor. Agent Slate, by pressing up against it, you have in a sense activated the pressure component, though it was already in a state of being activated remotely anyway. The second you pull away; the pin will drop and the entire thing goes kaboom."

"I don't understand what's happening here," Zara says.

"Who is this guy?" I ask.

"He worked for Simon—I mean, he helped me clear the federal building, and covered up a murder for me, and Simon shot him for it." Without letting go, Zara turns her face so she can see him. "How are you here? What is going on?"

"I understand your confusion, but I really think the best thing would be for me to help you disarm that device before we all end up little bits scattered halfway to Manhattan, hm?"

"But you got shot!" she exclaims. Clearly the two of them have some history, though I'm not entirely sure what's happening.

"Have you been here this entire time?" I ask.

"No, I just arrived a moment ago, unfortunately," he replies. "I was hoping to beat you here, so I might help Zara with the vest. Now things are a little more...complicated. Though I will say you did manage to at least stave off Simon's hand for a moment longer." He looks above us and does a little wave. "This has to be driving him crazy. I can just see him now, pressing the button on his phone over and over, trying to make it blow." Theodore glances back up again. "It won't work, mate! You've done put a failsafe in this thing."

"Okay," I say. "I'm not sure of what's going on, but I'm assuming you're not here to blow us up."

"Quite the opposite."

"And as long as we don't let go, the pressure sensor won't release?"

"Correct."

"So what? Are we just supposed to stay like this forever?"

"Fortunately for you birds, I happen to be an expert in explosive devices," he says, taking a cursory look at the unit between us, before circling around Zara and inspecting the back on her back. "Yep, standard plates…wires wrap around to blow the C4 wrapped in the back. Pins are in so no getting those out. We're going to have to disarm it *and* disconnect it at exactly the same time."

"How do we do that?" Zara asks.

"The unit has three different buckles. Clipping all three armed the bomb. But Simon is no dummy. He's going to have a contingency; in the event the vest was activated by mistake. Remember all those munitions he had stockpiled? He wouldn't have wanted this going off anywhere near them. We're going to need to unlock all three at once while still holding the unit as tight as you can between each other. I'm afraid you might be feeling each other up for this part."

For the first time, Zara cracks a smile, even though her cheeks are tear-stained. At some point, I have been crying as well, though I don't even remember it. I just know my own cheeks have that salty residue on them that only comes from a few tears.

"Well, if I have to do it to someone…" she says. "Where are the buckles?"

"You've got two in the front, one above the main unit and one below. And then another one on your back here. I'll handle that one."

I don't have the slightest clue who this guy is or where he came from, and right now I don't care. All that matters to me is getting this damn vest off her and making sure it's not going to explode.

"What about the other buildings?" I ask. "Aren't they all individually wired?"

"Now that would have been the smart thing to do, wouldn't it?" Theodore asks, walking around the back of Zara. "But Simon is a bit too narcissistic for his own good. Thought it would be much showier if everything was kicked off by this little beauty right here." He glances up. "I mean the bomb, not Agent Foley. Though, of course, she's quite beautiful as well—I mean, well, anyway let's focus on the job at hand, shall we?"

Zara's eyes meet mine and while I'm sure I look like a deer caught in the headlights, I see that smile return, crinkling the skin up her face. "You think I'm beautiful?" she asks in that signature cocky voice of hers. If nothing else, this distraction has brought her back to herself.

"I think it's best we try not to die right now," he says, drawing out the first word. His voice is a little higher than before, as he's clearly embarrassed.

"Sure, then you can tell me how you survived a gunshot wound to the stomach," she replies.

"Do you trust this guy?" I ask.

"Well, he's had more than one opportunity to kill me, so either he's really bad at this stuff or he's being honest about his intentions." I'm really going to have to get the full story when this is all over. Assuming we don't blow ourselves to bits.

Theodore clears his throat. "Are we all ready?"

"Wait," I say, feeling around for the bottom buckle. "I think so."

"Ready," Zara says.

"Okay, now what's going to happen is we'll pull the buckles, then you two will separate, and I'll remove the detonator from the explosives. It will all need to be done very quickly, and we must be perfectly in sync. I'll countdown from three, and on *pull*, we pull, got it?"

We both nod.

"Here we go. Three. Two. One. *PULL*."

We all pull at the same time. The buckles come loose, and Zara and I step back as Theodore takes the unit in his hands, laying it down on the ground. He roots around on the detonator for a second or two, removing the attaching clamps before taking the detonator off the packs of explosives and stepping back.

"Ha!" he says. "Well done!"

"Wait," I say, looking at the unit itself. I'm no engineer, but something about the configuration looks familiar. I reach down and pull back a strap of cloth, to reveal a second detonator, which is still armed. Before I know what I'm doing, I pull the wire connecting it and the detonator dies in my hand.

"Sneaky bugger," Theodore says. He gets back down and feels around the vest for anything else. "I think you got it. How'd you know that would be there?"

"Because we're dealing with a man who covers his bases," I say. "He'll have something else planned, I'm sure of it." Now that the bomb has been disabled, I can take an actual breath. Zara is standing close, looking at the vest like it still might explode. I grab her and pull her into a hug again, this time without death standing between us.

"Thank you for coming for me," she says.

"I never even considered anything else," I tell her. "Against everyone else's advice."

"Brilliant," Theodore says. "Now that that's sorted, I do believe introductions are in order." He holds out a hand to Zara. "Theodore Arquenest. MI6. But you can call me Theo."

She takes his hand. "Like the James Bond MI6?"

"Well, to be honest I'm retired. I do freelance work now."

"Freelance work," I say, flatly.

"Independent Contractor."

I narrow my eyes. "Employed by who?"

"Myself. See, there's only so much you can get done when

working for a large, government-sponsored organization. I find I'm much more effective on my own."

"You don't mind if we check your credentials," I say.

He waves a hand. "Be my guest, love. I was part of the Royal Navy for five years before joining Her Majesty's Service, and worked there until just last year, when I took an indefinite sabbatical."

"What does that mean?" I ask.

"It means I can return at any time, but until then, I'm on…vacation."

I exchange a glance with Zara. "So you just infiltrate threats against the state because why? You're bored?"

He shrugs. "Everyone needs a hobby. But seeing as things are about to get very crowded in here, I think I'll take my leave." He tips an imaginary hat at us, before throwing Zara another wink. "I'll see you around."

"Wait, you can't just—" Before I can say anything else, the doors behind us burst open and about fifty soldiers file in, all their weapons trained on us. Both Zara and I hold up our hands. "The bomb is disabled!" I yell.

"Stand down!" I cock my head at the familiar voice. Janice appears in the middle of the crowd, heading directly for us. I glance behind me, but Arquenest is already gone. Like he was never even here.

"You're okay?" she asks.

I exchange another glance with Zara. "We were able to disarm the vest. But we'll still need to remove all the explosives…we believe this vest is remotely tied to explosives in the other data centers."

Janice motions behind her and a group of people dressed head to toe in bomb suits come running up while Zara and I are ushered back outside.

"We'll let the bomb squad deal with this," she says, leading us back to the SUVs where Liam, Elliott and Nadia are all waiting. Liam runs forward and grabs me in a hug before I can even say anything.

"I thought you were dead," he says.

"I couldn't leave her alone in there," I say.

He nods. "I know. Just…" He doesn't say anything else, only holds me tighter before pulling Zara into the hug as well. She chuckles, but at the same time I can feel the tension leaving her.

"All this attention all at once, gives me the fuzzies," Zara says.

"We'll need to debrief all of you," Janice says.

Liam lets go of me and I turn to her. "How are you here?"

"I was in a meeting in Manhattan when I got the news," she replies, pulling her vape out of her blazer and taking a puff. "I thought you might try something stupid. The Marines almost shot you when you ran in that building, you know."

I can't *wait* for Wallace to hear about that one. "We still need to locate Larson. He'll have another play. Every time we've gone after him, he's had something in his back pocket. I'm betting this is no different."

"He's in the wind," Janice replies.

"What?"

"I located that camera signal." Nadia says. "It's broadcasting to a warehouse about fifteen miles from here."

"While the two of you have been stopping the financial apocalypse, Cohen and his men went ahead, but Larson was long gone. He left a few of his followers there, however, which was nice of him," Janice adds.

"You don't have any clue where he could have gone?" I ask.

"None. But that's not your concern. The two of you have done enough. Get yourselves and your team back to DC. We'll have a national manhunt out for Larson." She stows the vape again.

"But—" Zara begins but a stern look from Janice silences her. "Yes, ma'am."

"C'mon," I say. "I think this is one time a rest is warranted."

"Book yourselves the next flight out of Newark," she says. "I've rescinded your...travel restrictions, Slate."

"Oh," I say. "Thanks."

"Mm," is all she says, turning back to the other agents on site. Obviously she's going to finish coordinating things here herself.

"What the hell happened in there?" Liam says, leading all of us back to the SUV.

I exchange a knowing look with Zara. "Why don't you tell it?"

"Oh, no. I'm a mess, it's all you."

We slide into the backseat of the vehicle as Elliott takes up being the driver yet again. "You know what? Maybe some things are just better left unsaid."

Chapter Twenty-Nine

NEWARK AIRPORT IS LITERALLY RIGHT across the road from us, so we're booking flights back to DC in record time. Everyone seems exhausted, and I can't blame them. Elliott, Nadia and Liam have all been up as long as I have, working straight through ever since before the incident in Philly yesterday. God, was that yesterday? It feels like a month ago.

I can tell Zara is worn down as well. She's been through a lot and has been uncharacteristically quiet while we check in and get through security. I only now notice what she's wearing and the faint smell coming from her.

"Have you had those clothes on all week?"

"It wasn't like I had my wardrobe with me," she replies, headed for the bathroom. "I just want to go back home and take a long, hot shower."

"That goes for both of us." She uses the sink to throw some water on her face, which comes away dirty. She scrubs for a good minute before finally shutting the water off and grabbing a paper towel.

"I can't do undercover work again, Em. I'm no good at it." She rubs her face with the scratchy paper towel.

"From what I understand, you never broke cover. If Agent Crowne hadn't—"

"That doesn't matter," she snaps before taking a deep breath. "I couldn't—I couldn't handle it. I tried to maintain that hard exterior, but I just—ugh. I miss the days when the most dangerous thing I had to do was make sure a file was uploaded to the right server."

I lean against the counter, studying her. "You don't mean that. You're a great field agent."

"Then why do I feel so shitty?"

"Because he got away," I say. "Because he toyed with you, played psychological games with you, tortured you and still slipped through our grasp. He's a coward, that's what they do. One thing is for sure, he'll never be able to operate in the US ever again. Now that we know what he looks like and his M.O., he'll have to stay in hiding forever."

Zara stares off into the distance. "He won't. He needs that validation too much. You should have seen him when he was surrounded by people that 'worshiped' him. It was like he was performing for them, creating this big show just for his ego."

"And yet he abandoned them all to save himself."

She looks like she's contemplating something, but eventually it passes, and she goes to use the bathroom before rejoining me and washing her hands. "Let's just get home."

We head back out into the atrium, and I spot Liam and the others already sitting at the gate, all three of them with their heads back and eyes closed. I can't wait to slip into my own bed. I'll have to call Tess and let her know I'll be home in a few hours.

Just as I'm dialing, Zara tugs on my arm. "Em." I look over to where her attention has been drawn to see she's staring at the *International Departures* gates. "You're right. He won't ever be able to operate in the US again. But that doesn't mean he's planning on staying here."

"He can't take a commercial flight anywhere," I say. "TSA has been notified; he's on the no-fly list."

She turns back to me. "No, he talked about being a pilot back when he was in the Marines. And I think he has access to a private plane. It'll be something small, a puddle jumper."

"That could be anywhere though," I say, thinking back. Then I remember passing the sign for that small airport while we were on our way out to that farm belonging to his family. "Unless he's sticking close to what he knows."

"What do you mean?"

"I spoke with his uncle while we were trying to find him. The family owns a farm out in New Brunswick, right next to a private airport. What are the odds he has a plane there?"

"He had the funds for it, the Simonites weren't hard up for money," she says. "If he's there, we need to go, now."

I look back at the others. Liam is going to kill me for this, but she's right. If he is trying to flee the country, that would be the quickest. It hasn't been that long since we traced the signal, we might not be too late.

"Let's move."

Twenty-five minutes later we're back on the same rural roads Sandel was driving on earlier. I decided to drive, despite not being cleared, since Zara has been through hell this past week and a half. Both of us haven't said a word the entire trip, instead we're both focused on getting there as fast as possible. We grabbed the car we left in the parking lot for the local agents to pick up. The same one with the additional firepower in the back. Zara has taken the assault rifle for herself, while I'm sticking with my sidearm. She looks out of place wielding such a large weapon.

We hit the single-lane road and I make the turn for the airport, spotting it in the distance. It's kind of up on an artificial hill, which provides for a long, flat runway across the terrain. A couple of small hangars sit off the primary runway, all of them with prop planes in them except for one.

A single plane sits on the runway, though it's not running yet. The engine cover is up and the door to the plane stands open. A figure is on the runway, running back and forth from a box of tools to the open engine cover.

"It's him," Zara says.

"You were right, nice call." I gun the engine and jump the small barrier at the end of the runway, the tires of the SUV squealing as we peel down the runway. I stop about a hundred yards from the plane and get out, aiming my weapon at the man working on the engine.

"Larson, it's over! Put your hands in the air, turn toward me, and walk forward." Zara is out of the other side of the car, using the door as a shield as she levels the assault rifle at the man.

The man stops working, raising both hands, one of which has a wrench in it. He turns and walks toward me, smirking. "Well, if it isn't the instrument of my shame. How are you Zara?"

"Better now that I have you in my sights," she calls out. Larson doesn't appear armed, at least not that I can see.

"Drop the wrench!" I yell.

He does and it clatters on the pavement. "The very fact that you are here means I have sorely underestimated you. The both of you," he says. "Did you know, Emily, that Zara here killed one of my men by strangling him with the chain of her own handcuffs?"

"Too bad she didn't do it to you."

He chuckles. "Yes, but then again, I never turned my back on her. I knew the moment I did; I would be dead. And so here we are."

"Get down on your knees and place your hands behind your head. No sudden movements."

He drops his hands. "Let's just not, how about that, Agent Slate? We both know you need me alive. I think we can skip all this posturing, don't you?"

"Alive doesn't mean pristine," Zara calls out. "You can stand trial with shattered kneecaps."

"I really thought I could change you," he says, like she hasn't said anything. "When I found out you were a federal agent, Clint told me to shoot you and be done with it. But no, I thought I could *turn* you. I have turned everyone from the homeless to a CEO of a fortune 500."

Zara pinches her features. "Mitch?"

Larson chuckles. "You're good. But I've never had much success bringing women to my cause. For some reason, our philosophy just doesn't resonate with you. I resolved for it to be different with you. After all, you can't have a new world order without women to help propagate the believers."

"So what, we're nothing more than vessels to you?" she asks.

He kind of shrugs, like the question isn't important. "Vessels of life. Or death, in your case."

"In other words, you needed her skills," I say. "You couldn't complete your plans without her so you changed your rules so you could still use her. That's ironic."

"You're right, Agent Slate, you're right," he says. "Ironic that the only person who could help me obtain my ultimate goal would also be the first person to turn on me. I knew it wouldn't be easy, but I didn't anticipate you using your powers on Theodore as well."

"I didn't do a thing to him," she calls back. "He made those choices himself."

"Are you blind, woman? It's obvious the man was in love with you. Thankfully I relieved him of any future worries. I should have seen it. I should have done a lot of things differently." He reaches into his back pocket and immediately I readjust my weapon.

"Freeze!" he could be going for anything.

But when he pulls his hand out, he's holding a small control pad. There's no telling what that might detonate, but I can't say I'm surprised. Larson always has had a backup plan in his pocket. "It may not be the world economy, but at least it's some—"

Before he can finish a shot rings out and at the exact same time, Larson's hand explodes from the palm up. I shoot a glance at Zara who is still looking through the sight, her weapon trained on him.

Larson is rolling on the ground, screaming as he holds his mutilated hand and we round the vehicle, coming up on him. I check to make sure he's not armed, finding nothing on him but his ID. He's screaming for help, but Zara just looks down at him while I check all his pockets.

"He's going to need surgery," she says.

"Call it in," I tell her. "I'll try to stop the bleeding." She doesn't move. "Z! Call it in."

She seems to snap out of it. "Right." She runs back to the SUV to make the call. Larson is still squirming as I take off my blazer and wrap it around his stump.

"You should have known better, Larson. You can't change people who don't want to be changed."

Chapter Thirty

"TELL ME, Emily, how are you doing?"

I sit up and level my gaze at Dr. Frost. "Better. I think."

"That's great to hear."

"Zara's alive. That's what matters."

"Is that *all* that matters?"

I take a deep breath, reminding myself that he's only doing his job. The past few days have felt like a blur. Larson managed to pull through, despite losing a lot of blood, and will be charged with terrorism and sedition against the state, as well as conspiracy, destruction of government property and about a dozen other charges. He's putting up a fight, insisting he was working for the betterment of humanity, but no one is buying it. The sad thing is he probably actually believes it himself. Regardless, he's going away for a long time.

"Well, my boyfriend is pissed at me," I add. "So…no?"

"And why is he mad?"

"Because I may have left him and the rest of my team so Zara and I could confront Larson alone. We…we haven't talked about moving in anymore."

"How do you feel about that?" Frost crosses one of his legs over the other.

"Like he needs to cut me some slack," I say. "I was sleep-deprived, I'd just survived almost being blown into a million pieces and I'd just gotten my best friend back. Maybe I wasn't thinking completely straight."

"It was a big risk, going after Larson alone," he replies.

"Not really. The odds that he would even be there were low. Maybe that's why I did it; because I didn't actually believe we could catch up to him. I've been wrong about so many other aspects of this case…"

"That's what it always comes back to, isn't it? Your self-confidence. You've talked before about how your hesitation has put people at risk," he says.

"This is different. This time I was *too* sure. I was too willing to accept Agent Cohen was involved when he had nothing to do with Larson or his followers. I was too eager to accept that I knew exactly what Zara was trying to tell me. I didn't consider that she didn't have full control of the situation."

"Would you say your love for your friend blinded you?"

I screw up my features. "What are you saying? I can only rely on myself?"

He sets his pad on the desk and leans forward, uncrossing his legs. "Not at all. Emily, you have made a lot of progress since we began seeing each other. Especially over these past few days now that you've begun opening up a little more. Do you remember telling me how there was a point in time when you didn't feel close with anyone, *including* Agent Foley?"

"I do," I say. "It was right after Matt."

"But she was there for you. And now, you were there for her, championing her to your superiors, fighting for her. Can you say that you would have done that a year ago?"

I can't say that I would, but I don't verbalize it. We both already know.

"Your connection to Zara and, by extension, your other co-workers, friends and even Liam were all made possible by you being willing to open yourself up again after suffering a devastating loss. Emily, we can't go around in this world only relying on ourselves. And yeah, sometimes we may get it wrong. But that's not the point. The point is that we fight for the ones we love, no matter what the circumstances. *That's* what you did. And you should be very proud of yourself."

Now that he says it aloud, it hits me. I hadn't even realized how much I'd changed; I'd forgotten just how lonely and self-reliant I had been. There had been a time there when I thought that nothing would ever be different.

"I would have done anything to get her back."

"Which just goes to show how important those connections have become to you. You shouldn't blame yourself, you're only human. And as humans, we fight for the ones we love."

That's true. Zara never gave up on me when I needed her. She gave me space, but never abandoned me. "I'm lucky to have her."

"I'd say you're both lucky to have each other," he says. "As for Liam, give him some time. From what you've told me about him, I'm sure he'll come around."

"I'm sure he will," I say. "I'm just not sure I want to move in together. Not yet. I think I still need more time."

"Then just be honest with him," Frost says. "That's all you can do. And it's always served you well in the past."

I scoff. "Yeah, sometimes a little *too* well."

"Emily, these experiences are helping you to become a *whole* person again. Embrace them." Normally I would let a statement like that slide right off my back. But I've decided to make an effort here and Frost seems genuine enough, so I guess I can't ignore his advice. We made it out alive. That's what matters. I give him a less than emphatic nod.

"Great." He glances at the small clock on his desk. "Let's leave it there for today. I'll see you next week?"

"Actually," I say. "I've decided to take that time off everyone has been hounding me about. *Really* take it this time." And I mean it. I fully intend to head off on vacation. I just need to tie up one loose end first.

"Well, let me know when you plan on coming back and we'll set up your next appointment."

"I will," I say, standing.

"Be well, Emily. And enjoy your vacation."

"Thanks, doc." I head out, feeling somewhat vindicated.

When I get back to the office, I head straight for Wallace's office, only to see Zara sitting right back at her desk, her feet up on it as she works on her computer.

"What the hell are you doing?" I ask.

"What?" she asks, innocently. "I'm just working."

"You're supposed to be on leave!" I practically yell, garnering the attention of everyone around us. Before she can protest I take her by the arm and pull her along with me toward Wallace's office.

"Em, what's going on? What are you—" She's trying to fight me, but not doing a very good job of it.

I burst into his office, still holding Zara. "We're taking a vacation." Wallace looks up, nonplussed before sitting back, silent. "I'm finally taking that time you've been hounding me about and Zara needs at least two weeks leave. I think she's deserved that much after everything she had to go through."

"No, really, I'm okay," Zara protests weakly. "It's no big deal—"

"Approved," Wallace says before going back to whatever he was working on.

For a moment I'm thrown. I thought for sure he'd fight me, seeing as I just got back from a "vacation" in Virginia that didn't turn out to be a vacation. Maybe he still feels bad about the whole knocking me out thing when I was still in the hospital.

Before he can change his mind, I pull Zara back out into the hallway. "Em, really, I'm okay. I can keep wor—"

"Take it from someone who knows," I say, finally letting go of her arm. "Take the time when you can get it. All of this has made me realize just how precious time can be. And you and me, we haven't had significant time off since when? Savannah? And even then we were still trying to track down Camille."

"Are you saying you want a girls trip?" Her eyes light up.

"Yes. And I know the perfect place. Pack your bathing suit. I'll make all the arrangements."

"Oh, you have no idea what you've just signed up for. A real *vacation*? Is Liam coming?"

I glance over in the direction of his desk, but he's not there. He's probably off working on a case. Coming back from this one finally convinced Wallace to start giving Liam his own caseload, for which I'm grateful. He's been the "new guy" long enough. "I don't know. Are you bringing Raoul?"

"Ugh," she says, turning her face down at the sound of his name. "God, no. He called me yesterday, after I finally got my normal phone back, asking how I'd been. Left me one message the entire time I was undercover. He said he'd been too busy at work to check in, but 'hoped I was well'." She uses air quotes.

"Yeah, he called me once while we were still tracking you, asked if you were coming to some event or another."

"See, this is why I don't date. Because every guy I find is a certified creep. I should have known it way back at your birthday party, but I was too stubborn. It's just been downhill from there."

"Yeah, I think Liam is still pissed we went after Larson ourselves, without backup. I'll try to talk to him tonight, but I think it's better if we keep this a girl's trip exclusively."

"What else do I need to pack?" she asks, her eyes alight with excitement.

"Just plan for warm weather. I don't know about you, but I'm ready to feel the sun on my skin."

"After spending two weeks locked in a bunker, I can't think of anything better," she says.

"Me either. There's just one thing I need to go do first."

Chapter Thirty-One

"Thanks for coming along," I say as we pull off the main road. "I know I'm not your favorite person at the moment."

Liam glances over at me from the passenger's seat. "I'm not mad that you did it, I just wish you could have trusted me to help."

"I do trust you," I say, winding along the one-lane drive that finally ends in a dirt parking lot. "But everyone was so tired, you were already asleep and to be perfectly honest, I didn't even think he'd be there. I thought we'd get there, and it would be nothing but an empty field. The fact that his plane had engine trouble was the only thing that saved us. If not for that, Larson would have gone underground and never popped back up."

"I know. But I can't help but worry about you. Especially when you're being impulsive."

I shoot him a grin, hoping to break him out of his bad mood. "C'mon, you love my impulsiveness."

He's quiet for a moment. "Sometimes."

I nudge him with my elbow. "C'mon."

"Don't push your luck," he adds, though there's something

of a smile in his voice. "But Em, I swear to god if you pull that ever again, I'll stop cooking for you for a month."

I hit the brakes, turning to him. "Don't even joke about something like that."

"Oh, I'm being dead serious. You should be on probation right now. If not for almost getting yourself blown up, you already would be."

I take his hand in mine. "I really am sorry. Things were moving fast. And I wasn't thinking clearly. I hadn't slept in thirty hours, at least? Zara was there, and the possibility just seemed so remote. I think...I think too I just needed to make sure that she was real. That it all wasn't some elaborate ruse."

"How—"

I shake my head. "I don't know. I spent so much time building up the scenario in my head that she was gone and then she wasn't, and I think my brain had a hard time reconciling it. I just needed to be with her a minute to make sure she was real."

He's quiet, probably unsure how to respond to something like that. Hell, *I* don't know how to respond to something like that. But his hand does tighten around mine.

"I know I screwed up. I didn't do it to hurt you."

"I know," he replies.

"And..." Might as well get it all out at once. "I'm not ready to move in together." He crinkles his brow and looks down for a moment.

"Absolutely, don't blame you at all." He's trying to cover it up, but I can still hear the disappointment in his voice.

"It's not because I don't want to; I just need some more time. To be on my own. Establish my own footing and find out who I am. I've been defining myself so much by other people's expectations. Wife, special agent, girlfriend, best friend. I just need the time to figure out who I am on my own two feet."

"Did Dr. Frost suggest that?" he asks.

"No, but he did encourage me," I reply.

He nods. "Then I hope I can support you as much as he has. I know we don't have what anyone would call a... normal...relationship, and I'm fine if we do things differently. And I don't plan on going anywhere."

I reach up and stroke his cheek, bringing my lips to his. It's a soft reminder of what we have together, and how well we fit. I pull back just enough so that I can still feel his breath on my lips. "And Liam," I say. "I love you, too."

I can almost feel the smile before his lips are on mine again. Everything of promise is in that kiss, and we hold in the moment for what feels like a lifetime, and yet, it's also fleeting. "I would take you into that backseat right now, you know, if we weren't...well, if we were literally anywhere else."

That produces a laugh out of me. "Yeah, maybe this isn't the best for setting the mood." I turn my attention back to the snow-dusted dirt lot and woods beyond. A light blanket of white covers the entire area. It's actually quite beautiful, and no doubt more than one couple has driven out here for a little one-on-one time. In fact, I'm sure of it. This was the first place Matt and I made love.

"Do you want me to get out with you?" he asks.

"No, I've got this one," I say. "I won't be long." I hop out, pulling my coat tight against me as the snow begins to fall a little harder. It's the first snow DC has seen this year and it's just barely enough to have covered the brown grass. The tree line is about twenty feet from the edge of the parking lot and my boots leave shallow prints in the snow. I make my way past the first few trees until I find the one I'm looking for: a gnarled oak tree that looks to be taller than the rest. There's no marker, no indication to anyone in the outside world that this was where I scattered my ex-husband's ashes. To anyone else, it's just a tree. But he loved this place—told me time and time again it was his favorite spot in the entire world, because it always reminded him of us.

Despite everything he did, I still love him. That will never change. But I have to move forward. There's an old Zen proverb I heard once: *let go, or be dragged*. And I'm tired of having dirt in my mouth.

I reach into my pocket and pull out the ring that adorned my left ring finger for almost four years. I've been carrying it around all this time because I thought I needed it to keep me attached to the one person I believed understood me better than anyone else. Even after I learned about his betrayal, I couldn't find the strength to let it go. But now I realize I have forged stronger and more authentic connections than I ever had with Matt.

I set the ring at the base of the tree and step back, watching as the tiny flakes begin covering it, causing it to disappear into the white. "I hope you find the same kind of peace I've found," I say softly. "But I can't hold on to you anymore." Exactly one year ago today my world crumbled. And yet here I am, still standing. I take a deep breath, allowing the cool air to fill my lungs and the flakes to land on my head.

It's peaceful here. Beautiful.

I smile, then head back to the car, looking to the white sky.

∿

"So what's the story with this Theo guy?" Liam says as we head back to my apartment. I've already made the arrangements for my trip with Zara, all I need to do is finish packing my suitcase and then Liam is going to drop me off at her place after we pick up Timber.

"No one knows. We can't find anything about him, but then again MI6 is notoriously tight-lipped about their operatives. My bet is he wasn't even *with* MI6, it was just another cover." I pull into my parking spot and get out. "I can tell you one thing though, Zara was smitten."

"No way," he replies, closing his door.

"Practically swooning," I say. "Then again, we did have an explosive that could have leveled a city block between us at the time, but you should have seen her light up. I bet you anything she's doing a deep dive right now, trying to find him again."

"Maybe that's just what she needs," he says as we make our way up the stairs to my door. "Someone who can challenge her."

"I'm sure it's all we'll talk about on our trip." I shoot him a wink.

"You know, you keep taking these 'vacations' without me. A guy can only take so much." He stands by the door, leaning up against the frame and giving me that little bit of swagger he manages somehow to pull off.

"Tell you what, as soon as Wallace approves you a week, we'll take a trip north. I hear it's nice up there in the summer. Not too hot, plenty of activities. Could be romantic."

"Yeah?" he asks. "Good for dogs?"

"Great for dogs," I say, opening my door. As if on cue, a ball of wiggles slams into me, licking me up and down. Timber is so excited he's practically shaking. "Hey, there buddy. God, you are so wired." I look to Liam. "Maybe I should think about getting him a friend. Someone to help keep him company during the day. Even with Tess here for a few hours, I feel like he's got so much energy these days."

"Maybe he's just feeding off you," Liam says. "He knows you're happy."

I smile, giving Timber a couple more pats on the side. "Yeah, I guess I am." I drop my stuff on the counter and head for my bedroom. I need to pack my bag and grab stuff quick; I'm supposed to be at Zara's in half an hour. We want to try and get out before this snow gets any worse. But before I manage to reach my room my phone buzzes in my pocket.

"Slate," I say, putting it up to my ear as I enter the

bedroom, catching sight of all the photographs still piled on the box in the corner. If this is Wallace trying to pull me back in for another assignment, he's got a surprise coming.

"Emily Slate?" A strong male voice says.

"Yes."

"This is Dr. Ruben Archer. You left me a series of messages? I'm sorry for taking so long to return your calls, I've been overseas."

Suddenly my heart is in my chest. "Yes, thank you for calling me back. A friend of mine gave me your number. I was looking for more information about my mother, who I believe was one of your patients." I take a seat on the edge of the bed. I've left Dr. Archer half a dozen messages. Part of me thought he'd never call back. Judy's mom back in Fernview warned that she wasn't supposed to talk about the group to anyone.

"Margaret," he says, his tone full of foreboding. Just the tone itself is enough to make me think he already knows something.

"That's right." There's a pause on the other end, long enough that I'm afraid he may have hung up. "Dr. Archer, are you still there?"

"Yes. I'm sorry, but I can't help you. I know what you're looking for, but I will not violate your mother's confidence. That extends even past her death."

"Then you're aware she died," I say.

"I am, and I know it's a bit late, but I'm very sorry for your loss."

I take a deep breath. "I think in this case, you may need to make an exception."

"Why is that?" There's no accusation in his voice, only curiosity.

"Because I've received two letters from someone pretending to be her, written in her handwriting." As I say the words, Liam appears at the door, his face grim and drawn. In his hand he holds a sealed envelope, with my name written across it in script. "Actually, make that *three* letters." My eyes meet his. He doesn't need to speak for me to know what he's thinking. This is getting serious.

Dr. Archer is quiet for another moment before speaking again. "When can you meet?"

I stand back up. "Right away."

"Good. We have a lot to discuss."

The End?

To be continued...

Want to read more about Emily?

SOMETIMES THE SCARS WE CAN'T SEE ARE THE ONES THAT RUN the deepest.

Fresh off barely stopping a plot to derail the world's economy, Special Agent Emily Slate finds herself faced with a new and strange case: a body found drained of all its blood in a small Louisiana town. The local police can't seem to make heads or tails of it and Emily's boss insists this is the perfect case for her, despite her desire to find the person continuing to send her letters claiming they're from her dead mother.

But when Emily arrives to begin her investigation, without her ride-or-die fellow Agent Zara Foley to boot, she discovers superstition embedded deep in the small community of Bellefleur. Superstition which only grows when a second body is discovered.

Emily has never had to face a supernatural killer before, though everyone keeps insisting that's what's out there, terrorizing people. But Emily isn't willing to accept anything on face value, and she will do whatever it takes to get to the truth behind these deaths.

It will take all of Emily's wits to uncover the secrets behind these killings, secrets that reach back hundreds of years and speak to the very heart of what it means for one person to be connected to another.

Will she find the truth before it's too late? Or will Bellefleur's secrets swallow her up, like the rest of the town?

You don't belong here, little sister. Run home before it's too late.

To get your copy of THE VANISHING EYES, CLICK HERE or scan the code below!

Start Reading

FREE book offer!
Where did it all go wrong for Emily?

I HOPE YOU ENJOYED *HIS FINAL ACT*. IF YOU'D LIKE TO LEARN more about Emily's backstory and what happened in the days following her husband's unfortunate death, including what almost got her kicked out of the FBI, then you're in luck! *Her Last Shot* introduces Emily and tells the story of the case that almost ended her career. Interested? CLICK HERE to get your free copy now!

Not Available Anywhere Else!

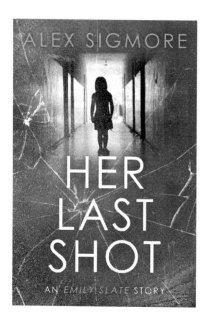

You'll also be the first to know when each book in the Emily Slate series is available!

Download for **FREE HERE** or scan the code below!

The Emily Slate FBI Mystery Series

Free Prequel - Her Last Shot (Emily Slate Bonus Story)

His Perfect Crime - (Emily Slate Series Book One)

The Collection Girls - (Emily Slate Series Book Two)

Smoke and Ashes - (Emily Slate Series Book Three)

Her Final Words - (Emily Slate Series Book Four)

Can't Miss Her - (Emily Slate Series Book Five)

The Lost Daughter - (Emily Slate Series Book Six)

The Secret Seven - (Emily Slate Series Book Seven)

A Liar's Grave - (Emily Slate Series Book Eight)

The Girl in the Wall - (Emily Slate Series Book Nine)

His Final Act - (Emily Slate Series Book Ten)

The Vanishing Eyes - (Emily Slate Series Book Eleven)

Coming Soon!

Edge of the Woods - (Emily Slate Series Book Twelve)

The Missing Bones - (Emily Slate Series Book Thirteen)

A Note from Alex

Hi there!

Thanks so much for reading *His Final Act*! This was such a fun story for me to come up with and it was a privilege to deliver it to you. I hope you've enjoyed all of Emily's adventures so far. The response to this series has been incredible, and as long as you, the reader, continue to ask for Emily Slate stories, you can be rest assured I will deliver them!

As I've always said, you are the reason I write!

If you haven't already, please take a moment to leave a review or recommend this series to a fellow book lover. It really helps me as a writer and is the best way to make sure there are plenty more *Emily Slate* books in the future.

As always, thank you for being a loyal reader,

Alex

Made in the USA
Middletown, DE
11 February 2024

49556515R00156